Twice Upon A Time

Erica Lee

D1519026

Dedication

Dedicated to my Twitter family. Your constant love and support means more to me than you'll ever know. I hope this story fills you with as much joy as you give me everyday! Love you all!

Table of Contents

Prologue

"I can't stay here, Kar."

I stared across the table at Kacey, my girlfriend of three years, trying to decipher what those words meant. She had a knack for cryptic one-liners. Her mysteriousness could be frustrating, but it was also part of what made her so damn sexy. It was what first attracted me to her and what led me to kiss her for the first time two months later — an anniversary we were currently celebrating since we considered that kiss to be the beginning of our fairytale romance. And it was a fairytale. I felt like there was still a lot I didn't know about Kacey, but from that very first kiss, I knew she was the person I would spend the rest of my life with.

That didn't mean she wasn't absolutely infuriating sometimes, now being one of them. "Are you sick?" I asked, reaching out to take her hand. "I can have them pack our food up and we'll go back to the apartment."

Kacey shook her head. "I'm not sick. I didn't mean here, as in the restaurant. I meant here as in Bellman. I can't stay in Bellman anymore. I have to go back home."

My eyebrows furrowed. "You mean once we graduate?"

I wasn't sure why she was being so weird about it. Sure, we had discussed where we would live after graduation and agreed that staying in Bellman was what we both preferred, but if she had a reason to go back home, I wouldn't be opposed to that. It would put us a little farther from my family than I'd like, but I was willing to go anywhere with Kacey.

"No. I mean right now. I'm not finishing out this semester."

My heart pounded in my chest. "What are you talking about? You're a semester-and-a-half away from graduating. You can't just drop out now."

Kacey shrugged, picking up a salt shaker and staring at it, rather than looking at me. "I don't really have a choice. I have to get home."

I shook my head in frustration. "What does that even mean, Kacey? Why do you have to go home?"

"It's complicated."

I stared across the table at her, dumbfounded, not even sure what to say, and praying this was some sick joke.

After a minute of complete silence, Kacey brought her cool, dark eyes to mine. "Don't worry. I'll still pay my half of the bills."

I threw my hands up. "I don't care about the freaking bills, Kacey. I care about you. I care about us. What does this mean for our future?"

"I still want a future with you."

I waited for her to say more, but quickly realized that wasn't happening. I closed my eyes and ran a hand over my temple. "When do you leave?"

Kacey put the salt shaker down and reached across the table to take my hand. "I leave tonight."

A mixture of anger and sadness built up inside of me. "Tonight? What the hell, Kacey? Why are you just telling me this now? Why wouldn't you talk about this with me?"

Kacey shrugged again. "I didn't want to ruin our anniversary. Plus, it was sudden. Kind of a family emergency."

A family emergency? In the three years we'd been dating, Kacey had told me almost nothing about her family. All I knew was that she lived with her little sister and grandma growing up. While she spoke to her grandma on the phone every once in a while, she didn't seem to have much of a relationship with either of them. Now, she was dropping out of school for them?

"Can we just enjoy our dinner?" Kacey asked, interrupting my thoughts. "I love you, Kari Adelberg. Nothing will ever change that. Believe me."

I did believe her. In our whole relationship, Kacey had never done anything to betray my trust. Enjoying dinner would be the hard part.

It would have been even harder if I had realized that night would be the last time I saw Kacey Caldwell.

Chapter 1

"Pst. Pst. Wake up." A finger tapped on my shoulder at a rapid pace. "Kari, get up."

I opened one eye and looked at the clock on my nightstand, groaning when I realized it was only 8 a.m. I rubbed my eyes and looked toward the person who dared to wake me up so early on my day off. I groaned again when my best friend's shaggy brown hair and boyish grin came into focus. "Bo, what the hell are you doing in my house?"

"Your new next-door neighbor is moving in and she is smoking hot."

I rolled my eyes and turned away from him. "Cool. Go bug her."

Instead of leaving, Bo pulled my comforter off of me. "Dude, I'm trying to bro out with you right now. Don't leave me hanging."

I sat up, realizing sleep wasn't happening anymore. I raised one eyebrow at Bo. "How did you even get into my house?"

"You gave me a key when I watched this little guy," he said, patting my fifteen-pound white mutt, Duke, on the head.

Duke lazily licked his hand, and I rolled my eyes at my "attack dog." I shook my head when Bo's words registered. "I took that key back from you."

Bo lifted one shoulder and let it drop. "I made myself a copy. You know. For emergencies."

"And this is an emergency?"

"Um yeah. We're over thirty and both still single."

I picked up a pillow and tossed it at him. "You can have her, man. The chances of her being gay are slim to none."

"Hey, now. You never know. Plus, she would just be a dine and dash for me, anyway. She's a single mom. I can't be going down that road. Kids aren't my thing."

That comment earned him a punch to his shoulder. "First of all, she's a human being, so you can stop talking about her like she's a meal at a diner. Second, how do you know all of this?"

"You know my buddy, Derek?"

"Douchey Derek?"

Bo's face lit up as if he was proud of his friend's nickname. "You know it! He was her realtor, so he learned all this shit about her. I thought he was exaggerating, but nah. I caught a glimpse of her when I was coming in here. Dark hair. Dark eyes. Derek says she really has the whole dark and mysterious thing going on. You're into that right?"

I groaned at his description. "Ugh. Not since college."

This time, Bo rolled his eyes at me. "Yeah, yeah. I get it. Your college girlfriend broke your heart. Come on, Kari. I didn't even meet you until like five years after things ended between you two, and I've still heard about her multiple times."

"She was the one," I breathed out.

"If she was the one, she would still be here." Bo raised both eyebrows as if he were a father lecturing his teenage daughter.

I glared at him, and he patted me on the head the same way he'd done to the dog. "Who knows? Maybe the hottie next door is *actually* the one."

No. Of course she isn't the one. The point of the one is that they are the one and only. Kacey Caldwell was my soul mate, and even if the only feelings I harbored toward her at this point were anger and hatred, it still didn't change that. "Doubtful. Plus, I don't really think it's the best idea to start a relationship that is destined to fail with the person who *literally* shares a driveway with me."

I loved the townhouse community I lived in with its small matching houses and community center and pool, but it wasn't easy to avoid people when all the houses had no space between them and no private backyards. Not that it was a bad thing. Because of this, I had made friends with a bunch of my neighbors, Bo being one of them.

Soon after moving in, he and I bonded over the fact that we were the only people our age in the development

9

who didn't have kids or weren't trying to conceive them. It was a great place for building lasting friendships. But it was not a good place for love, unless awkward run-ins with an ex-lover were your thing.

I looked back at Bo, and he was still staring at me with big puppy dog eyes. I couldn't help but smile at his persistence. "Fine. I'll check her out with you. Are you happy?"

"Very," he said, hopping off the bed.

When I stood up, he gave me a once-over and grimaced, waving a hand in front of me. "You need to do something about all of this though."

I looked down at my wrinkled pj's and could only imagine the mess that my dirty blonde hair was right now. Still, I had no interest in getting dolled up for the straight, dark, and mysterious single mother next door. Not that I had a problem with kids. The kid wouldn't be the issue. It would be my stupid heart that never seemed to want to give anyone a chance. That and the fact that she was most likely straight, just like almost everyone else in this small town.

I stared at Bo and crossed my arms in front of my chest. "Contrary to what you might think, I don't care how good looking this girl is. I'm not trying to get with her, so it really doesn't matter how I look."

Bo grabbed me by the shoulders and directed me to the bathroom. "At least brush your teeth. It's called having a little pride. Sheesh."

Once I was standing in front of my bathroom mirror with my toothbrush in my mouth, I realized Bo was right. I hadn't taken the time to wash off my makeup the night before, and my hair was now sticking in every direction. I sighed, then washed my face, put on a little eyeliner, and pulled my hair back into a messy bun.

When I walked out of the bathroom, Bo let out a low whistle. "See. That wasn't so hard, was it? Now get changed, so we can go meet this bombshell."

I did as he said, and within a few minutes, I was following him as he skipped down the stairs and out my front door. I shielded my eyes from the bright August sun and looked to my left where a big U-Haul sat in the driveway. I walked a few more steps across my short sidewalk and spotted a little girl sitting on the back of the truck, staring down at an iPad. As we approached, her head shot up and she smiled over at us, waving excitedly. "Bonjour! Hola! Guten Tag! Are you my new neighbors?"

Bo chuckled, not trying to hide his amusement over our young neighbor's multilingual greeting. He bent down so he was at her level. "I'm Bo. I live on the other side of the neighborhood, but this is Kari. She lives right next door."

Her dark brown eyes lit up when she looked over at me, and there was something about her smile that seemed familiar. Then a voice that was also strangely familiar came from the front of the house. "Bailey, what did I tell you about talking to…"

The words were cut short when those big dark eyes latched onto mine. The eyes I hadn't seen in a decade, but never forgot. My mind immediately flashed back to the first night I saw them.

It was the weekend following our first week of classes and like any good college freshman, I was sufficiently drunk. After spending most of high school as the closeted girl, I had vowed to be my authentic self in college and was celebrating this newfound freedom by partying with my floormates who hadn't even flinched when I told them I was a lesbian. The only problem was, unlike most of them, I could count the amount of times I had drank on one hand.

Walking out of my dorm room where we'd been pregaming, I realized I was already way too drunk. That's when I saw her. She walked out of the bathroom at the same moment I was stumbling by. Her long dark hair was soaking wet from the shower. She was holding a bathroom tote and was wearing tight cotton shorts and a black tank top that showed off her ripped biceps, one that had a large tattoo of some sort of symbol. My eyes not-so-subtly traced the length of her whole body, but it was her eyes that stopped me in my tracks.

I stopped so quickly that my roommate ran into me from behind, pushing me forward right into the pretty girl. Her strong arms grabbing my shoulders helped break my fall, but my eyes never left hers. I giggled uncontrollably as I stared up at the girl who was just a couple inches taller than me. "Your eyes are really pretty. Like, really, really pretty. What color are they?"

To my surprise, the girl in front of me, still holding onto my arms, chuckled softly. "Dark brown, I guess. You could probably give me a better idea though. I don't think I've ever stared at them as much as you are right now."

Her joke brought me back to reality, sobering me enough to realize I was embarrassing myself. "Shit. Sorry. I'm being weird, right?"

My embarrassment didn't stop me from giggling again as I heard my friends laugh at the show I was putting on.

"Don't worry about it," the girl said cooly. "I'm not one to complain about a pretty girl staring at me."

"Are you a lesbian?" I asked in wonder, as if I had just found out she was a unicorn. Although, in my drunken state, finding another lesbian at my small university a week into the school year felt like finding a unicorn.

Her lips quirked up into a slight smirk. "I don't like to label myself."

"Wow, who are y—?" The sudden urge to throw up cut off my question.

I ran into the bathroom to avoid losing the contents of my stomach on some hot girl's feet. I made it to the toilet just in time, and after a minute of upchucking my dinner, turned to see that not only had all of my friends followed me in, but also the hot mystery girl. Great.

I stood and walked to the sink to wash my hands, praying that the room would stop spinning soon. When I stumbled away from the sink, the same strong arms from earlier

---

grabbed ahold of me. Those big dark eyes bore into me so hard, I thought I might melt into a puddle right there in the bathroom.

"We should probably get you back to your room." My knight in shining armor removed her eyes from mine to look toward my friends. "You guys can go. I'll take her back to her room to make sure she doesn't get cited for underage drinking."

My friends quickly agreed and left the two of us standing alone in the bathroom. I felt the strong tattooed arm slip around my waist as its owner stared down at me. "I'm Kacey Caldwell, by the way."

I couldn't respond because we had started walking and all of my focus was on trying to put one foot in front of the other. When we got to my door, I stopped and fumbled for my keys, clumsily dropping them on the ground. Kacey reached down and picked them up, unlocking the door for me, before leading me inside.

"Which bed is yours?" she asked calmly.

I pointed to the bed on the right side of the room with the white and pink striped bedding. Kacey's lips tilted up on just one side and she lifted her eyebrow ever so slightly. "Cute bed."

I knew she didn't mean anything by it, but that didn't stop my intoxicated body from heating up at the possible implication.

Before I could say anything else, Kacey directed me toward the bed. She helped me get settled under the covers, then searched around the room, grabbing a small trash can and putting a new bag in it before setting it beside the bed.

"Do you have any bottles of water or Tylenol?"

I shook my head. "Probably not. I have no idea though."

Kacey nodded slowly, as if she was pondering something. "I have some. I'll be right back."

Just like that, she was out the door. Part of me figured she wouldn't come back, but a few minutes later, she returned with a bottle of water and two pills. She bent down by my bed and held them out. "Take these pills and make sure you drink the whole bottle of water before you pass out. Otherwise, I have a feeling you won't be too happy in the morning."

I blinked at the girl in front of me, trying to bring her into focus. "Why are you being so nice to me?"

Kacey brushed me off with a small shrug. "I guess I just have a lot of experience taking care of drunk people, so it's kind of instinctual for me."

In my drunken state, I didn't think about what she'd said too much. I was only worried about how I appeared to this enigma of a girl in front of me.

"I'm not normally messy like this, you know. If you can believe it, this is only like my fifth time drinking."

Kacey chuckled lightly. "Yeah. That wasn't too hard to figure out."

She looked toward the door and I worried she was about to leave, so I said the first thing that came to my mind. "I've never kissed a girl." My eyes widened when I realized what I had just admitted, but my drunken brain couldn't tell my mouth to shut up. "I mean… I know I'm gay. I just… haven't had the opportunity. Not that I couldn't. I just wasn't out. Have you kissed a girl?"

An amused grin surfaced on Kacey's face. "I have."

"I'm Kari Adelberg, by the way."

Kacey lifted an eyebrow at that. "Adelberg as in the Adelberg dining hall?"

I groaned internally. I didn't want to be known as the girl whose parents donated so much money to the university, their alma mater, that they had a dining hall named after them. That's exactly who I was though.

I put a hand over my face. "That would be correct."

"It's the better dining hall by far, so that's cool."

I wasn't sure if she was being serious or sarcastic, but I was too awestruck (and drunk) to care.

Much to my disappointment, Kacey chose that moment to stand up fully and take a few steps away from the bed. "I better get going, but take care of yourself, Kari Adelberg."

It looked like she was about to move toward the door, but then she turned and came back to the bed instead, bending down to place a quick kiss on my cheek. I stared at her as she pulled back, and she simply shrugged one shoulder. "Now you can say you've been kissed by a girl."

"Yo, Kari. You're being awfully rude right now."

My mind snapped back to the present moment, and I looked toward Bo. He was talking, but I couldn't register what he was saying.

He put one arm around me and looked at Kacey. "You'll have to excuse my friend here. Since she looks like she just saw a ghost, I'm going to guess it's because you somewhat resemble her ex. Seems about right given the detailed descriptions she's—" Bo paused and quickly moved his eyes between the two of us. "No shit. You're Kacey Caldwell, aren't you? Well, shit." He ran a hand through his hair then looked down at Bailey. "I mean crap. Or… umm… poop. Hell, what are kids your age allowed to say?"

Bailey put a hand over her mouth and giggled. "You could say caca. It's Spanish."

Kacey put her hand on the young girl's shoulder and smiled down at her, rather than looking at us. "She has a word of the day app and one of the latest words had something to do with being multilingual, so now she is trying to learn multiple languages in addition to being very well-versed in the English language. My daughter, the child prodigy."

Hearing her say the word daughter felt like a punch in the gut. There was a time when Kacey Caldwell and I talked about starting a family together. Now, here I was ten years later, heart beating rapidly at the sight of her, while she stood there with *her* daughter. Her daughter who couldn't have been younger than seven or eight, which meant Kacey had moved on much more quickly than me.

"I'm a polyglot." Bailey's voice interrupted my thoughts.

"A poly-what?" Bo asked.

Bailey smiled proudly. "A polyglot. It's someone who can speak more than one language. I just think it's a really cool word."

"Well, I agree," Bo said, bending down and reaching out his hand to give Bailey a high five.

When he stood back up, we all continued to stare down at the little girl. Bailey looked between all three of us, her face scrunched up in thought as if trying to solve a mystery. After what felt like a lifetime of awkward silence, Kacey cleared her throat and reached out a hand toward Bo. "My name is Kacey Caldwell. This is my daughter, Bailey. As you can see, we're moving in." She looked toward the house, then her dark eyes landed on me again. "Kari, it's nice to see you. It's been a while."

Nice to see you? Ten years ago, she dropped out of school with no explanation, then barely talked to me for months before dumping me over a text message and now all she had to say was that it was nice to see me? I could have screamed. All of the years I spent thinking about what it would be like to see her again, I never imagined it would be like this. I knew this wasn't the time or place to bring up old wounds though, so I straightened my shoulders and put on my best fake smile. "*Nice* to see you too, Kacey."

Clearly catching on to my sarcasm, Kacey lifted one eyebrow, so subtle that it'd be missed by most people, but I noticed. Of course I noticed, and I hated that I did. I hated the effect that one slight movement was having on me, causing a feeling that started in my gut and spread throughout my whole body.

"You know my mom?" Bailey asked, tilting her head.

I blew out a breath as I thought about how to answer. She had no idea just how loaded that question really was. I smiled down at Bailey, hoping she wouldn't realize how hard this was for me. How much I would give to be anywhere but here right now. "I do," I answered simply.

When I looked from Bailey to Kacey, her eyes were studying me in a way that only Kacey's could, and I felt like I might melt. I hated it and loved it, which only made me hate it even more. I refused to let her have this effect on me. Not after all these years. Not without any explanation as to why she left me brokenhearted. I forced my eyes away from hers before I spoke again. "Well, I did. But that was a long time ago. I don't know her anymore." I glanced down at my phone as though I had somewhere to be. "Now, if you'll excuse me, I have to get going. It was great to meet you, Bailey."

Without saying another word, I turned on my heels and headed toward the house. After closing the door, I pressed my back against it and took big heaving breaths, trying to gain any semblance of control. Kacey was gone. Out of my life. I was never going to see her again. It took me years to accept that. Now that she was back, what was I supposed to do? How was I supposed to feel?

I couldn't think about anything right now. I just needed to go back to bed and escape from reality for a bit. But I knew the truth. I could never escape Kacey Caldwell. Not even in my dreams.

***

I sat up in my dorm room bed, head spinning, and immediately regretted how much I drank the night prior.

"Glad to see you're alive," my roommate said with a laugh. "I thought I was going to have to check for a pulse."

I rubbed my eyes and stretched my arms into the air, yawning loudly. "What time is it?"

"12:30. We're about to head to lunch if you want to go."

I shook my head. The thought of eating anything turned my stomach. "Thanks, but I think I'll just shower and try to feel human again."

"Great plan. Get yourself feeling better so you can actually make it out tonight."

"Again? I don't think I can handle that."

"You have to. Stacey's older brother is on the football team and they're having a party tonight. We can't miss it. There's going to be a bunch of hot older guys…" She paused as if she just realized who she was talking to. "Okay. So, you don't care about that, but you should totally invite your new girlfriend."

My eyes shot up. "Girlfriend?"

"Yeah, you know, the girl you were making googly eyes at last night."

I crossed my arms over my chest trying my best to feign naïveté. "I don't know what you're talking about."

"Sure you do. She walked you back here. I think someone said her name is Katie."

"It's Kacey," I answered way too quickly, causing a big smile to spread across my roommate's face.

"Exactly. Get yourself looking pretty, then go knock on her door and invite her to come tonight."

———

My roommate left the room before I had the chance to argue. I slid out of bed and got my shower stuff together before heading into the hall. I stared down at my phone, catching up on all of the texts from my friends until I was stopped dead by something, or rather someone.

The same strong arms from last night grabbed onto me again. "We really need to stop bumping into each other like this," Kacey said, keeping her hands firmly on my arms.

I swallowed hard trying to ignore the feeling that simple touch sent through my whole body. I stared at her hands, then moved my eyes up to rest on her tattoo, which was way too sexy and cool for a freshman going to college in rural Pennsylvania.

"If you're lucky, I'll tell you what it means someday."

When I finally made eye contact with Kacey, she had the slightest hint of a smirk on her face.

I felt my face turning red. It was so unlike me to get tongue-tied. I was normally a social butterfly, comfortable talking to anyone, especially since embracing my true identity. But not this girl. There was something so intimidating about her, and I had a feeling part of it had to do with the way my body responded just to being around her. "Sorry. I'm still hungover from last night. Thanks for taking care of me, by the way. You really didn't have to."

Kacey squeezed my arms, then let go and shrugged her shoulders. "It's no big deal."

"Well, to me it was, so thank you." I paused for a brief moment, wondering if I had the guts to ask my next question. "How would you feel about going to a party tonight? Since you didn't drink last night, I thought maybe you would want to tonight."

"I don't drink." Her answer was so quick and firm that I figured it was an excuse not to come. When my eyes dropped from hers, she bent her head, forcing me to look at her again. "I'm down to go though. I just won't be drinking."

I couldn't help the smile that came to my face. "Oh. That's great. If I'm being honest, the thought of going out again makes me want to hurl."

"If I remember correctly, you didn't actually go out last night."

"Touché. Still. I'm only going because I feel like a loser staying in by myself."

"We could stay in together if you want." Kacey shrugged nonchalantly, as if the thought of the two of us hanging out didn't stir up her insides the way it did mine. "My original plan was to go to the library to get a head start on studying. Any interest in that?"

I scrunched up my nose. "Or we could go to the arcade at the mall."

"The arcade sounds great. Meet you in the lobby at six?"

"It's a…" I cut myself off before the word date could slip out. This was just two new friends getting to know each other. College was about new experiences and living it up. It wasn't about falling for the first girl who gave me any sort of attention… even if that girl was ridiculously sexy.

Chapter 2

I woke to the feeling of warm breath on my neck. I wrapped the comforter around my body tighter and enjoyed the serenity of the warmth mixed with my current dreamy state. "That feels…" My head snapped up and crashed right into Bo's. "Shit, Bo. What the hell are you doing?"

Bo rubbed his head. "Apparently getting a concussion."

"Well, you'd deserve it. You can't just walk into someone's house whenever you want and crawl into bed with them. What are you even doing here?"

"I'll have you know, I came over so I could take Duke for a walk because I assumed you were taking a pity nap. He peed and pooped so you're welcome."

"That's surprisingly sweet, but it still doesn't explain why you crawled into bed with me."

"I wanted to whisper sweet nothings in your ear to get you to talk in your sleep, so I could figure out what you were dreaming about."

I shook my head. "And that is very unsurprisingly weird of you."

Bo laughed much louder than necessary. "So, are you going to tell me what you were dreaming about?"

"No."

Bo smiled knowingly. "Ah. So, you were dreaming about her. I knew it. I don't blame you. She's hot. I don't think you gave her level of hotness justice. Was she this hot in college?"

I glared at Bo. "I'm not answering that." Kacey had always been sexy to me, but somehow she had gotten even better looking since college. It was so unfair. "We're not talking about her. That's the plan. Pretend she doesn't live next door. She's just another neighbor as far as I'm concerned. I'll just avoid her."

"That'll be hard since she's going to the back to school barbecue next week."

I cringed. The back to school barbecue was a big party in our development to celebrate the end of summer and give kids one last hoorah before they headed back to school. It was also a way to welcome new residents, and I had stupidly volunteered to be on the welcoming committee.

"How do you know she's going?"

Bo averted his gaze. "I told her about it."

I let out a low growl. "And why would you do that, Bo?"

Bo shrugged. "Because she's hot."

When I rolled my eyes, the look on his face became more sincere. "She also has a daughter who is the same age as a bunch of kids in the neighborhood and I thought it would be nice to help her make some friends." He reached out and squeezed my hand. "Plus, this will give you a chance for closure, which you desperately need. Never in my life have I been hung up on a girl like you are with this one. Well, at least not since Susan Delanco kissed me behind the bleachers in fifth grade, then told me I couldn't be her boyfriend because we weren't in the same math class."

"Isn't Susan Delanco the girl you told me you lost your virginity to after your junior prom?"

A smirk appeared on Bo's face. "Exactly. Closure."

"I really hope you're not suggesting I have sex with her because that's not happening."

Bo's face lit up. "That's totally *not* where I was going with that, but it's a great idea. Who needs to talk when you could have one last passion filled angry f—"

I put up my hand. "Absolutely not."

Just the mention of sex with Kacey had my body in overdrive. My mind drifted to what it felt like to touch her. How it felt when she touched me. The way her every move was strong yet delicate.

The sound of Bo clearing his throat brought me back to reality. When I looked at him, he had a goofy smile on his face. "I feel like you could use some alone time." He made an obscene gesture with his hand while wiggling his eyebrows.

"Ew. Stop."

Bo held both hands in the air and stood from the bed, slowly backing away. "Hey, I'm just saying. You have to work out all of this frustration in one way or another. Just think about how much better Kacey Caldwell would be than your hand."

I threw a pillow at him just as he dashed out my bedroom door and closed it behind him. I listened as he laughed all the way down the stairs until he left.

I shook my head, but knew he was right. Not about the sex, but about the closure. If I was going to make it through being her next-door neighbor, I had to find a way to get closure with Kacey.

***

I stood behind a table filled with community information pamphlets and event calendars and watched as Mr. Prince, the homeowners' association president, made his way over to me. He was a short, graying man in his late seventies and had been the only president since the first houses were built twenty years ago. Every few years, someone new would try to take over, but he refused to back down. His wife was gone and his kids had moved away, so I think the community felt like family to him, and he worried about losing that.

I stepped around the table and gave him a big hug. "Mr. Prince, it's so nice to see you."

He nodded his head seriously, the way he always did, as if he were the president of the country, rather than just the neighborhood. He scanned the table before looking back at me. "Everything looks great. It turns out Tom won't be around to help you today, but there's only one house that sold over the last few months so you shouldn't be too busy. I visited your new neighbors yesterday. Girl looks to be about your age. Seems nice. Not very talkative, but that's okay. Her daughter makes up for that. Cutest little girl. Quite the chatterbox. Reminds me of my youngest granddaughter. Speak of the devil. Here they come."

I turned to look in the direction of Mr. Prince's stare, hoping my body's reaction to Kacey would have simmered down in the past week of avoiding her. Maybe I could see her as just another neighbor.

That wasn't the case though. Of course it wasn't. Kacey had her long dark hair pulled into a ponytail and hidden underneath a hat. She was wearing jean shorts and a white V-neck T-shirt, that revealed the very top of her blue bikini. I relished the view, but cursed it at the same time. Why did I have to have such a hot ex? Why wasn't I one of those people whose tastes had gotten better with time? Nope, my taste was spot-on when I fell for Kacey.

"Kacey. Bailey. It's great to see you both," Mr. Prince said cheerfully after they reached us.

Kacey gave him a polite smile. "It's nice to see you too." She looked toward me and her smile faltered. "Kari."

That was it. Not even a *nice to see you* this time around. I tried not to think about it too much and looked toward Bailey instead. "How's it going, kiddo?"

Bailey shrugged and smiled sweetly at me. "Everything is copacetic here."

Mr. Prince chuckled. "That's a big word for such a little girl."

"Let me guess. Was that a word of the day?" I asked as cheerfully as possible, trying to ignore the fact that Kacey had yet to take her eyes off of me.

"Sure was," Bailey answered proudly. "In case you were wondering, it means *all is well.*"

This time, the smile that came to my face was sincere. "I'm very happy to hear that. Are you excited for school to start tomorrow?"

Bailey's smile dropped for the first time since walking over to us, and she looked toward the ground. "I'm a little nervous. Mom says I'm going to love it here. She calls it a fresh start, but I'm worried about making friends."

I knelt down so I was eye to eye with the little girl. "You'll have no problem making friends. In fact, I would bet money that by the end of the day, you're already running around and playing with the neighborhood kids."

Bailey lifted an eyebrow as the grin returned to her face. "How much money?"

"Bailey Grace Caldwell, don't—"

24

"Five dollars," I said, interrupting Kacey's words. I'm not sure why I was bent on befriending Bailey. Maybe it was because it was easier to face her than her mom. Or maybe part of me believed she was my key to closure. If I could see Kacey as Bailey's mom, I'd no longer see her as the girl I fell in love with in college, because she clearly wasn't that girl anymore.

Bailey stuck her hand out toward me and giggled as I shook it. "At the end of the day, I'm going to have five dollars or new friends. Either way I win."

"You're a very smart girl."

Bailey nodded enthusiastically. "Yeah. I get that from my mom. She's the smartest person I know."

Kacey cleared her throat and finally tore her eyes away from me. "Come on, Bailey. I'm sure Miss Adelberg has her own friends to hang out with, and we get to explore the neighborhood with the welcoming committee."

"Actually, I am the welcoming committee," I said softly.

Kacey's eyes snapped toward mine again, but I couldn't read her thoughts. We stared at each other for a moment before Mr. Prince interrupted, oblivious to the tension palpating between the two of us. "You're going to love this town. The college kids get a bit rowdy at times, but there are plenty of places where you can go to escape from them. I can tell you the best restaurants to go to if you want me to."

"I actually know what's around. I went to Bellman University. It was a long time ago, but it doesn't look like things have changed too much."

Mr. Prince looked between the two of us. "Kari, didn't you go to Bellman? I'm surprised the two of you didn't know each other, being right around the same age and all."

"They did know each other," Bailey answered before either of us could. "They *used* to know each other, but they don't anymore."

"Well, why didn't anyone tell me that?" Mr. Prince asked with a chuckle. "I'm going to get out of your hair so you ladies have a chance to catch up."

I watched him walk away, unsure what to say next.

25

Luckily, Bailey never seemed to be at a loss for words. "Miss Adelberg, are you going to show us around?"

"I sure am."

We walked around the neighborhood and I talked to them about the pool and community center hours and the different activities we had throughout the year. Kacey was quiet while Bailey asked questions about everything. As we made our way back to where we started, I was happy to see Bo approaching us.

"How's it going, ladies?" he asked coolly.

"It's awesome! I got to see the whole neighborhood," Bailey answered excitedly.

"Oh yeah? That's awesome." Bo looked between Kacey and me, then back toward Bailey. "I actually came over here because I need a little help. I'm supposed to be grilling hamburgers, but I need a super special helper to tell me when to flip them."

Bailey pointed to herself. "I can do that!"

Bo clapped his hands together. "Perfect! There's only space for one special helper though, so we have to make sure it's okay with your mom if I steal you for a little bit." Bo ignored my glare as he and Bailey both smile at Kacey.

"Please, Mommy, can I go?"

"Yes. Please, Mommy," Bo repeated, putting his hands together in a praying motion.

"Um. Of course. Just be careful. Don't touch anything hot."

Bo winked at me before grabbing Bailey's hand and walking away from us.

Kacey looked over at me and raised both eyebrows before averting her eyes to look at the table. She ran her hands over the pamphlets sitting out, feigning interest in them. When she finally looked up, there was a sadness in her eyes that wasn't there before. "Listen, I know this is really weird. I'm sorry. I want you to know that I had no idea you owned the house next door to ours. I didn't even know if you were still in Bellman."

I scoffed. "Well, yeah, I figured that. I didn't think someone who broke up with me over a text message after ignoring me for months would then stalk me and buy the house next door just to be close to me."

Kacey cringed as if my words hurt her and I almost felt bad. Except I knew I shouldn't. Nothing I did could hurt her as much as she hurt me. "I wanted to apologize for how I ended things."

I waved my hand as nonchalantly as possible. "That's in the past."

Kacey studied me the same way she always used to as if she was searching for the truth somewhere within my blatant lies. "I—"

"Ladies!" Mr. Prince's voice interrupted. "I hope the tour went well. Kacey, make sure you take a copy of each of those pamphlets."

He picked one up that had information about local restaurants and pointed at something. "Have you been to the Bellman Bar and Grill? Best burgers in town if you ask me." He hitched a thumb toward me and I could feel my stomach drop, dreading his next words. "This one right here doesn't like it. Says she had a bad experience there."

I avoided eye contact with Kacey, knowing she was fully aware of what that bad experience was. "Mr. Prince, could you finish up for me? I'm not feeling well."

"Of… of course, dear. Are you okay? You look very pale suddenly."

I nodded my head, but walked away without saying another word. *Bellman Bar and Grill* was where I had one of the worst nights of my life, but that memory wasn't the one that hurt so bad. It was the memory of one of the best nights of my life that haunted me and kept me from ever walking through that door again.

***

As Kacey held the door to the restaurant open for me, I wondered for the millionth time since becoming friends two months earlier if this was a date. Her very simple 'want to check out that new restaurant? I hear they have good milkshakes' while we were studying certainly didn't sound like a date invitation.

But Kacey and I had grown closer—so much closer—since the beginning of the school year. She was by far my best friend at college, and we spent most of our time together. Lunch during the day. Studying at night. On some weekends, I could even drag her out to whatever party the girls were going to, or she'd convince me to stay in. We spent most Sundays lying in one of our beds and switching between studying and watching TV. Our bodies would always end up pushed close together, but that was kind of unavoidable in a small twin bed. What wasn't necessary were the little touches we shared. A finger running along bare skin here. An arm draped across a stomach there. These things were happening more and more often as time passed, but we never spoke about them or took things any further.

Kacey was so cool and confident, I figured she'd make the first move, but waiting for her was killing me and also causing me to wonder if the chemistry between us was just my imagination.

"Table or booth?"

Kacey's question brought me back to reality, and I shook my head to get my bearings back. "A booth sounds great."

"Are you okay?" Kacey asked as she gently squeezed my arm.

"I'm great. Just a little stressed about the two exams I have this week."

Kacey's brow wrinkled. "We didn't have to come. We can just go back to the dorms and study if you want. We'll pick up food or have something delivered."

"No!" I answered way too quickly. "I need the break. I just let my mind wander for a minute there."

A smile split Kacey's face. "Okay then. After you." Kacey put out her hand and motioned for me to take a seat in the booth. Once I slid in, she sat down on the other side. She looked around, then let out a contented sigh. "It's so nice to get out every once in a while."

"I'm sure. Between your job in the admissions office and all the time you spend studying, I'm surprised you even know what sunlight looks like."

Kacey stuck her lip out into a pout that was way too sexy. "Don't make fun. I happen to enjoy both of those things."

"Didn't you say all you do in the admissions office is file things away and clean?"

"Yeah, but most days people bring donuts." Kacey's smile took on a childlike appearance, which made butterflies take flight in my stomach. I was learning that was one of my favorite smiles of hers, albeit being one of the less frequent ones.

We spent the meal talking about our classes, the tests we had coming up, and fall break.

"When are you heading home for break?" I asked Kacey, feeling sad thinking about spending a few days away from her.

Kacey shook her head and looked down toward the water in front of her, slowly stirring it around with the straw. "I'm not going home."

"No? Why not?"

Kacey shrugged. "It's over three hours from here. It seems like a waste for just a long weekend."

"Your parents aren't upset about you staying?"

Kacey continued to stare at her water, but briefly squeezed her eyes shut as if the question had upset her. "It's just my grandma and sister and they don't really care."

Shit. Kari Adelberg puts her foot in her mouth once again. I instinctively reached out my hand and grabbed Kacey's to comfort her. To my surprise, instead of pulling away, Kacey turned her hand over so her palm could rest against mine. I opened my mouth to say something, but the waiter interrupted me.

"Would you ladies like any dessert tonight?"

Kacey looked from the waiter, then over toward me. "I'm stuffed, but I don't want to miss out on trying one of the delicious milkshakes I've heard so much about. Maybe we could get one to go and split it?"

I nodded. "That sounds great."

"Perfect. I'll get you a milkshake and the check." The waiter's eyes landed on my hand, still resting on top of Kacey's in the middle of the table. "Will you two be paying together or separate tonight?"

"Together," Kacey answered before I had the chance to respond.

When the waiter returned, Kacey quickly reached for the check and dug into her pockets to pull out cash. When I opened my mouth to ask about helping to pay, she stuck up her hand as if she knew what was coming. "Tonight is on me."

I nodded my head, then followed her outside where we passed the milkshake back and forth as we walked back toward campus and into our dorm. I was quiet as I considered what I wanted to say. Whether or not I wanted to ask the question I was dying to know the answer to. When we got to the door to my room, I couldn't take it anymore. "So, was this a date?"

Kacey casually shrugged her shoulders. "It was a nice night out shared between two people who clearly enjoy each other's company. You can call it whatever you'd like."

This girl and her damn aversion to labeling anything. She was making this all so much harder than it had to be. "You see, the problem is… I need to know if this is a date, so I know if it's okay to… Oh, shit. Screw it." I threw my hands in the air, then wrapped them around Kacey's neck to pull her closer to me. Before I could overthink it, I leaned in and brought my lips to hers. I felt Kacey's lips twitch into a smile for a moment, before pushing harder against mine. Our mouths moved in tandem, until mine instinctually opened to hers and she slipped her tongue in, sending sensations through my whole body that I'd never felt before. Kacey slipped her hands around my waist and pulled our bodies even closer together as our tongues continued their dance.

I didn't know if seconds had passed or minutes as the whole world around us seemed to melt away. All I knew was that I was pretty sure Kacey Caldwell was the only person I wanted to kiss for the rest of my life.

When we finally pulled apart, I smiled as I touched my now swollen lips. "Wow. That was… wow."

Kacey smiled and rested her forehead against mine. "Those were my thoughts exactly." She chuckled lightly. "It took you long enough though."

I pulled back so I could look her in the eye. "Me? I was waiting for you to make the first move."

Kacey tilted her head ever-so-slightly. "That's the thing. I did make the first move. Did you forget that I kissed you the night we first met?"

I couldn't help but laugh at this. "You mean the pity kiss on my cheek?"

Kacey's face became serious. "It was far from a pity kiss. I wanted to kiss you from the moment you drunkenly stumbled into my arms, but I was trying to be considerate and wait on you. You told me you never kissed a girl before and I wanted to make sure that the first time you did, it was completely your choice." She shrugged as if what she had just said wasn't the sweetest thing in the world.

My lips curled into a half smile. "So, what you're saying is that we've both been waiting for that for far too long?"

Kacey smirked back at me. "That's exactly what I'm saying."

Feeling emboldened, I reached out and grabbed the drawstrings of her hoodie to pull her in close. "You know what that means, don't you?"

Kacey lifted one eyebrow, the smile never leaving her face. "Tell me."

I moved in even closer, so my mouth was just inches from hers. "It means we have to make up for lost time." And just like that, the second of many kisses with Kacey was underway.

***

I leapt from my spot on the couch, startled by the sound of the doorbell. Groggily, I pulled out my phone to check the time and found that it was already six o'clock. Since my dramatic exit from the barbecue hours earlier, I had immersed myself in a marathon of romantic comedies.

As I made my way to the door, I looked down at my tattered Bellman University sweats. I would've been embarrassed by my appearance if I thought it could be anyone else but Bo ringing my doorbell. I swung the door open, ready to yell at him for what he pulled with Bailey, when I realized he wasn't the one standing there.

32

My eyes first landed on Bailey, then moved up to focus on Kacey. My eyes drifted between her and my outfit, which now seemed like a terrible idea. "Sorry. I wasn't expecting company."

Luckily, Kacey seemed to be just as flustered and embarrassed as me. She cleared her throat a few times as she ran her eyes up and down my outfit. "No, we're sorry. We shouldn't have just stopped by, but Bailey insisted."

I looked back at Bailey, who was now thrusting a five-dollar bill toward me. "You won the bet. A group of kids asked me to play soccer with them. I'm glad you were right, even if it meant giving up my life savings."

I knelt down so I was on her level and pushed the money away. "I couldn't possibly take your life savings. I'm just happy to hear that you made friends."

Bailey looked like she might argue with me until her eyes went wide as she focused on something behind me. "Puppy!" she exclaimed as she pushed past me into the house.

Kacey shook her head and followed closely behind. "Bailey, you can't just walk into someone's house without being invited or asking them first."

Bailey looked up from where she was already seated beside Duke giving him belly rubs. "But Kari is my friend. Bo told me that when you're friends with someone in this neighborhood, you can just walk right in."

Of course he did. "Normally, I wouldn't suggest listening to anything Bo says, but in this case he was right. We are friends. So, my house is your house."

"Mi casa es tu casa," Bailey repeated in Spanish, earning a laugh from both Kacey and me. "What's his name?"

I could feel my face turning red just from the question and cursed myself for thinking this was a good idea for a name. "His name? Umm… it's… his name is… Duke."

Kacey's eyes immediately landed on mine following this confession. "You named your dog Duke?"

I tried to blow off her question as if it was a coincidence that I had given my dog the name she once told me she wanted to name our future son. "It's a good name for a dog."

33

"It's a good name for a person too," she mumbled under her breath, although I couldn't tell if her voice was more of annoyance or pain. Not that it mattered. She had no right to feel either.

I stared at Kacey trying to think of a snarky comment to make in reply. Because that's what I had to do, right? Say something to keep me from looking like the pathetic schmuck who couldn't let go of the past. My thoughts were interrupted by the sound of Bailey's laughter. I looked down to see Duke licking her face while she giggled and rolled around on her back.

"He likes you," I said with a laugh.

"I like him too," Bailey said as she sat up and placed kisses all over his face.

I looked toward Kacey, who also had a slight smile on her face now. I smiled back at her, and for a moment, I was transported back to a time when things were so much easier. Back when I had no question where I belonged and who I belonged with. I hadn't felt like that for years and I wanted to hang onto the moment forever.

Unfortunately, Kacey must not have felt the same way. She removed her eyes from mine, so she could look toward Bailey. "Sorry to break this up, sweetie, but we have to get home so we can get everything ready for your first day of school tomorrow."

Bailey's face dropped into a pout. "Aw, really?" When Kacey nodded in return, Bailey patted Duke on the head, then walked past Kacey out the front door.

Kacey turned to follow, but turned around before she was fully out the door. "I'm sorry for just stopping by. When that girl gets an idea in her head, there's no way to stop her. I promise we'll give you space though. I truly am sorry... for everything." Before I could respond, she turned around and walked away from me once again.

Chapter 3

"Where have you been?"

I had to pull the phone away from my ear as Bo's voice boomed from the other end. "Dude, volume. We've talked about this."

"Oh. Does it sound like I'm shouting? Because I totally am. I haven't seen you since the barbecue. It's been almost two weeks."

"I picked up more clients. I've barely been home," I lied. Barely left the house was more like it.

"Bullshit."

"Excuse me?"

"That's bullshit. I see your car in the driveway all the time. You're hermiting away to hide from Miss Dark and Mysterious from college." I opened my mouth to say something, but Bo started talking before I had the chance. "Don't even try to fight me on that. I'm your best friend. I know you. Have you thought anymore about my suggestion?"

"I'm not having sex with her, Bo."

Bo let out a low growl as if I had somehow hurt him with those words. "Fine. But have you at least tried talking to her?"

"Define *talk*."

"Ask her what happened. Tell her you're pissed off about what she did. Let it all out. I don't know. Do whatever you need to do so you can move on from this and maybe someday we can all be friends."

"You only want to be friends with her because you think she's hot."

"First of all, I don't *think* she's hot. It's a fact that she's hot. But no, that's not why I want to be friends with her. I've talked to her a few times, and she's actually really cool."

"Traitor," I mumbled, starting to become annoyed with Bo's pushiness. He had the habit of getting on my nerves, but it was unlike him to push things this much.

"Whatever. I just think—"

His words were cut off by the sound of my doorbell. For a second, I worried it might be Kacey, but that didn't make sense since she had been respectful of the space she promised to give me. I looked through the peephole to see my sister, Kylie, on the other side.

"Sorry, Bo. I have to go. Kylie's here." I rested the phone between my ear and shoulder as I opened the door for her and mouthed the word sorry.

"Kylie? Maybe I should come over."

"You shouldn't."

"Fine. But at least tell her I said hello."

"I won't."

Bo cackled, clearly entertained by our usual game. "You can't keep us apart forever, you know. Romeo and Juliet found a way and thus so shall I."

I shook my head, but laughed along with him. "Yes, but Juliet didn't have me as a sister, and you're far from being Romeo. Now, please let me go before I have to hang up on you."

"I'll let you go if you promise to come over for dinner tomorrow night."

That was strange. Bo almost never invited me over to his house and he certainly never cooked for me. Most of the time he showed up at my house and insisted that I cook for him. "*You're* inviting *me* over for dinner?"

Bo scoffed. "Yeah. Is that so hard to believe?"

"It is, but I'm ready for you to shut up, so you have a deal. I'll see you then."

I hung up the phone before Bo could say anything else. "Sorry, that was Bo."

Kylie's face lit up at the mention of Bo's name. "Yeah. I figured that out. How is Bo?"

I rolled my eyes at my little sister's blatant crush on my best friend. "Still too old and too douchey for you."

Kylie snarled and stuck her tongue out at me, showing her immaturity. "I'm twenty-six. That's only five

---

36

years younger than you. Plus, girls mature faster than boys."

"And I have no doubt that you are a million times more mature than Bo. Hence, why that is *never* going to happen."

Kylie pushed past me and threw herself onto my couch, sighing dramatically. "You used to be the fun one. What happened to the sister who used to sneak me into college parties when I was only fifteen?"

She had her heart shattered. "She grew up." I pushed Kylie's feet off of my coffee table where she had them resting. "So, what's up with you?"

"You know, just missing my big sis. Also, Mom and Dad are driving me nuts, so I had to get out." She nodded her head toward my front door. "Cute neighbor, by the way."

I felt my face turning red. "You saw my neighbor?"

Kylie looked at me in wonder. "You mean the little girl? Probably nine or ten? Yeah. She was outside playing."

I shook my head. "I don't think she's nine or ten. Probably more like seven or eight if I had to guess."

Kylie laughed out loud. "You always were terrible at determining ages. There's no way that girl is younger than nine."

I shook my head even harder this time. "No. That's not right. She's definitely not nine. I'm positive of that." Even I was surprised by how shaky my voice sounded.

Kylie stopped laughing and tilted her head at me. "Okay. I'm confused. What's going on?"

I let out a long breath and sat down on the couch beside her. "My new neighbor." I had to stop and blink my eyes a few times to stop the tears from falling. My sister was the one person I could never hide my emotions around. "It's Kacey."

"Kacey Caldwell is your new neighbor? Who's the little girl?"

This time, a few tears fell. I wiped my eyes on the sleeve of my sweatshirt before looking back at Kylie. "It's her daughter."

Kylie's eyes went wide and her smile fell completely. "That bitch." She shook her head and stared up toward the ceiling. "You know, I never liked her."

37

"That's a lie. You used to tell me Kacey was the cool older sister you always wanted."

"Yeah, well, I was wrong." Kylie reached out and placed her hand on top of mine. "I hope you know that was a joke. I always thought you were a cool older sister. Granted, you were a little cooler before that bitch broke your heart, but I guess you're still alright." She flashed me a wide grin to show it was all in good fun, then a silence fell over us.

"So, have you talked to her?" Kylie asked.

I groaned. "Now you sound like Bo."

Kylie smiled mischievously and wiggled her eyebrows. "That's because we're soul mates."

"Ew. Stop. That will never be a thing, so you need to get that idea out of your head. We've talked sparingly. We've avoided the topic of the past for the most part, but she apologized for breaking up with me over a text message."

"Did she also apologize for never talking to you again after sending that text? God, I feel like she owes *me* an apology too. I'm the one who had to talk you down every time she ignored another text or call from you. I'm the one who finally had to figure out how to block her number from your phone so you stopped trying to reach her."

I rolled my eyes. If this was my sister's way of trying to make me feel better, she was failing miserably. "I get it. I was awful to deal with after that breakup."

She waved a hand at me. "Nah. I'm just giving you a hard time. It was understandable. You and Kacey had plans. You had your future all figured out. Then she suddenly changed the game with no explanation. That would mess anyone up. You've had some great girlfriends since her though and I feel like you haven't really given them a chance because you're still holding on to what you *thought* your life would be like. So, talk to her, please. That way you can finally move on."

I wanted to argue that I had moved on, but we both knew that was a lie. Instead, I leaned further into the couch and closed my eyes. "I'll talk to her. I promise. I just need time."

***

As soon as I walked into Bo's house and smelled an actual home cooked meal, I knew something was up. Even Duke seemed to stick his nose up in surprise at the smell he wasn't used to inside this house.

"Okay. Who did you kill?" I asked as I entered Bo's kitchen, where he was stirring pots of spaghetti and meat sauce.

"What do you mean?" Bo asked in a singsong voice.

"I mean you never cook so clearly you killed someone and are buttering me up so I'll help you move the body."

Bo leaned in and placed a kiss on my cheek. "Oh come on. I'd sure hope I wouldn't have to butter you up to get you to move a body with me. That's a rule in the best friend handbook. Why do you think I'm up to something? Can't a guy just cook his friend a meal without having some ulterior motive?"

"Not when that guy is you," I said with a laugh. "So, what did you do?"

Like clockwork, there was a knock at his door that very moment. *But who would he possibly have invited…?* If looks could kill, I'm pretty sure Bo would have been dead as my eyes shot toward his, silently begging that I was wrong about who was knocking. "Who's at the door, Bo?"

Bo ducked his head, then slipped past me. "You know, someday you'll find this all really funny."

"Bo…"

He stuck both hands in the air as he headed toward the front door. "I swear this is for your own good."

I stood frozen in place as he opened the door and motioned for Bailey and Kacey to come inside. As soon as Kacey saw me, I knew she was as much in the dark about all of this as I had been. Her eyes went wide and she opened and closed her mouth a few times as though she wasn't sure what to say.

"The more the merrier, right?" Bo asked, giggling awkwardly into the silence.

To my surprise, Bailey ran over to me and wrapped me in a tight hug. "Definitely. I'm so excited you're here, Miss Adelberg."

I had to laugh at her innocence. Leave it to a child to totally miss the tension in a room. "Hey, kiddo. I'm excited you're here too. But I thought we were friends. All of my friends call me Kari."

"My mom says I should never call grown-ups by their first name."

I bent down so I was on her level. "Can I tell you a secret?"

Bailey nodded her head, then looked around as if she was checking to make sure no one else could hear us.

I put my mouth close to her ear so I could whisper. "I don't see any adults here." I then looked toward Bo and spoke louder so he could hear. "Especially not Bo. I think you know more words than him."

Bailey put her hand over her mouth, trying to hide her laughter, then looked toward Bo. "It's okay, Mr. Bo. You're very gregarious."

Bo put his hands on his hips and his nose up in the air. "Did you hear that, Kari? I'm gregarious. I'm pretty sure that means I'm stunningly handsome."

I grabbed Duke's toy that he had left on the kitchen floor and threw it at Bo. "I'm pretty sure it doesn't, which only further proves my point."

Bo took the toy that had just bounced off of his shoulder and tossed it across the room at Duke, who just watched it fall to the ground as he lazily licked at his foot. "Whatever. Shall we eat, ladies? I made chicken parmigiana because a little birdy told me that is Bailey's favorite."

"It is!" Bailey answered excitedly.

As Bailey skipped to the table, Kacey placed a hand on Bo's shoulder and gave it a squeeze. "Thanks for doing that. It was really sweet."

I couldn't take my eyes off of her hand that seemed to rest there just a little too long for my liking. I hated the pang of jealousy it sent through my whole body. There was no reason to be jealous of Kacey and Bo. I might not have any idea what type of person Kacey would go for nowadays, but I knew that Bo would never cross that line with my ex-girlfriend. So, why was I even jealous? Except, I knew exactly why I was jealous. It was because, whether or not I wanted to admit it, I had spent the past ten years missing that very touch that Bo was now experiencing.

As if reading my mind, Bo slipped away and headed toward the kitchen. "Let's do this."

Once we were all seated at the table, the awkward silence took back over. "So, Kacey, what do you do for a living?" Bo asked, trying to fill the void.

Kacey looked at me briefly before looking over at Bo. "I work for Bellman Interface. It's an IT services firm that provides IT services to small and mid-sized businesses in this area and some surrounding towns. I'm one of the IT consultants."

When Bo just stared at her dumbfounded, she shrugged. "Pretty much I'm a nerd who's good with computers." She laughed at herself, and I couldn't stop myself from staring. The way her eyes crinkled and her lips turned up slightly, immediately took me back to college and all the nights spent snuggled up in bed laughing together. Just one laugh was already chipping away at years of pent up anger. God, I was pathetic.

"So, what about you two?" Kacey directed her question to both Bo and I, but never took her eyes off of me.

Oblivious to this, Bo began talking with a mouth full of food. "I'm an academic advisor to student athletes at Bellman."

Kacey still hadn't taken her eyes off of me and it was making me feel like I wanted to crawl out of my own skin. It was so unfair for her to look at me like that. "That's awesome, Bo. I'm sure that's a very rewarding job." Kacey's eyes studied mine even more closely now. "And... umm... what about you, Kari?"

I looked down at the table, her stare too much for me to take. "I'm a BCBA," I answered softly, hoping no one noticed the way my voice cracked because of the sudden attention I was receiving.

Apparently Bailey didn't. "What's a BCBA?" she asked, her voice sounding both confused and excited.

Before I could respond, Kacey answered for me. "It's a Board Certified Behavior Analyst, sweetheart."

I looked up so my eyes met Kacey's, a bolt of electricity shooting through me as soon as we connected. "You remembered." My voice was barely above a whisper, and now my eyes were studying hers the same way she had been studying mine.

A look of absolute sincerity took over her face. "Of course I remember." I thought the room might go up in flames from the heated stare passing between us across the table, but just like that Kacey looked away, suddenly interested in the food on her plate. She made a sound that seemed to be somewhat between a cough and a laugh. "I mean, you talked about it all the time in college. How could I forget? It's cool that you did it though. Does that mean you got your master's degree? Where are you working?"

Kacey was rambling now, something she rarely did. She only rambled when she got really nervous, which hardly ever happened, or at least it didn't when I knew her ten years ago. I tried not to think about what that meant and focused on her questions instead.

"Yeah. I started the master's program a year after I graduated. I work as an independent contractor for a behavioral health company. I mostly work with kids on the autism spectrum."

Bo pointed his fork, that still had spaghetti hanging from it, toward me. "She's pretty badass." He then looked toward Bailey and dropped his fork. "Shit. Sorry, kid."

Bailey giggled at his double slip-up. "Don't worry about it, Mr. Bo. I'm in fourth grade. I've heard all of the swear words by now."

I quickly tried to do the math in my head. *Fourth grade? How old is someone in fourth grade?* I thought hard, but it just didn't seem to add up. "Fourth grade, huh?" I asked. "Aren't you pretty young for fourth grade?"

Bailey nodded her head excitedly as if it was a point of pride for her. "I am. I don't turn ten until June eighteenth. All of my friends in my class turn ten during the school year. My friend, Sally, is already ten. I still got the highest grade on the last spelling test though."

I felt like the whole room was spinning as the reality crashed into me. I stood from the table, but had to rest my hand on it to stabilize myself. "Sorry. I have to use the restroom." I wasn't even sure if I'd spoken these words out loud, but I wasted no time heading up the stairs to Bo's master bathroom, needing to get as far away as possible.

Once inside, I shut the door and took a few deep breaths. June eighteenth. I would never forget that date. Specifically, the June eighteenth just over nine years ago. The day my entire world shattered once and for all. The day that after months of wondering what was going on, I was left with even more questions in the form of a simple 'We need to break up' text.

With shaky hands, I scrolled through the calendar in my phone over and over again, hoping I was figuring this all out wrong. Wishing and praying that somehow this wasn't what it looked like.

My thoughts were interrupted by the sound of a soft knock on the bathroom door. "Kari?" Kacey's voice echoed across the room and made me feel sick to my stomach. "Could you please open up? I need to talk to you. I need to explain some things."

No. This wasn't happening. Not right here in Bo's bathroom with my best friend and Kacey's daughter downstairs. I leaned my head against the door, wanting to feel closer and further from her all at once. "We can't have this talk right now."

"Please," Kacey begged, so much desperation in her voice that every ounce of me was aching to cave. "Bo and Bailey took Duke for a walk. It's just the two of us."

I reluctantly opened the door, surprised to find Kacey so close that she came stumbling into the bathroom. This time, it was her who stumbled into my arms. The same way I had stumbled into hers that night we first met. I shook these thoughts from my head and removed my hands from her arms, crossing them in front of my chest and staring daggers into her eyes.

"Listen. I can explain. It's not what it seems." Kacey tried to reach toward me, but I moved my arm away before she could and shook my head. I didn't want to hear her explanation. I didn't want to hear how this was somehow my fault. How she felt trapped or claustrophobic and made a mistake because of her fear. No. That wasn't going to work for me. I couldn't stand here and listen to that. I wouldn't.

43

"It's not what it seems, Kacey?" I snarled, finally bringing all of my anger from the past ten years up to the surface. "Because it *seems* like you cheated on me. *You* had sex with a guy while we were dating. Hell, while we were planning our future together, you screwed some guy and got yourself knocked up. And instead of being honest with me, you ran away like a coward. You ran away, but continued to lead me on for months. Continued to make me believe that we had a future. And for what? To dump me in a text message the day your daughter was born. Let me tell you. That's rich."

Kacey tried to say something, but I shook my head as the tears ran down my cheeks. "No. I have no interest in hearing anything you have to say." I laughed sardonically through my tears. "You know what? This is actually a good thing. As much as I hate to admit it, I couldn't move on from you, Kacey. Having you back here only proved just how much I hadn't moved on over the past ten years. That's not a problem anymore though. I have nothing to hold on to. Our relationship clearly meant nothing to you, and now, you mean nothing to me. So, thank you. You may be the world's biggest asshole, but at least now I know that and can move on."

Kacey's eyes dropped to the floor, and she no longer looked like she had anything to say. She stared at the floor in silence for what felt like hours, never budging the way I wished she would. When she finally looked back up at me, her eyes were filled with tears and her face was pale. "I'm just happy you can move on now. You always deserved better than me. I hope now you can find that."

Without another word, she turned on her heels and walked out of the bathroom. I listened as she made her way down the stairs and out the front door. Not even a minute later, the door opened back up.

"Kari?" Bo called out hesitantly.

I rushed down the stairs, still fuming from what had just happened. When Bo saw me, he put both hands in the air, his face just as pale as Kacey's had been. "Listen, I had no idea. If I had any clue that was going to happen, I never would have -"

"Just stop," I interrupted. "I have no interest in anything you have to say to me right now. For once, just mind your own goddamn business and stay out of mine." I shoved past him and ran out the front door.

I should have felt bad for how I was treating him, but right now I only had one thing in my mind. The date June eighteenth and the events of that day and the days that followed, kept playing on repeat inside my head.

***

"We should go on a trip to celebrate you graduating and me starting my senior year." Kylie stared at me as I stared down at my phone.

This was what my life had become since Kacey dropped out of school and moved back home. Watching my phone and waiting for the call or text that didn't even come some days. When we did talk, it felt strained most of the time. I knew there was so much she wasn't sharing with me, and all the secrets were driving a wedge between us.

"Earth to Kari," my sister's voice interrupted. "I was saying we should take a trip together. Maybe a long weekend at the beach?"

When I reluctantly looked up from my phone, Kylie looked between the silent object and me. "You can ask Kacey to come if you want. Maybe it would be good for you guys to get away for a bit. If Kacey wants to come, I'll ask Jeremy to come along. I know things are pretty new between us, but I'm sure he'd love to come."

*Before I could answer, the sound of a text message coming through stole my attention. I smiled in spite of myself as Kacey's name popped up on the screen. My smile, and my phone, fell when I read her text. **We need to break up.** That was it. No explanation, no apologies. Just those five words.*

"Kari? What's going on?" Kylie's voice sounded so distant as I sat there frozen, unable to move or speak.

"I…" I shook my head, unable to say the words.

Kylie picked my phone up off the floor and read the text. "This has to be a joke, right?"

I shook my head again as my whole body started to shake. "I don't think it is."

Within seconds, Kylie was by my side with her arms wrapped tightly around me. "What can I do?"

My breaths came out ragged as I tried to swallow my tears. "I don't know. I think… I need… I need to call her."

I quickly stood from the couch and clicked on Kacey's name as I walked out of the room. The phone rang only a few times before sending me to voicemail. Thinking this must have been some kind of mistake, I hung up and called right back. This time, it rang even fewer times. I thought about leaving a voicemail but hung up when I heard a text come through. **It's for the best if we just cut this off completely. I'm sorry.**

I walked back into the room my sister was in, unsure what to say. How could I explain what had just happened? What I felt right now?

"How did it go?" my sister asked.

Only I couldn't answer. Tears streamed down my face as I continued to shake my head back and forth, unsure what else I could do. Before I knew it, my sister was standing right beside me and I fell into her arms and wept.

Chapter 4

I groaned when I heard my doorbell ring, assuming I didn't want to talk to whoever was on the other side of the door. A week had passed since dinner at Bo's and I had successfully avoided everyone in that time. Even all of the apologetic calls and texts from Bo weren't enough to get me to respond to him.

"Who is it?" I yelled through the door.

"It's me," Bo's voice answered. When I didn't immediately answer, he continued to yell from the other side. "Listen. I know you don't want to talk to me. It's pretty obvious since you've been ignoring me all week. But we need to talk, and I'll use my key if I have to."

I reluctantly opened the door and let him in. As soon as he was inside, I noticed how tired he looked. His hair was sticking out in every direction and his eyes had rings around them. I immediately wished that it wasn't because of me.

"Are you okay?" I asked.

Bo placed both hands in his pockets and rocked on his heels. "Well, my best friend won't talk to me because of a really stupid mistake I made, so I guess you could say I've been better."

"That's really why you look like you haven't slept in days?"

Bo looked at me, his expression more sincere than I had ever seen it in the past. "I look like I haven't slept in days because I really haven't. And, yes, it's because of you. I might act like an immature asshole about ninety-five percent of the time, but I really do have a heart."

I reached out and grabbed his hand, hating to see him look so fragile. "I know you have a heart, Bo. Why do you think I'm friends with you?"

A small smile finally came onto Bo's face. "I always thought it was because of the fact that I'm devilishly handsome."

47

I laughed, starting to feel good for the first time in days. "Well, that is a big part of it, but I also think you're pretty cool." My face became serious as I squeezed his hand again. "I'm the one who should apologize, though. I haven't been fair to you. I'm not too happy that you tricked me into that dinner, but I have to admit that it actually was going well before the bomb dropped. And it's not your fault that happened. You had no way of knowing that she cheated on me or that I would find that out during dinner."

Bo blew out a breath. "Yeah. I definitely didn't see that coming. I knew things ended badly between you two, but I didn't know it was that bad."

"You and me both. I was shocked when Kacey dumped me and even more shocked at how she completely cut me off after that. But never in my wildest dreams did it cross my mind that there was someone else involved. Never in a million years did I think she would be the type of person to cheat."

Bo shook his head and moved past me to sit down at my kitchen table. "I just don't get it. I don't know why she would go to some guy when she had a hottie like you. Don't get me wrong, I love what God blessed me with in my nether regions, and I do a good job with it—"

I put up my hand. "Please don't say *nether regions* ever again."

"Please don't interrupt me when I'm making a point. As I was saying, I'm very *well-endowed* and I think I do a pretty good job of pleasing the ladies, but I'm man enough to admit that I don't see why anyone would choose to have sex with guys over girls. There's no way it's better. No way."

I had to laugh at his thought process. Although, I wasn't surprised that's where his mind went. "I appreciate you saying that. You're absolutely right, by the way, and I'm happy you're able to admit that. But maybe it wasn't about the sex." I became more somber as I thought about it. "Maybe... Maybe it was love. Maybe she didn't love me anymore. Maybe she fell out of love with me when she fell in love with him. I have no idea." This thought brought tears to my eyes and I tried, and failed, to blink them away. I was so sick of crying. I had cried way too much this week.

Bo's face was serious as he shook his head. "I don't believe that. I've seen the way she looks at you even after all these years. I have a lot of trouble believing it was about more than just sex."

"Stop. Don't say that. I hate when people pull the whole *'I see the way she looks at you'* thing. It's so cliché. Such a Hollywood fabrication. Looks can be deceiving. Especially with Kacey. Don't let those big, dark eyes fool you. If she cared about me, she never would have done that." I couldn't let myself believe that Kacey had feelings when she really didn't. I finally felt like I could move on and believing a lie that she never stopped loving me would make that impossible.

"Either way, I think she's a bitch for doing that to you. No amount of hotness makes that okay. You know my alliances are with you. They always will be, and I'm sorry if I made you feel differently. I don't need more friends anyway."

"You don't have to cut her off just because of me. We're adults. Not teenagers. I think we're all mature enough to realize that we don't have to like all the same people." Even as I said the words, they felt like a lie. I *wanted* to be that mature. I knew I *should* be, but part of me was happy to hear Bo say those things.

"I'm just glad you're talking to me again. The only person I had to talk to was Derek, and God, he's annoying sometimes."

"Now you know how I feel," I joked.

"Speaking of Derek. We're hitting the town together tonight. He's coming over to my place soon and we're going to pre-game then go out and try to get ourselves some ladies. What do you say? Want to join us?"

I scrunched up my nose in disgust. "I don't think there's anything in this world that I want to do less than that. You know how I feel about Derek."

Bo groaned. "Yeah, yeah. I know. But he's funny and not so bad to deal with after you've been drinking. You said that yourself."

"I said that after you made me take way too many tequila shots and about an hour before I started throwing up

---

49

all over your floor. There is a reason I don't really drink anymore."

"Hmm. I thought it was because you're old and boring now."

I reached across the table and slapped his shoulder. "Whatever, dude. Some of us have just come to terms with the fact that we're not twenty-one anymore."

"Whatever, to you too. At least come over and do one shot with me before I get ready."

"Do I really have to walk all the way to your place to do a shot? I've been very content with barely going outside all week. Can't we do one here?"

Bo smiled knowingly. "Oh, yeah, sure. Do you have any alcohol here?"

"No," I mumbled, hanging my head in shame. I really was old and boring. I stood from the table, knowing that I owed Bo this one after how I treated him this past week.

A few minutes later, we were inside Bo's house with a shot glass sitting in front of each of us. I took a large sniff and had to keep myself from gagging just from the smell. "All right, let's just do this."

"Don't be so hasty. I need to toast first." He held his glass high in the air and cleared his throat. "Here's to you, and here's to me, and here's to all the girls that lick us where we—"

His words were cut off by the sound of the doorbell. Bo put down his glass and looked at his watch. "That's weird. Derek isn't supposed to be here for another half hour. He's never early." He lifted a finger. "Give me one second, and don't you dare think this gets you out of anything."

I stood in the kitchen just out of view of the front door and waited for Bo to open it, expecting to hear Derek's loud and obnoxious voice echoing throughout the house. To my surprise, it wasn't his voice. It was one that I dreaded even more.

"Hey, Bo. I'm really sorry to bother you. I have a feeling I'm the last person you want to see right now, and I don't blame you. I'm kind of in a bind though. One of the bigger businesses my company works with had a huge crash in their main computer system, and we kind of need all hands on deck right now. I wanted to see if you happened to be free to watch Bailey. I can pay you. I wouldn't expect you to do it for nothing."

"I actually have plans tonight. I'm sorry." Bo's voice sounded both apologetic and hesitant. I could tell he was hoping not to anger any of the women in his house.

I went to sit my shot glass down on the table, but my hands were shaky just from hearing Kacey's voice, and I ended up dropping it on its side instead. "Shit," I whispered as the glass clanked loudly against the table.

"Oh. I'm sorry," Kacey's voice said from doorway. "I didn't realize you had company."

"No big. It's just… ahh… Kari." Bo's unease was doing nothing to quell the current awkwardness.

"Miss Kari is here?" Bailey asked excitedly.

Before anyone could answer, she was rounding the corner into the kitchen with a wide grin on her face. "Miss Kari! Do you want to watch me tonight? You did say we were friends after all."

God, why did I have to have such a soft spot for kids? I wanted to say no, if for no other reason than to spite Kacey, but I was powerless to the sweet puppy dog eyes Bailey was giving me. "You know what? That sounds great. I would love to hang out with you tonight."

Everyone, aside from Bailey, looked surprised by my words. "Are you sure?" Kacey asked, her face so much more unsure than I had ever seen it in the past. "You really don't have to, Kari. I can tell them I can't come in."

"Of course I'm sure," I said as confidently as possible, hoping Bailey wouldn't realize how much of a lie that was.

Kacey smiled slightly, but also looked like she could cry. "I can't thank you enough for doing this for me, Kari."

Something about the way she said my name reminded me of how it used to sound all those years ago, but now the thought made me feel sick. All those times she whispered my name. All those times she told me she loved me and always would. It was all a lie. One big lie. I could feel my body stiffening. "I'm doing it for Bailey," I said firmly.

The trace of a smile immediately fell from Kacey's face. "Oh. Of course. I know." Kacey's eyes bored into mine and it was too much to handle.

I cleared my throat and looked toward Bailey. "What do you say, kiddo? Should we head over to my place? I was thinking I could make mac and cheese and then we could watch some movies. How does that sound?"

The grin on Bailey's face was wide as she smiled up at me. "That sounds awesome!"

I gave Bo a hug and nodded goodbye to Kacey before leaving the house with Bailey. Once back at my house, I immediately got to work on making macaroni and cheese. As I cooked, Bailey walked around my house, taking in all of my pictures.

After a few minutes, she walked up to me holding a picture of my sister and me standing on the beach, from the trip we took the same summer Kacey dumped me. She tilted her head and pointed to Kylie. "Who is this?"

"That's my sister."

Bailey looked at the picture really closely as if she were studying it, then she looked back at me with confusion written all over her face. "Does my mom know your sister?"

I laid down the spoon that I had been using to stir the macaroni and cheese and turned so I could focus on Bailey, unsure where she was going with this. "Yes. It's been a long time since she's seen any of them, but your mom used to know my whole family. Why do you ask, sweetie?"

"I think my mom has a picture of your sister."

"Excuse me?" I asked, trying to keep my voice from shaking.

"My mom has a picture that looks just like your sister. She doesn't know that I know about it. I think it's a secret. She keeps it in the nightstand right beside her bed. Even at the new house, it's still there. In the picture, she's leaning against a tree. It's kind of funny." Bailey laughed as she talked about it, and it reminded me of another laugh that sounded just like hers. My mind immediately went to the night I heard that laughter because of that exact picture.

"Wait a second. What is this?" Kacey asked as she pulled one of my senior pictures out of my wristlet.

52

I had made the mistake of asking her to grab some cash out of there so we could pay the delivery guy once he got to my dorm room with our pizza, completely forgetting that I still had that picture in there.

Kacey snickered as she stared at it. "What are you doing? Holding up this tree?"

I glared at her as I snatched the picture out of her hands. "You know, for someone so cool, you make really lame jokes. That's something my dad would say."

"I never claimed to be cool." Kacey lifted one eyebrow, then leaned in to kiss me. Since we were already lying on my bed, she easily slipped on top of me to deepen the kiss.

My body hummed at the feeling and I thought about all of the things we had yet to do together. All of the things I was dying to do. It had been a month since our first kiss, and while we made out a lot, it had yet to go beyond that. As Kacey ran her hand down my arm, I thought maybe this would be the moment that changed. When her fingers reached my hand, instead of grabbing onto it, she grabbed onto the picture I was still holding. All too quickly, she jumped off of me.

"Aha!" she said proudly. "This is mine now."

"Not fair," I pouted. "Why would you want that anyway? I look like a dork. My mom made me take that one and then insisted on buying it. I think I was supposed to give that copy to my grandma, and that's why it's in there."

"Well, send your grandma my deepest apologies, because she's not getting this." She looked down at the picture, her smile growing even wider. "And to answer your question—I want this because you look so cute. Also, I don't have any pictures of you, and all of the women who work in the admissions office have been begging to see a picture of my girlfriend."

53

"Girlfriend?" Butterflies fluttered in my stomach. Even though we acted like a couple, we had never explicitly stated that's what we were. I had almost brought it up countless times, but worried about how Kacey would feel about it.

Kacey ran one hand over my cheek. "Yeah. I mean, that's what you are, right?" Kacey's face became serious. "I don't act this way with just anyone, you know. It's hard for me to open up."

It made sense. Kacey was cool with my friends and they all loved her, but I saw a different side to her when we were alone. I leaned into her hand and sighed. "Yes, Kacey. That's exactly what I am."

"Miss Kari?" Bailey's voice pulled me from my daydream.

"Sorry, kiddo. I just let my mind wander for a second there. That picture your mom has is actually of me. I gave it to her a long time ago when we were friends." Why did she still have that picture and why was it right by her bed? It didn't make sense.

"You look a lot like your sister. My mom looks like her sister too. That's why I look so much like her even though she's not actually my biological mom."

My eyes snapped back to Bailey, who was now simply scratching Duke behind his ear, as if she hadn't just dropped a major bomb. "What did you say?"

"Ariana is the one who made me and carried me in her belly, but once I came into the world, she wasn't able to take care of me the way she needed to. So, she gave my mom the best gift ever—me." She laughed. "At least that's what my mom says. She says there's no greater gift in the world than being my mom. I don't know if I agree because the bike I got for Christmas last year was pretty cool."

I had to put my hand onto the counter to steady myself. If the thought of Kacey cheating on me had been a surprise, this new bit of information was an absolute shock. So, she hadn't cheated on me? Why hadn't she just told me that? More importantly, I still had no idea why she dumped me on the day Bailey was born.

"Miss Kari, I think the mac and cheese is done."

I looked down at the pot where the macaroni had started to get a little brown around the edges. I smiled down at Bailey, trying to move the new information I had just learned to the back of my mind. "What do you say we eat this on the couch while we watch a movie?"

Bailey's eyes lit up. "Really? My mom always makes us eat at the table. This is so exciting."

Less than an hour into the movie, Bailey had already finished two bowls of macaroni and cheese and was lying across the couch with her head on my lap. I could tell by her shallow breaths that she had fallen asleep and I took this opportunity to lay my head back against the couch cushion and shut my eyes.

I woke up to the sound of knocking at my door. I slowly opened my eyes and blinked a few times to take in my surroundings. It took a minute to get my bearings and make my way to the door. I wasn't surprised to find Kacey waiting on the other side. What I was surprised by was how my body reacted to the sight of her in khaki pants and a polo shirt with the words *Bellman Interface* written across the left side of the chest. I could see the very bottom of her tattoo sneaking out from underneath her sleeve and it made my mouth go dry. I shook these thoughts from my head and cursed myself for having them. "Sorry. We fell asleep watching a movie, so I'm a little out of it right now."

"No worries. Is Bailey still asleep?"

I turned around to see her still lying peacefully on the couch. Kacey followed the direction of my gaze and laughed. "I swear that girl can sleep through anything." She became serious again when her eyes landed back on mine. "I'm just going to grab her and we'll get out of your hair. Thanks for doing this. I promise it won't become a regular thing. I don't want to bother you."

She looked timid and unsure, which was so unlike her. I knew I should say something about what Bailey told me. The things I said when I thought she cheated on me were terrible, and no matter how much she hurt me, I felt the need to tell her that they weren't true. But there were still so many unanswered questions. Did I really want to dig into the past so much?

As these thoughts swirled in my head, Kacey went and picked Bailey up off the couch, her muscles bulging out of her shirt as she carried the little girl back toward the door. "This was much easier when she was a baby." She laughed slightly, but stopped when she realized that was probably a time she shouldn't bring up. Kacey gave me a slight nod. "Well, thanks again. Umm... take care."

I watched her walk away and questioned what I should do. "Kacey! Wait."

When she turned around to look at me, a sleeping Bailey hanging from her arms, I couldn't find the words I wanted to say. I pointed toward Bailey. "You got a good one there."

A look of sincere gratitude came onto Kacey's face. "Thanks, Kari. That really means a lot coming from you."

***

By the time Monday rolled around, I still hadn't gotten my conversation with Bailey out of my mind. I looked at the clock and saw that it was a quarter past eleven, which seemed like a good time to go knock on Kacey's door. I figured she probably wouldn't be home and I could at least tell myself that I tried.

When I walked outside and saw Kacey's car in the driveway, I hoped it was a fluke. Maybe she was close enough to work to walk. I knew there was no way I could get that lucky though, which was confirmed when I knocked on the door and heard footsteps on the other side.

Kacey opened the door and froze. "Kari. Hey. I wasn't expecting you." She had her hair up in a bun and was wearing pajama pants and an old Bellman University T-shirt that I wished I didn't recognize. She looked down at her outfit, then back at me. "I pretty much had to work all weekend, so I have today off. Clearly, I wasn't expecting company."

"No worries. You know what? I can just go." *This was such a stupid, stupid idea.* I moved to turn around, but Kacey reached out and grabbed my arm, this simple touch causing my skin to feel like it was on fire.

"Do you... want to come in?"

She looked as nervous about her invitation as I felt, easing some of my tension. "No. Actually, yes. I need to talk to you."

Kacey stepped to the side and motioned for me to come in. Having just moved in, her walls were still pretty bare, but she had already added a few personal touches. Pictures of her and Bailey were scattered upon shelves and above the fireplace.

"I'm still working on decorating," Kacey explained when she noticed me taking it all in.

"Don't worry. I've lived here for years and still feel like I'm trying to get the house looking exactly as I want it to." I laughed, but it came out sounding much more strained than I intended it to.

Kacey sighed as she studied my face. "What did you want to talk to me about, Kari?"

I pointed toward her family room. "Could we sit maybe?"

Kacey nodded and motioned for me to walk ahead of her. I sat down on the couch and she chose a seat on the adjacent love seat. I cracked my knuckles as I stared over at her, wondering where to start. My knee started to bounce up and down as my nerves became even worse. I couldn't take the unease I felt building throughout my body, so I stood from the couch and started pacing. "On second thought, I don't think I can sit." Instead of looking at Kacey, I stared at my feet as they moved across the carpet. "Bailey told me."

"Bailey told you what?" Kacey asked hesitantly.

I stopped my movements and finally looked up at Kacey, trying to ignore the way eye contact from her made me feel. "She told me you're not really her mom."

"Wait, she said that?" Kacey's voice dropped to barely a whisper as if the words had hurt her.

"I think I may have worded that wrong. I'm sorry. She never told me you weren't her mom. She just told me that it was your sister who was pregnant, not you. So, pretty much, I feel like a jackass for some of the things I said to you." I shook my head, feeling frustrated about all of the questions I

57

had. "Except, I also don't. I have so many questions. I tried to ignore them all and move on, but I can't. For once, I just want you to be honest with me about what happened." I could feel my blood boil the more I spoke, and it was showing in the rising of my voice.

"Maybe… you should sit," Kacey said softly. "This might take awhile."

I reluctantly sat down on the couch and stared over at her, motioning for her to continue.

Kacey took a deep breath and blew it out. "So, while we were dating, I never told you a ton about my family. It's because I was embarrassed. Your family is great. Your parents were always loving and supportive. Your sister was hilarious. I wanted to keep the life I knew growing up completely separate from the life I had at college. It was supposed to be a clean slate for me, a fresh start. You didn't see me as the girl with a deadbeat alcoholic mother or an out of control sister."

My eyes went wide. "I didn't know any of that."

"Of course you didn't. That's how I wanted it to be." A few tears came to Kacey's eyes and she quickly wiped them away, always having to be the tough one. "I wasn't happy growing up. My dad was never in the picture. My mom was in and out of my life until I was about ten and then she left for good. My grandma provided us with the essentials, but she wasn't the nurturing type by any means so I pretty much had to raise my sister. Instead of being thankful for everything I did, she resented me. She rebelled against everything I said to the point that I just couldn't take it anymore. I got a scholarship to Bellman and never looked back. I just wanted to leave that part of my life behind me."

"But you didn't leave it behind…"

Kacey shook her head, almost looking ashamed. "When my grandma called me during our senior year to tell me that my seventeen-year-old sister was pregnant, I wanted to tell her to deal with it and slam the phone. But something stopped me. Something told me I had to go home and help."

I put my head in my hands. I wanted to scream at Kacey and hug her at the same time. "So, you left…" I prompted.

Kacey stood and walked over to the couch, sitting down next to me and taking my hand. "You have to know that I never intended to break up with you. I still wanted to be with you. I wanted the life we had planned together."

I pulled my hand away, unable to handle the feelings coursing through me. "So, what changed?"

"It became obvious pretty quickly that my sister wasn't ready to raise a child and frankly had no interest in it. I figured we would put her up for adoption, but the day she was born, that all changed. One look at Bailey and my heart was gone."

"So, you only had space in your heart for one person, and it wasn't me?" I knew that wasn't a fair thing to say, but nothing about this situation was fair.

Kacey reached her hand toward mine again, but pulled it back, running it over her pants instead. "It wasn't like that. I wanted both of you in my life, but I couldn't do that. We were twenty-two, Kari. You were carefree and young and had so much of your life to live."

I stood back up from the couch and threw my hands in the air, angry at Kacey for thinking she had the right to make that decision for me. "Don't you think maybe that was for me to decide? Don't you think that just maybe I deserved the whole story? That I didn't deserve to have my world ripped apart all because *you* decided what I wanted?" At this point I was screaming, but I was too far gone to calm myself down.

Kacey jumped up from the couch, her voice just as loud as mine. "No, Kari. I couldn't give you that choice."

"Why not?"

"Because I knew what decision you would make, okay? I knew you would give up everything to be with me, and I loved you way too much to let you do that."

My head swung back and forth as the tears streamed down my face. "You loved me, Kacey? Really? Because you cut me off and never talked to me again. How is that love? It was like I never even existed to you."

Kacey took a bunch of rapid breaths as the sobs escaped from her throat. "That's not true. It was the hardest thing I ever did. I had to cut you off, so you could move on. I did it for you."

———

I threw both hands in the air, my frustration at an all-time high. "You did it so I could move on? How very noble of you. There's just one problem. You were my first love, Kacey. Every single person I've been with since, I've compared to you. Do you know how hard it is to move on when part of your heart is always with someone else?"

Kacey let out a sardonic laugh. "I do, actually. I know exactly what it's like to have your *whole* heart belong to someone. I was your first love? You were my only love, Kari. I never even tried to be with anyone else because I knew that no one could ever compare to you."

Wait. Was she saying...? My body was thrumming with so many emotions I felt like I might burst. I was confused. I was furious. I was so very turned on. Before I knew what was happening, I lunged my body forward, crashing my lips into Kacey's.

Chapter 5

I wasn't sure how Kacey would take my surprise assault, but she wasted no time wrapping her arms around me and pulling me tightly against her. My lips weren't only on her mouth, but on any part of her body I could reach. I kissed across her chin, licked across her neck, and nipped at her pulse point, doing anything I could to make up for the years I didn't have the chance to taste her.

When I brought my lips back to hers, she was ready for me. Our mouths moved in tandem until I ran my tongue along her bottom lip and she immediately granted me entrance. Just one touch of her tongue had every synapse in my body firing. I had no control of myself anymore and I didn't care.

I pushed her away from me and looked into the eyes that were burning with a desire that could bring me to my knees. "I would ask where your room is, but since the setup is the same, I'll lead the way."

"Kari, are you...?"

Instead of answering, I grabbed Kacey's arm and pulled her up the stairs, stopping once in the middle to push her against the wall to get another taste.

Once we were in her room, I didn't stop to look around. I pushed her onto the bed and crawled right on top of her. Never in my life had I been this ravenous, but I couldn't stop now. I drove my hips into hers as my hands reached for the bottom of her shirt, pulling it off in one swift motion and tossing it onto the floor.

I paused when I noticed the look on Kacey's face. Amidst the desire was also fear. She gulped audibly as she stared up at me. "Kari, I wasn't making things up downstairs, I haven't done this in..."

"Do you want this?" I interrupted, desperate to know if we could continue.

Kacey nodded her head rapidly. "More than anything in the entire world."

I moved my hand down her stomach and slipped my fingers underneath the waistband of her pants. "Good. I'll lead the way. Don't worry."

I ran one finger up her center, happy to see how wet she already was. Given her confession, I figured this wouldn't last very long, but I didn't care. I'd take whatever I could get.

Kacey whimpered as my finger slid away from her center. My hand returned right to the waistband of her pants and I pulled them off her legs as if both of our lives depended on it. At this point, I was almost convinced they did.

I took a moment to sit back and take in Kacey's near-naked body. It was still just as amazing as I remembered. She had the perfect mix of curves and muscles. She was feminine and strong all at once.

I traced my fingers along her tattoo, then bent down to have my tongue follow the same path. This simple touch must have brought something out in her because her hips bucked up against mine, and suddenly the little bit of clothes she was wearing was way too much. I directed her to sit up and wrapped my arms around her back, using one hand to unclip her bra and the other to remove it. I quickly moved my hands back to her underwear, which I didn't hesitate to strip away.

I started to move my hand back to where she needed me. Hell, back to where we both needed me. But Kacey stopped my path. She nodded toward my fully clothed body. "May I?"

"Please," I breathed.

Once given permission, it took her no time to strip off my clothes. Now that we were both naked, I moved my hand between our bodies and moved against her in a way that elicited the sexiest moan I had ever heard. Just the sound of Kacey Caldwell losing control was almost enough to send me over the edge.

Not wanting to waste any time, I pushed two fingers deep inside of her. I moved them in and out as our hips moved together. Kacey squirmed and squealed and desperately moved her hand between us as well, moaning again at the first touch of my wetness.

I bent down and took one of her nipples into my mouth as I continued to drive my fingers in and out of her. Kacey's body was shaking, but she still found a way to get two fingers inside of me as well. There was a bit of fumbling around on her part, but none of that mattered. One touch from Kacey was all it ever took to set my body on fire.

I licked across her chest and sucked her other nipple into my mouth, biting down onto it with a little more force than I originally intended.

Kacey cried out and I thought it might be in pain until she pulled me even tighter against her. Her breathing was ragged and she could barely push out the words she wanted to say. "Kari, I'm going to... I'm going to co—"

Her words were cut short when the orgasm shot through her. Just the sight of her reaching climax was enough to send me over the edge, and the two of us rode out our orgasms together.

Once everything subsided, I rolled off of her. I lay on my back and tried desperately to catch my breath, still not fully comprehending what just happened.

Kacey turned to face me, a slight smile playing on her lips. "Wow, Kari. That was... wow. Ten years and it honestly feels like nothing has changed."

If there were any words that could ruin the current moment, it was those. Reality suddenly came crashing down on me, and I found myself angry that the moment had been ruined so quickly. I shook my head and hopped out of the bed, desperately searching for my clothes which were scattered around the room. "No. Everything has changed."

Sadness took over Kacey's face when she realized we weren't on the same page, and even though I wished it wouldn't, it broke my heart. I put on my clothes, then walked over to the bed, bending down and taking her hand in mine. "Listen, I'm sorry. I know there's a lot we need to talk about, but I just... can't right now. I need to get away. I need to think."

Before Kacey could respond, I turned around and walked out of her room. I practically ran down the stairs and out the front door, afraid that if I slowed down, I would turn

---

63

back around. And I couldn't do that. She was wrong. The feelings might still be there, but nothing was the same. She wasn't the same girl I fell in love with. Hell, did I even really know who that girl was? I wasn't the same either. I was a completely different person than the girl who fell for her, naively believing that life was perfect and love never ends. Not even the way our bodies connected was the same.

***

"When are you heading home for Christmas break?"

Kacey looked up from her books and stared across the table at me as if I had just asked her a crazy question. "Oh. I don't know. I'm not in a hurry."

I was starting to realize Kacey never seemed to be in a hurry to get home to her family. She had skipped Fall break completely and had only been gone for twenty-four hours over Thanksgiving. I wasn't complaining. I enjoyed the fact that I got extra time with her, but I still hated that she didn't feel close enough to her family to want to spend time with them.

"Well, my parents are away this weekend because my sister has a basketball tournament. Would you want to stay at their house with me?" I shrugged, trying to act innocent, even though there was only one thing on my mind. "It beats a dorm room."

"You want to take me home?" Kacey swallowed hard.

"Yeah. I mean, I'm not asking you to meet my parents or anything. I just figured since it's only about twenty minutes from here, it would be a nice little getaway."

"I'm down," Kacey answered cooly.

*

A few days later, once we were all done with finals, we packed up my car and headed to my parents' house. When we pulled into the driveway, Kacey's eyes went wide. "Wow. Nice house."

Her reaction surprised me. The house was average for the area I lived in. Most of my friends lived in ones that were about the same size, if not a little bigger.

Once I'd given her a tour of the house, I started to feel anxious. I hadn't talked to Kacey about what I hoped would happen this weekend, but I didn't think she would have a problem with it. We were freshmen in college. Most of my friends had lost their virginity by now, so I figured the same was true for Kacey. I just hoped it didn't bother her that I really didn't know what I was doing.

"Want to have something to eat and then watch a movie in my room or something?" I asked as calmly as possible.

"Sounds great." Kacey's voice was smooth and her posture relaxed. If she had any idea what I really meant by 'watch a movie' she didn't seem to be worried about it.

After dinner, we put on a romantic comedy and made ourselves comfortable on the bed. Kacey draped one arm around my shoulder and I snuggled my head into her neck and let my arm lay across her stomach. About a half hour into the movie, I moved a hand onto her cheek and brought my lips to hers. It didn't take long for her to switch positions and move her body on top of mine.

I felt like I could barely breathe. This wasn't the first time we'd been in this position, but it somehow felt different tonight. Kacey moved a hand down my arm as she continued to kiss me. To my surprise, after reaching the bottom of my arm, she tentatively moved her hand underneath my shirt. As her hand slowly moved up higher, my breathing picked up. She stopped just below my bra, then pulled back to look at me, almost as if she was asking for permission to keep going. I nodded my head and let out a moan as her fingers snuck underneath my bra and across my breast. Her touch was soft and light, almost hesitant.

She leaned in so her lips were right by my ear. "I love the feeling of your skin underneath my fingers. Do you mind if I...?" Instead of finishing her question, she moved the hand that wasn't touching me to the bottom of my shirt and pulled it up slightly.

I nodded erratically. "Please."

She motioned for me to sit up, then slipped the shirt over my head. She then reached behind me and unclasped my bra. I shook it off of my arms and allowed it to fall to the bed. Kacey sat back and studied my body as if it were a piece of art. I had never felt so exposed, yet so seen all at once. "God, Kari, you're perfect."

I looked toward her shirt and wiggled my eyebrows, trying to act more confident than I felt. Kacey let out a light laugh and nodded her head. "Yes. I would very much like this off."

My hand trembled slightly as I pulled it over her head and I hoped she wouldn't notice. The trembling intensified when I tried to take off her bra and my hands fumbled with the clasp.

Kacey grabbed my arms and pulled my hands away from her bra. She squeezed my hands and gave me a serious look. "We don't have to do anything you don't want to."

I shook my head. "I want to do everything with you, Kacey. I really do. I'm ready. It's just..." I closed my eyes, not wanting to see her reaction to my confession. "I've never had sex before. I'm a... virgin."

To my surprise, Kacey laughed softly, but it was sweet rather than judgmental. "I kind of figured that. You told me on the first night we met that you never kissed a girl. Most people don't have sex without kissing."

I groaned and put my face into my hands, but Kacey pulled them away, forcing me to look at her. "Hey, I've never been with anyone either. If we move forward with this, it'll be my first time too."

"Really?" I couldn't believe Kacey didn't have people falling all over her in high school.

"Yes. I wanted to wait for the right time. And here with you—nothing feels more right than that."

I pulled Kacey back in for a kiss and relished the way our bodies felt pressed up against each other. Her hands moved to my pants at the same time mine moved to hers and I knew it was happening. I was going to have sex with Kacey and just as she had pointed out, nothing had ever felt so right.

*

The sex was far from perfect. There was fumbling around and fingers going places they didn't belong, but we figured it out together. Kacey led the way and made me feel protected the whole time. It might not have been perfect, but it was beautiful and breathtaking and better than anything I could have ever dreamed of. Reaching climax together was just the icing on the cake.

I ran my hand over Kacey's tattoo as we lay naked in bed together, working to come down from the high we were on. "So, can you tell me what this means yet?"

"It's a Celtic symbol—the Dara Knot. It represents strength. I got it to remind myself that my strength comes from within."

"Well, you're the strongest person I know," I said sincerely, and she really was. Every part of Kacey exuded strength, *down to something as simple as the way she carried herself.*

She kissed my forehead and ran a hand through my hair. "Thanks for telling me that. I don't always feel strong."

"You should. Think of all the nights you've had to carry me home after a party." I joked to try to lighten the mood. "Speaking of which, why don't you drink? I don't think you've ever actually told me." I figured now was the time I could ask these questions since we'd just given ourselves to each other so completely.

"Just bad experiences, I guess."

"So, you used to drink?"

"No." Kacey's answer was short and sharp. I wanted to find out more, but could tell she didn't want to talk about it, so I let it drop.

I sighed and laid my head on her chest, snuggling as close as possible. "This is nice."

Kacey hummed contently. "It really is. As much as I loved the sex, lying here with you right now and feeling completely connected, body and soul, is about as good as it gets."

She was right. I couldn't remember a moment in my life that felt so perfect. But I had a feeling the best was yet to come with Kacey.

***

"Kari. Hey."

I jumped at the sound of Kacey's voice as I got out of my car. It had been such a long day of work that I didn't even notice her standing there. "Hey. What are you doing out here?"

Kacey pointed to the trash can in front of her. "Just putting this out. They come way too early for me to do it in the morning."

I nodded my head and looked around, unable to handle the tension in the air between us. "So, where's Bailey?"

"She went to a friend's house after school. I'm going to pick her up in about an hour."

"That's awesome that she's making friends."

Kacey let out a long breath. "Are we really going to do this?"

"Do what?" I knew it was an unfair question. I knew exactly what she was referring to. It just wasn't something I felt like diving into.

"Oh, you know, pretend that we didn't have sex on Monday. Pretend that you haven't been ignoring me the past two days since it happened."

"I haven't been ignor—" Kacey gave me a look that told me there was no reason to lie. "Okay. I have. I'm just not sure what to say. Monday was great. It was wonderful, actually. I don't regret it at all, and I hope you don't either. But I still don't think it should happen again. I think we should just be friends."

"Friends," Kacey repeated softly, cringing as if the word left a bad taste in her mouth.

"Friends," I said once again.

Kacey pointed her thumb toward her house. "Do you think we could talk about this inside?"

I looked to her house and my mind immediately went to what happened the last time I was there. "I don't think that's the best idea."

Kacey crossed her arms in front of her chest. "Why not?"

"I think you know why not."

The air grew thick between us and it took everything in me not to reach out and touch Kacey. Now that I had gotten a taste, I needed more. I was like an addict, ready to fall back into my old habits.

"Friends should be able to be alone together without ripping each other's clothes off, and that's what you want, right? Friendship?"

No. What I actually wanted was to rip her clothes off. But I knew I couldn't go down that road again. It had taken way too long to get a semblance of my life back. "You're right," I conceded. "Take that trash down and then we'll talk."

Kacey nodded her head and quickly pushed the trash can to the edge of the driveway. Once she was back beside me, she motioned for me to go into the house. I stood just inside the door and rocked back and forth on my feet, already feeling more tension than outside.

Kacey chuckled. "Why don't we head to the family room and have a seat? I promise to sit as far away from you as possible."

We took the same seats we had two days earlier, and I had to laugh. "Why do I feel like I'm having a weird case of deja vu?"

Kacey groaned and laid her head back on the couch. "Will this ever stop being weird?"

"That's the goal." I let out a sigh and forced myself to look at Kacey. "Listen, I'm sorry if what happened gave you the wrong idea."

"I'm a big girl. I can handle it," Kacey replied flatly. Her face softened slightly and she sat up. "Could I ask you a question, though?"

"Anything."

"Why?"

"Why what?"

"Why can't we give this a chance and see where it goes?"

I sat forward in my seat and prepared myself to name all the reasons I had come up with in the past few days. "It's been ten years. We don't really even know each other anymore."

"But that's the point. We could get to know each other again."

"And that's what I want. I want us to get to know each other as friends."

To my surprise, Kacey let out a low growl. "Could you stop saying that word?"

70

"It's not just the fact that it's been so long, Kacey. When you broke up with me, you shattered my whole world, and I haven't been the same since."

A look of regret took over Kacey's face, and I wondered if she might cry. "I really never meant to hurt you. I thought between all of your friends and family, you would be okay."

"I believe that. I really do, but it still doesn't change anything. We talked about spending our lives together. I realize a lot of college romances don't last, but I really believed ours would. And then you were gone with no explanation. I'm not sure I can get past that. I don't know if I can see you as anything other than the girl who broke my heart. And even if I get to that point, how could I trust that you wouldn't do it again?"

"I won't," Kacey said quickly.

I shook my head, wishing I could believe that. "You might say that now, but what about when things get hard? How do I know that right when something goes wrong, you're not going to decide you know what's best for me again?"

"It's about trust." As soon as the words left Kacey's lips, she hung her head. "Which is exactly the problem. You don't trust me."

Even after everything that happened between us and our years apart, I still couldn't stand to see her upset. I moved from my spot and took a seat next to her, placing a hand lightly on top of hers. "I want to be in your life, Kacey. I didn't think I did, but I was wrong. Just being around you again makes me feel like a part of me that was missing is back."

Kacey wiped the lone tear running down her cheek and smiled over at me. "I feel that way too."

I squeezed her hand and smiled back at her. "I think we're at a good place. We don't have to pretend that we don't have a past or lie to ourselves or each other about lingering feelings that might still be there. I think if we accept that, developing a friendship shouldn't be a problem at all."

Kacey looked down, where my thumb was now gently caressing the back of her hand. It was so natural to me that I hadn't even noticed I was doing it. I forced myself to stop and slowly pulled my hand away.

"Well, it's time for me to pick up Bailey," Kacey said, jumping from the couch.

I stood, but didn't budge, unsure how I was supposed to act now.

"So, since we're doing this friend thing now, can we hug?" Kacey asked hesitantly.

I swallowed hard but nodded, hoping she couldn't see how nervous I was over something as simple as a hug. I'm not sure who moved in first, but soon Kacey's arms were wrapped around my body and mine around hers. This felt so much different than the sex. It was more intimate. It wasn't rushed or intense. It was simply two bodies melted together. Two bodies that fit perfectly. This spot, right between Kacey's arms, felt like exactly where I was meant to be, which was precisely why I had to force myself to pull away. It wasn't easy, especially since Kacey didn't seem to be showing any signs of letting go. Her arms were holding me so tightly that my head was pressed against her chest, the same way it always did when we hugged back in college. I shook these thoughts from my head and let my arms drop to my side. The loss of contact on my end finally caused Kacey to loosen her grip, and I slipped away.

Kacey looked to the floor as I set my sights on her front door, already planning my escape route. "Well, this was a great talk. Feel free to text me or something if you still have my number. And umm… tell Bailey I said hi."

Kacey stayed still as I turned to walk down the hallway and out the front door. I took a deep breath as soon as I was outside. *Yep, this friendship thing wasn't going to be a problem at all.*

Chapter 6

"You're avoiding me again." Bo didn't wait for an invitation as he slid past me and into my house.

"What? No, I'm not."

Bo walked right into my kitchen and opened up the snack cabinet. He pulled out a bag of chips, tore it open, and grabbed a big handful, shoving it right into his mouth. "Oh yeah? Then why haven't I seen or heard from you all week? You never even told me how babysitting the enemy's daughter went."

I rolled my eyes at his complete lack of manners. "Maybe because you're disgusting and still haven't learned how to chew with your mouth closed."

"Don't change the subject. I know you. The only time you go without talking to me is if you're mad at me or if you realized I was right about something and don't want to admit it." His face lit up as if he'd given himself the answer to his own question. "Oh my God. You totally had hate sex with Kacey, didn't you?"

How the hell did he always do that? "No... I... It wasn't hate sex."

A wide grin took over Bo's face. "But you had sex? Wow. I underestimated you. I didn't actually think you would do it."

I forced myself to stand a little taller, doing whatever I could to keep my pride. "It was a one time thing. We decided to be friends."

Bo looked surprised. "Friends? Really?"

"Yes. Even though I don't like admitting this, I think you were right. I think I just needed to get that out of my system and now I can move on."

"Huh. I was just spewing bullshit as usual, but I'm glad it worked out for you." Bo's eyes went wide as if he had just come up with a great idea. "Some of the teams at Bellman are hosting an activities night for kids from the

73

community next Friday. My student athletes have been begging me to go, but I didn't have any interest I think it could be fun for Bailey though, so the four of us should go."

"You would really give up your Friday night to do that?"

Bo shrugged his shoulders. "Yeah. Why not?"

"Sometimes I think I underestimate you, Bo. No matter how much you try to hide it, deep down you're a big sweetheart."

"That's not the only thing big about me." Bo moved his hips in a humping motion.

"And then you do something like that and completely ruin it."

My phone vibrating in my pocket grabbed my attention. I pulled it out to see a text from an unknown number. *Hey. It's Kacey. I'm not sure if this is still your number, but I wanted to text you so you could have mine. I got a new number a few years ago.*

I tried not to smile as I typed out my reply. *It's me :) I'm surprised you actually still have my number.*

I always had it memorized. It's one of the many things about you I never forgot.

I felt my face flush from Kacey's words. While I contemplated what to say in return, another text came through from her.

Sorry if that was too forward. Still figuring out how this 'friend' thing works.

A slight giggle escaped my lips in response. God, why was a stupid text making me so giddy?

"Is that Kacey?" Bo asked, finally getting my eyes to leave my phone.

"It is, but how did you know?"

"Because you're looking at the phone as if you wish you could somehow rip her clothes off through it."

I felt my face turn even redder at his annoyingly accurate observation. "I told you. I already did that. Now I'm over it."

Bo scoffed. "I'm your best friend. Lying to me is useless, you know."

"Okay, fine. You're right. Sex with Kacey was great, and it brought up a lot of feelings I was trying to deny. But I'll

74

tell you the same thing I told her. After everything that happened between us in the past, I just don't think we could make a future together work. She hurt me too much and I don't think I can ever trust her again."

"Yeah. I can't imagine trusting someone who cheated on me."

His words surprised me. I had totally forgotten that I didn't update him on any of that. "She didn't cheat on me."

"I'm confused. I thought Bailey was born on the day she dumped you. I might not know a ton about kids, but I do know how long it takes to cook a baby."

"Bailey is biologically her niece. Apparently, her sister is a mess so Kacey adopted Bailey pretty much right after she was born."

Bo raised both eyebrows and let out a low whistle. "That's very noble of her."

"It is. But she should've told me."

"Would you have wanted to take on all that responsibility right out of college?"

I groaned. Now, he sounded just like Kacey. "It wasn't something I ever planned on, but for Kacey, I would have definitely done that. She didn't give me a choice though."

Bo nodded his head slowly as if contemplating something. "You know, you probably wouldn't have gotten your master's degree or taken your boards if that were the case."

I crossed my arms in front of my chest. I knew Bo was right, but that didn't mean I wanted to admit it. "You don't know that for sure. I could have figured it out."

"I'm just saying. I really do think Kacey wanted what was best for you, and maybe she was right to let you go."

I tried my best to smile. "Well, none of that matters anymore. We just weren't meant to be anything more than friends."

Bo walked away from me and started searching my kitchen for something. He opened the cabinet that held alcohol if I ever actually had it and let out a frustrated sigh, then settled for water. He lifted his glass in the air and smiled at me. "To friendship."

To friendship, indeed…

***

"This looks so cool." Bailey beamed as we walked into the Bellman gymnasium. There were multiple stands set up. Some were filled with information about a healthy lifestyle or Bellman athletics, but most of them had activities set up.

"Bo! You came!" a voice yelled from across the gym.

I turned to see Joey Hopkins walking toward us. I had spoken to Joey and her wife a few times at get-togethers at Bo's house. They had apparently been at Bellman around the same time as Kacey and me, but we had never crossed paths.

Once she reached us, Bo pulled her into a hug. "Long time, no see. I haven't seen you in the office lately." He pulled back and searched the gym. "Is Faith here tonight?"

"No. She's at home with Naomi." Joey turned toward Kacey and me. "Naomi is our third. She's a month old." She held a hand out toward Kacey. "I'm Joey, by the way. I'm the head track and field coach here at Bellman. My sister-in-law, Susan, is also one of the coaches. You might see her around at some point tonight. She's currently entertaining my children, which is much appreciated."

"Yo, Coach Hopkins, we need you!" one of the student athletes yelled.

She gave us an apologetic look. "Sorry. Duty calls. Will I be seeing all of you at Friendsgiving at Bo's house?"

"All three ladies will most definitely be there," Bo answered before anyone else could.

"Awesome! We'll see you guys then."

"Friendsgiving, huh?" Kacey asked.

Bo gave her his charming boyish grin that no girl could resist. Not even the biggest lesbian. "Oh yeah. You can't miss it. It's the day after Thanksgiving. Everyone brings their leftovers to my house, and we have a big feast. Tons of fun." He moved his gaze down to Bailey. "*And* I put up my Christmas tree that day and we all decorate it together."

Kacey smiled at Bo as she put a hand on Bailey's shoulder. "Sounds wonderful."

Thinking of spending more time with Kacey made me feel excited and nervous all at once. Being around her made me feel lighter somehow, as if the weight of this world wasn't so harsh. Yet, I couldn't help but worry about it all being ripped away from me again. I looked toward Kacey and her eyes were already on me. When she noticed my stare, her lips curved up on just one side and I could tell she knew exactly what I was thinking. Somehow, she always knew. As if sensing what I needed, she reached out and squeezed my hand, quickly dropping it rather than holding on. It didn't matter though. I felt that quick touch not just in my hand but throughout my whole body. As if that wasn't torture enough, Kacey leaned in close to whisper in my ear, her breath causing the hair on my neck to stand up. "If any of this is too much for you, just say the word and I'll back off."

I closed my eyes and inhaled deeply, hoping to regain some control over my body. But her scent lingered between us, making it even harder to breathe. I pushed the air back out of my lungs and forced myself to look down at Bailey. "What do you want to do first?" I asked, hoping no one noticed the slight crack in my voice.

Bailey pointed to a stand a few feet away from us with a sign that said, *Bellman Pigskin Potato Sack Races*. A bunch of burly guys sat behind the table, and I figured they must be football players. We all followed behind Bailey as she skipped toward the stand. Once there, she turned around and placed her hands on her hips. "All right. Who's racing me?"

We all laughed, but it was Kacey who spoke up. "I bet Kari loves a good potato sack race."

I scoffed. "As if. There's no way you're getting me in one of those."

Kacey playfully threw her arm over my shoulder. "Aw come on. Back in the day, you wouldn't have even hesitated to do it."

"Well, I'm not the same girl I was back then." I tried to keep the bite out of my voice, but as soon as the words were out, I could tell it didn't work. I laughed awkwardly. "I mean, I'm not even sure I could fit into that potato sack."

77

"You could try," Bailey said enthusiastically. "Mom always says you never know until you try"

"All right fine," I conceded. "Let's do this."

Kacey used the arm that was still around my neck to pull me closer to her. "All right. That's the girl I know and—" she quickly cut herself off. "I mean... that's my gi— have fun you two."

It would have been fun to watch Kacey cutely fumble over her words if I wasn't so caught up in what she almost said. *Did she really almost say love?* I shook the thought from my head. It was a saying. Bo had said it to me countless times, and I never thought anything of it. The only reason Kacey got weird about it was because of our past, not because she actually meant it.

"You know what? I'll do it, kiddo." Bo's voice interrupted my thoughts. He let his voice drop as he looked between Kacey and me. "These two are going to learn how to act like humans."

I watched as the two of them grabbed potato sacks and had to laugh watching Bo fumble around until he could somewhat shove his body into one. My laughter ceased when my gaze settled on Kacey. "He's right, you know. We're being weird."

Kacey sighed. "I know. I'm trying not to be. It's just hard to keep myself from falling into my old habits."

So, there it was. She was just falling into old habits. Her words didn't actually mean anything. I tried to keep this fact from upsetting me, because it shouldn't, but a heavy feeling settled in my gut. I forced my eyes back to Bailey and Bo. Bailey was laughing as she pulled way ahead of Bo, who still hadn't figured out how to keep his body inside the sack. She crossed the finish line and laughed even harder when Bo fell face first onto the ground. This brought a laugh from both Kacey and me too. He quickly jumped up, clearly hoping the student athletes he worked with didn't notice. He walked up to Bailey, bent down beside her, and pointed to something across the room. The two talked back and forth until Bo put up his hand and Bailey gave him a high five, before skipping back over to us. She put her hands on her hips and tried her best to keep a serious face, the corners of her mouth curving slightly. "We would like to challenge you to a three-legged race."

"Who?" Kacey and I asked in unison.

Bo walked up to us, still breathing heavily from the potato sack race. "You two. It's you guys against the kiddo and me. No backing out. We already decided."

I looked between Bailey and Bo. "Don't you think the height difference will make it a little tough for you guys?"

Bo scoffed. "As if. You're just scared because you know we'll win."

I was about to protest when Kacey spoke up. "Bring it on, you two." She looked at me and nodded her head seriously. "We got this."

Within a few minutes, we were over at the track and field booth where someone used an exercise band to tie my right leg tightly to Kacey's left. The band forced us close, and I hoped we weren't close enough for Kacey to realize how fast my heart was beating from the contact. The feeling of her body close to mine brought me back to just a few weeks ago, her clothed body somehow able to have just as much of an effect on me as her naked body.

Kacey wrapped one arm around my shoulder, pulling me even closer, then leaned in to whisper in my ear. "Are you okay? You seem on edge."

I let out a strained laugh. "Is this not affecting you the same way it's affecting me?"

Kacey rested her forehead against my temple and I could feel her warm breath on my skin, making it even harder to breathe. "What kind of question is that? Of course it is. We're trying not to be weird, remember?"

I forced a smile onto my face and draped an arm around her shoulders. "You're right. No weirdness. Just pure domination."

Kacey laughed, causing her body to rock against mine in the most delightfully torturous way possible. "Still just as competitive, I see."

"It always seems to work out in your favor, though." I smirked at her while I lifted an eyebrow, finally relaxing enough to not stress over the implications of my statement.

—

"All right, racers, are you ready?" one of the athletes asked. All four of us nodded our heads in unison. "On your marks. Get set. Go!"

Kacey and I both started to run, not paying attention to what the other person was doing, and ended up stumbling a little. Kacey tightened the grip on my shoulder to keep me upright. "Maybe we should try to work together."

"You're right. Outside leg first, then inside. Outside. Inside." I repeated my directions as we continued to move in tandem. Once we finally got our rhythm down, I stopped my commands and snuck a peak at our competition. Bo and Bailey were doing surprisingly well for their height difference and were just about even with us. "I think we have some real competition here," I whispered as I nodded my head toward the two of them.

"Does it make me a terrible mom if I really want to beat them?" Kacey asked.

"She's gotta learn to lose sometime. Might as well be now."

A devious grin took over Kacey's face. "I was hoping you'd say that. Let's do it." She picked up her pace, and I did my best to stay in step with her. The faster we went, the harder it became. Our arms moved to each other's waists where we both held on for dear life, laughing as we struggled to stay on our feet.

Right when we were about to reach the finish line, Bo came sprinting past us. Bailey's leg was still attached to his, but he was holding her in the air so he was the only one actually running. "Suckers," he yelled as Bailey stuck her tongue out at us, all the while laughing hysterically.

When we stopped, I rested my head against Kacey's and laughed. "We got played."

Bo put both of his hands in the air. "Hey, they only said that we had to stay tied together. I didn't hear any rules about how many legs actually had to stay on the ground."

"Whatever. We know who the real winners are. At least we know we still make a great team. K Squared forever, right?"

I felt my body stiffen at Kacey's words, and I let my arms drop away from her. Without responding, I bent down and took off the exercise band. K Squared was a dumb nickname I had made up one night in college when I was drunk. Kacey thought it was funny and wrote "P.S. K²forever" on every card she gave me after that. Cards and notes were the one place where Kacey would open up about her feelings for me. During college, they had the ability to make my heart beat faster and slower all at once. Now, thinking about it made me feel sick instead.

Noticing my change in demeanor, Kacey's smile dropped. She reached out and gently grabbed ahold of my arm, speaking low so only I could hear. "Sorry. I shouldn't have said that."

"No problem at all. Totally not going to make things weird tonight." Although, as I wiggled out of her grip and focused all of my attention on Bo and Bailey, I knew that was exactly what I was doing.

***

"You have really pretty eyes. Have I told you that?" I asked as Kacey wrapped a strong arm around my waist and helped me walk down the sidewalk toward her car.

"Only about five times in the past two minutes. Maybe you should tell me some more."

"They're so pretty. And so dark, like you're hiding a bunch of secrets inside of them." I leaned in closer to her and attempted a whisper that came out slightly above my normal speaking volume. "You're also so sexy when you're naked."

Kacey let out a noise that was somewhat between a cough and a laugh, then actually whispered back. "Thanks, babe. I don't think you need to let everyone at the party know that we've had sex, though."

"She already told me about it!" my roommate, who was walking to my car a few steps behind us, yelled.

I ignored her and kept my eyes plastered on Kacey. "But it was amazing. Don't you think it was amazing?" It had been almost a month since our first time, and aside from the

81

multiple times we had done it that weekend, it hadn't happened since because Kacey had gone home for Christmas break. This was her first weekend back, and she had somehow convinced me that we should go out with friends rather than stay in.

"Yes, babe. It was perfect." Kacey opened the passenger door of her car and helped me in, then opened the back door for my roommate. She shut both of our doors before walking over to the driver's side and slipping in.

I reached my hand across the middle console and rested it high up on her thigh. "It was so perfect, wasn't it? We were like one… like..." I paused as I tried to combine our names together, laughing out loud at myself. "Karci. Ha. No. That's stupid. K… K Squared. Yeah. When our bodies connected, we were like K Squared."

Kacey laughed and shook her head as she removed my hand from her thigh and intertwined our fingers together instead. "K Squared? Really, babe?"

I pushed my bottom lip out into a pout. "What? You don't like it?"

"It's… interesting."

My roommate snorted in the backseat. "She's lying to you. That's the lamest thing I've ever heard. I'm sure cool girl Kacey with her cool tat and cool car from the eighties would agree with me if she wasn't trying to get in your pants again."

Kacey laughed as the two of us continued to argue the rest of the way back to our dorm. Once back in the room, I pulled Kacey into my arms and sloppily kissed her. "Will you stay over tonight? I miss you." I looked over to my roommate's side of the room where she was already passed out and snoring in her bed. "She's out. We could totally have sex and she'd never even know it happened."

82

Kacey picked me up and carried me over to my own bed. She carefully laid me down and pulled the comforter over me. "I have a feeling you might not remember that it happened either, so what do you say I just snuggle with you until you fall asleep?"

I nodded my head as I let out a big yawn, then pulled down the covers so she could crawl in. Once she was in the bed, I laid my head on her chest and listened to her heartbeat, saying a prayer that it would somehow always beat for me. "Goodnight. Don't forget. K Squared for..." I drifted off to sleep before I could finish my sentence.

When I woke up the next day, Kacey was no longer in my bed, but there was a note from her on my nightstand. My heart melted as I read the words she had written over and over:

Good morning, beautiful! I hope you're feeling okay this morning. Sorry I didn't stay over. I didn't want your roommate to be sick of me before the semester even starts. I just wanted to let you know how good` it felt to be back in your arms. I can't wait to experience this semester (and hopefully many more) with you.

Kacey
P.S. K Squared Forever <3

***

    I stared down at the flyer on my kitchen table. The Bellman Community Carnival was a week away. It had been years since I went to the carnival—ten to be exact—but I started to re-think sitting it out again as I read the words that seemed to pop off the page at me. After ending the previous night with Kacey on a weird note, I contemplated whether I should ask if she wanted to go to the carnival with me. If I was determined to make this friendship work, I had to try to let go of what happened in the past, and that wouldn't be possible if we didn't spend time together. Avoiding Kacey wasn't an option, so I took out my phone and dialed her number.

Much to my surprise, she picked up after just two rings. "Kari. Hey. I didn't expect to hear from you again so soon."

I cleared my throat, trying to buy myself some time to figure out what I wanted to say. "Um… yeah. I don't know if you saw the flyer that came in the mail, but the Bellman carnival is next week."

"I did. Man, it's been a while since I've gone to that. We didn't miss a year in college."

"Yeah. That's what I'm calling about, actually. I was wondering if you wanted to go with me. I thought it could be fun… for Bailey."

"Oh. Of course. We would both love that."

"Awesome. It's a…" I cut myself off before I made the mistake of saying date. "A thing." I cringed at myself. A thing? Really? What was wrong with me?

To my surprise, Kacey let out a lighthearted laugh. "All right, then. If I don't see you sooner, I'll see you next weekend for our *thing*."

As soon as I hung up, I clicked on Bo's name to send him a text. *Bellman carnival with me, Kacey, and Bailey next weekend?*

Bo's reply came back almost immediately. *Depends. Are you going to make it weird?*

One thing I loved about Bo was his pull-no-punches attitude, even if it resulted in me getting called out. *I'm going to try really hard not to. No guarantees.*

Good enough for me. I'll be there, weirdo.

***

Two hours into the carnival, and it was going surprisingly well. We had played a few games, stuffed our faces with way too much food, and had successfully avoided bringing up the past. The sun was setting and the air was getting cooler, signaling that it was almost time for us to go. That's when my eyes settled on the Ferris wheel. I loved

Ferris wheels from the time I was a little girl, but hadn't been on one in ten years.

"You want to go on the Ferris wheel, don't you?" Kacey asked.

"No, that's okay. It's getting late. We should probably go."

"Kari hates Ferris wheels," Bo said with a laugh. "The few times we've been somewhere with a Ferris wheel, she refused to go on it."

Kacey looked between Bo and me, confusion written all over her face. "What? That's not right. We couldn't leave anywhere with a Ferris wheel until we went on it at least once." As she said the words, a realization seemed to settle over her face, and she gave me a look I couldn't quite read. "We should go on the Ferris wheel. I know you want to."

I tried to blow it off with a laugh. "Really. I'm fine."

"Kacey's right. We should definitely go on the Ferris wheel." Bo snapped his fingers over dramatically as if he just had an epiphany. "On second thought, I promised Bailey we would go get cotton candy, so you two should go."

I laughed awkwardly. "Oh, I don't—"

"Don't be weird, remember?" Bo leaned in close and whispered softly so only I could hear.

I smiled at Kacey. "What do you say? Wanna go on the Ferris wheel with me?"

She nodded in response and we headed toward the Ferris wheel while Bo and Bailey went in the opposite direction to find cotton candy. There was barely a line, so it wasn't long before we were seated across from each other and starting to move. I looked around as our cart climbed higher and higher, keeping my eyes on the setting sun rather than looking at Kacey. When we reached the top, we came to a stop.

"This brings back some good memories, doesn't it?" Kacey asked, breaking the silence between us.

I winced as I thought about the last time we were at this carnival and on this Ferris wheel. The memory wasn't a happy one for me. "I wouldn't exactly call it a good memory. This carnival was one of the last nights we ever spent together. You left less than a week later."

———

85

Kacey's smile dropped. She stared at me and rubbed tho back of her neck as if she was suddenly nervous "Why do you insist on doing that?"

"Doing what?" I asked, even though I had an idea of what she was referring to.

"Why do you have to take every positive thing that happened between us and turn it into a negative? I know I hurt you, but that doesn't mean that the time we had together wasn't amazing."

I put my head into my hands and gently massaged my forehead, wishing I could be doing anything other than having this conversation. When I finally looked up, Kacey was still staring at me expectantly. "Everything is tainted. I'll think of a good time, but my mind automatically goes to the heartbreak that followed. I think part of it was a defense mechanism I developed. It wouldn't hurt so bad being without you if I didn't think about how perfect it was with you."

Kacey reached across the cart and took my hand, the warmth from her touch spreading throughout my body as if she were a blanket covering me on a cold fall night. "I'm here now."

Her words were simple, but I felt my body relax from just that one sentence. She was right. She was here. It might not be in the same capacity she was before, but whose fault was that? The only thing holding Kacey back from me was myself. If I wanted to truly be friends with her, I couldn't keep holding her at arms length, because what was the point? I let my thoughts drift back to the last time we were in this exact spot together, and for the first time in a long time, smiled as the memories washed over me.

Chapter 7

Kacey looked down from where we sat at the highest point on the Ferris wheel. "What do you think is going on down there? I feel like we've been stuck up here for a while."

I stared down at the two men who were pointing at different parts of the Ferris wheel, then scratching at their heads as if they were confused. A woman walked over from another part of the fairgrounds and handed the one man something I couldn't quite see. When he held it up in front of his mouth, I realized it was a megaphone.

"Hey, folks. We seem to be having some technical difficulties. If you'll just be patient with us, we'll get you moving again shortly."

Kacey laughed. "Of course. This is what we get for going on a ride at a carnival."

"Hey, this is our fourth year riding the Ferris wheel and the first time anything went wrong. Three out of four ain't bad. Just ask Meatloaf."

Kacey laughed even harder now. "That's two out of three, babe, but good try."

I crossed my arms in front of me in mock anger. "Whatever. I can't think straight. I'm too cold."

Kacey opened up her backpack sitting next to her and pulled out a blanket. A proud smile played on her lips as she handed it over to me. "I knew you would get cold eventually. I told you that you didn't wear enough layers."

I looked down at the T-shirt and thin leather jacket I was wearing with a ripped pair of jeans. "I was trying to look cute for you."

"Yes. And you achieved it. Your purple lips are very cute." Kacey ran her thumb across my bottom lip, causing a shiver that had nothing to do with the cold.

I pulled her closer to me and put the blanket over both of us. "We're old and boring now, aren't we?"

Kacey scoffed. "We're not even twenty-two yet, and I would hardly call us boring."

"I'm just saying. We're not nearly as adventurous as we used to be." I ran my hand up Kacey's thigh as I said the words, causing her to sit up straighter.

"What do you mean by adventurous exactly?"

I moved my hand to the button of her jeans. "Wanna find out?"

Kacey took a deep breath and I could feel her heartbeat pick up beside me. "You know they could get us moving at any point, right?"

I smirked and undid the button. "That's the fun part."

"You're thinking about our last time on this Ferris wheel, aren't you?" Kacey asked, interrupting my thoughts.

I couldn't help the smile that bloomed across my face. "I think we were stuck for close to an hour, and we were the only two people who weren't pissed about it."

Kacey's face lit up as she started to laugh. "Yep. When we got off, the one worker was shocked that we were still smiling and asked what our secret was and you said—"

"What happens on the Ferris wheel stays on the Ferris wheel," we both said in unison as we broke into a fit of laughter.

Kacey shook her head playfully. "You were always such a dork."

I put a hand over my chest. "Me? I was the fun one. You were the one who always had her nose in a book."

"Fine. Whatever. You were crazy."

I lifted an eyebrow as a smirk came to my face. "You certainly didn't seem to mind my craziness that night, did you?"

Kacey's face turned the slightest bit red and I could tell she was thinking about the very same moment I was. I could still picture it perfectly. The way she bit her lip and stared up at the night sky as her body squirmed underneath my touch. She looked absolutely breathtaking in that moment. I remember thinking about how I loved her more and more with each passing day and wondering if my heart would burst eventually as we spent forever together.

Even though I tried to ignore it, the thought caused my heart to ache. I didn't want to ruin the lightheartedness of the moment, but a question started burning in the back of my mind. "Did you know? That night at the carnival. Did you know you were going to be leaving?"

A somber appearance overtook Kacey's face as she shook her head. "My grandma called me that night after we got back. You were already asleep. I knew something was up when she called that late, but I honestly thought one of them had run into money issues and wanted me to use the little that I had to help them out. Then she told me my sister was pregnant, and it all happened so fast after that. I didn't even really give myself time to think about the implications of everything. Less than a week later, I was back in my hometown living the life I had tried so desperately to escape from."

"Can I ask you something?" I asked quietly.

"You can ask me anything, Kari."

"Why did you do it? Why did you give up everything to help your grandma and sister? You never told me much, but from what I knew then combined with what I know now, it doesn't seem like you were very close with either of them. So, why drop everything to help?"

Kacey shrugged. "I honestly don't know. When I talked to my grandma that night, I actually went off on her for even calling and asking me for help. I told her I didn't owe them anything, and I meant it. They only ever came to me when they needed things. Never once did anyone ask what I needed. I told her never to call me again and had every intention of just cutting them out of my life completely. Then that night, I couldn't sleep at all because something was telling me I needed to go. I didn't understand it, but I knew there was a reason I needed to be there."

"Bailey," I said breathlessly.

"Bailey," Kacey repeated with a slight smile. "I have a lot of regrets, but I'll never regret going home. Bailey loves me in the way I always wished a family member would. You know how there are those people who make you feel at home whenever you're around them, no matter where you are or what's going on? Bailey makes me feel that way, and there's only one other person who has ever done that. I can't regret anything that brought me her."

It was heartbreaking to hear Kacey talk about her past. What was even more heartbreaking was the fact that I never fully understood the extent of it when we were together. I was young and naive and lived with my head in the clouds, completely oblivious to the world around me.

I wiped away the tears that had run down my cheeks and Kacey did the same to her own. To my surprise, she started to chuckle through her tears. "God, we're a mess. Can't say this is exactly how I wanted this ride to go."

Ready to lighten the mood, I tilted my head and kicked my foot against hers. "I hope you weren't expecting the same treatment as last time. I *am* an adult now."

I could see Kacey's whole body relax in response to my joke, and the sight brought a smile to my face. She shook her head and kicked back at my foot. "Trust me, I don't think anyone expects to get fingered on a Ferris wheel."

I felt a slight blush creeping up my neck in response to Kacey's bluntness, which I had to assume matched the tinge of red dotting her cheeks. "It was pretty crazy, wasn't it?" I said with a laugh.

"So very you, though. You always kept me on my toes." Kacey grew the slightest bit more serious, but one side of her lips remained curved into a half-smile. "That was one of the best nights of my life."

"Glad to see all it takes is a little hand action under a blanket to make you so happy."

"Although that was great, it wasn't because of that. Maybe it's because it was one of the last nights we spent together, but I've always remembered it as one of the last times I felt light and free."

I understood that feeling completely. Ever since losing Kacey, it felt like the weight of the world somehow became heavier, like we were two people splitting the load, and once she was gone, I had to learn how to do it alone. It seemed I still hadn't mastered that one. Before I could respond, the Ferris wheel came to a stop and the man working it let us off. Bo and Bailey were waiting by the exit, taking the last few bites of their cotton candy.

A small smirk played on Bo's lips as he looked between Kacey and me. "What's with the blush? Do I want to know what happened on the Ferris wheel?"

I put an arm around his shoulder and pulled him tight, acting like I was about to whisper into his ear. When he giggled like a middle school girl about to hear about her friend's first kiss, I playfully pushed him away. "What happens on the Ferris wheel stays on the Ferris wheel, dude."

Kacey and I burst into a fit of laughter just as we had ten years earlier. Bo and Bailey exchanged a look, then Bailey rolled her eyes at us. "You two are incorrigible."

"Another word of the day?" I asked as I continued to laugh.

Bailey shook her head. "Nope. Bo taught me it. He was right, though. You really are."

***

After the carnival, things became easier with Kacey. It felt the way it did at the beginning of our freshman year when I was just getting to know her. Only this time, Kacey wasn't holding back and showing me just the pieces she thought I would want to see. I was slowly learning about every part of her, even the past she wanted to leave behind. Granted, we didn't have nearly as much time as adults as we did as college students so most of our conversations took place over text message or in the driveway when we happened to be coming or going at the same time.

The text messages were becoming more consistent. Kacey would talk about some geeky technical thing that I didn't understand and send me pictures of Bailey. I talked about my clients and the latest ridiculous thing Bo did.

On the morning of Halloween, I walked out of my front door at the same time Bailey and Kacey emerged from theirs. Bailey skipped over to me, her ever-present smile plastered to her face. "Kari! It's Halloween!" She struck a pose in the Batwoman costume she was wearing. "Like my costume?"

"I love it! It's a nice change from all of the princesses I'm sure I'll see parading the neighborhood tonight."

Bailey scrunched up her nose like she was disgusted. "I don't dress up as princesses. I don't need someone to save me. I do the saving."

I pointed toward Bailey as I smiled over at Kacey. "Very smart little girl you have here."

The smile on Kacey's face warmed me from the inside out. "What can I say? She takes after her mom."

I found myself lost in Kacey's eyes that were staring right back into mine. The darkness in them seemed to shimmer against the morning sunlight. The moment was interrupted when I felt a tug on my coat. "Do you want to go trick or treating with us tonight?" Bailey asked.

"That depends if it's okay with your mom." I looked back at Kacey who nodded her head, but gave me a look that said I didn't have to if I had something better to do. "I can't turn down Batwoman. I'm in."

Bailey did a little hop and threw her fist in the air. When she landed, her face became serious again. "Meet us out here at five o'clock sharp. That's when trick or treating starts, and I want to get the best candy. If you have any type of superhero outfit, wear it." She looked down at the watch she was wearing on her wrist. "Well, we have to go. Can't be late on Parade Day. See you at five."

Before I could respond, she was skipping back to the car. Once she was inside, Kacey turned to me. "You really don't have to come if you don't want to."

I gave her a reassuring smile. "I haven't been trick or treating in years. It sounds fun."

"All right, then I'll see you at five sharp." Kacey pointed a finger at me in mock lecture.

I watched as she climbed into the car and backed out of the driveway. Once I was inside my car, I smiled at myself in the rearview mirror and sighed contently. I felt happy in a way I hadn't felt in a very long time.

***

Just before five o'clock, I headed outside wearing a rainbow cape I had worn to a Pride parade a few years earlier. When Bailey saw me, her eyes went wide. "You wore a cape! That's so much cooler than my mom's costume."

I let my eyes linger over Kacey's outfit. She was wearing black skinny jeans that hugged her body perfectly and a Wonder Woman sweatshirt. When our eyes met, her lips curled into a smile, and I allowed myself a moment to soak it in. "Your mom looks great." The words slipped from my tongue before I could overthink them, but I wouldn't have taken them back if I could. Kacey really did look great. She always did, but there was something about her relaxed demeanor that made her look even better.

"Can you guys stop staring at each other so we can trick or treat?"

I forced my eyes away from Kacey and glanced down at the ground before looking back at Bailey. "You're right. Let's do this. Time to save the world one candy bar at a time."

Bailey quickly made her way from house to house, joining in with some other kids when we were about halfway through the neighborhood. I watched as she pretended to fly and laughed along with her friends and felt a strange sense of pride even though she wasn't mine. I always thought I would have kids at this point in my life, and being around Bailey gave me a sense of longing to be a mom.

Kacey bumped her shoulder up against mine. "You've been awfully quiet tonight. Are you okay?"

Her sincere concern and acute sense of awareness brought a smile to my face. "I'm fine. I'm great actually. This, is really nice." Our arms bumped as we walked close beside each other and the sameness in that simple touch made me feel right at home.

Kacey looked up at the night sky, a wide grin adorning her face. She took a deep breath and closed her eyes as if she were taking it all in. "It is. I wasn't sure how it would be for Bailey. You know, uprooting life as she knows it and moving her to an unfamiliar area, but she's doing great. She's always been happy, but this is the happiest I've ever seen her. I think this is the fresh start we both needed."

"You don't have to answer this if you don't want to, but what made you decide to move here?"

Kacey stopped walking and turned to face me completely, her expression becoming more serious. "You can ask me anything, Kari. I want us to get to know each other the right way this time. I don't want to hold anything back." She moved a strand of hair behind her ear before letting her hand drop back down to her side. "My grandma died in January, so there wasn't really anything keeping us there anymore."

I reached out and gave Kacey's hand a gentle squeeze, not sure how to respond to everything she had just said. "I'm sorry." Simple, but safe.

Kacey lifted one shoulder and let it drop. "Losing someone is hard no matter what, but my relationship with my grandma was strained at best. She tried harder the past few years, especially after becoming sick, but so much had happened by then that I could never fully let my guard down around her or let her in. She did help with Bailey while I finished my degree, so I'm thankful for that. But once she was gone, it didn't feel like there was anything left to keep us in that town. I was still living in the house I grew up in and needed a change."

"So, why Bellman?"

Kacey shrugged again. "As you know, I don't really let people in, and since we don't have family, we didn't have any connections. So, really, we could've gone anywhere, but

94

I didn't want to go anywhere other than Bellman. Throughout my whole life, Bellman was the one place that felt like home. I wanted to feel that again."

I could kind of understand what she meant. Bellman was twenty minutes from my hometown, but it felt like the only choice when I was deciding where to buy a house. Although, I was learning that Bellman felt a lot more like home with Kacey around. I opened my mouth to say something but was interrupted by Bailey talking quickly as she ran back over to us.

"You should see all the candy I got. I can't believe I made it to every house in just an hour. This means we have time to watch a movie, right? Kari, do you want to come over and watch a Halloween movie with us? A fun one. Not a scary one. Don't worry."

Her excitement made me chuckle. "As long as it's not too late to start a movie, I'd love to." This time, I didn't wait for Kacey's approval. After our conversation, I knew she would be okay with it.

Kacey took Bailey's hand in hers and rested her other hand on my arm. "It's Halloween. I think popcorn, candy, and a movie is a must."

Once we were back at their house, Kacey made some popcorn while Bailey rooted through her candy, deciding which she was going to eat that night. Kacey put on a newer Halloween movie that I had never heard of, then took a seat beside Bailey on the couch. Bailey patted the other side of her and looked at me. "Kari, can you sit here? I want to be in the middle of my two favorite people."

"I'm totally going to tell Bo you said that. He'll be so jealous." I tickled her playfully as I sat down to keep myself from getting choked up over her words.

"He's number five," Bailey said matter-of-factly. "Right after Addison and Michael from my class." She held her mom's hand and rested her other hand on top of mine, then put all of her attention onto the TV.

About an hour into the movie, Bailey's legs were stretched across Kacey and her head was resting on my shoulder. I looked down to find her starting to doze off and ran my fingers through her hair to relax her. I smiled as I watched her drift off completely. After a few minutes, I could feel eyes on me and looked up to see Kacey watching the two of us. Her smile was content, but her eyes were intense. She barely even blinked as her eyes bore into me. "You're really good with her," she said so quietly I barely heard it.

I got lost in her eyes and the sincerity I saw in them as I stared back at her. The moment was so intense I wanted to look away, but also stay lost in it all at once. "She's a good kid." My words came out in a breathy whisper and I forced myself to look away.

Kacey cleared her throat and stood up. "I guess I should get her to bed." She lifted Bailey off of me and carried her to the stairs.

For whatever reason, my body felt compelled to stand up and follow her as she made her way up the stairs and down the hall to Bailey's room. I leaned against the doorframe, watching in awe as she pulled the covers over her daughter and placed a kiss on her forehead. Kacey always had a natural instinct for taking care of people, but the softness in the way she took care of Bailey was different. It was, quite literally, breathtaking. "You're really good with her too."

Kacey turned around quickly, clearly surprised to hear my voice. A slow smile spread across her face as our eyes met. "I didn't realize you were up here."

"Yeah. Sorry about that. I just wanted to say goodbye. I should head home."

Kacey walked over to me and put an arm lightly around my waist. "Let me walk you out."

Her hand remained on my hip as we made our way down the stairs. She didn't let it drop until we were at the front door, and I immediately found myself missing her touch. "Thanks for coming tonight. I had a really nice time, and I could tell Bailey did too."

"I had a great time too. Best Halloween I've had in years."

"Better than the time you insisted we dress up as Beauty and the Beast, then threw up all over your dress?" Kacey teased.

"It's close, but I'd say tonight topped that."

We both laughed lightly, but neither of us moved from our place. "Well, thanks again," Kacey said, her voice becoming more serious.

I hesitated slightly before reaching out and pulling her into my arms. Kacey melted into my touch and our bodies molded together. I held on as I took in the scent of her shampoo, reveling in the familiarity. I don't know how long we stayed like this, but eventually we reluctantly pulled away, our bodies slowly disconnecting until just our hands lingered. The touch was so light that it would have gone unnoticed if my body wasn't so hyper aware of Kacey's. I allowed my finger to continue to brush against her, not ready to break that connection. After a while, I forced myself to let go as I moved my hand to open the door. The feeling of the brisk fall air as I walked outside was in direct contrast to the warmth I felt throughout my body. I turned around one more time so I could take Kacey in once more before leaving.

"Goodnight, Kacey," I said breathlessly.

"Goodnight, Kari."

I willed myself to walk away this time, but felt Kacey's eyes on me until I disappeared into my house. I closed the door and leaned against the wall, feeling the need to catch my breath to calm down what was happening throughout my body. I wasn't sure if I liked this feeling or hated it, but I knew I couldn't stop smiling.

***

"I feel like I never see you anymore," Bo said before taking a big gulp from his glass of beer.

"That's not true. I saw you like a week ago on Halloween."

Bo scoffed, then took another sip. "For like two minutes when you guys came to my house for candy." He sighed dramatically as he set his empty glass back on the table and wiped at his mouth. "I'm just saying, I'm really happy that you're finally getting your lady bits rubbed, but don't forget about little old me."

I spit out the cocktail that I had just taken a sip of. "Excuse me?"

"I mean, that's what's happening, right? You and Kacey are hooking up now?"

"No. We're just friends," I answered quickly, confused where he would have gotten that idea.

"Huh. I was sure that's what was happening. You two totally look at each other like two people who are boning." His face suddenly lit up as if he had just had an epiphany that made him extremely happy. "Unless, that is the look of two people in lo—"

"Don't even think about it," I interrupted. "Kacey and I are friends. Nothing more."

Bo put his hands in the air and started to laugh. "Got it. Just friends."

I studied him for a minute and noticed that something seemed to be off. "Are you doing okay? Normally you're not one to get jealous of me hanging out with someone else, and you seem pretty peeved over Kacey."

Bo rubbed at his neck. "Sorry about that. I really am happy that you and Kacey are reconnecting. I guess it's just had me thinking about what I'm doing with my life."

"What do you mean?"

Bo picked up the new glass of beer that had been placed in front of him, studied it, and set it back down without taking a sip. Then he looked across the table and studied me in the same way he had just done with his beer. "You've been my person these past few years and that's great, but I'm almost thirty-five. I should probably have a different type of person by now."

"Like a girlfriend type of person?"

Bo scrunched up his nose and this time did take a big gulp of his beer. "You know I hate that word, but for lack of a better one, yes." I watched as Bo squirmed in his chair, as if he was uncomfortable with the conversation.

"What changed? You've never mentioned being interested in anything serious before now."

"Honestly? Seeing you and Kacey together. Call it friendship, call it lust, call it that word we're not allowed to say, but you guys light up when you're around each other. I guess I never realized how much I wanted that until I saw it right in front of me."

"Aww. My little Bo Bo's growing up." I reached across the table and ruffled his hair.

Bo glared at me while running a hand through his hair to get it back into place. "Okay, okay. Let's not make it a big thing."

"Seriously though, if you want a relationship, just get out there and start meeting girls."

Bo crossed his arms in front of his chest and leaned back in his chair, a sly grin overtaking his face. "Oh. I meet girls all the time. I have no problem with that."

I rolled my eyes at his cockiness. "I didn't say bang girls. I said *meet* girls. Talk to them. Get to know them."

"Well, that doesn't sound like very much fun."

"And you called me incorrigible? Ha!"

Bo's smile grew as his eyes focused on something behind me. I turned around to see Kylie waving excitedly as she walked toward us. When she reached the table, she picked up Bo's beer and drank half of it without even asking. "What's up, guys? Fancy meeting you here."

"We should be saying that to you. This is our territory. What are you doing around here?" I asked.

Kylie put her elbows onto the table and rested her chin on her hand. "I decided to try online dating. Tonight was my first date. It was lame."

Bo grunted. "That's because online dating is stupid."

Kylie turned her attention to Bo. "I'm only stuck doing it because *you* won't date me, Bozey."

Bo hitched his thumb toward me. "You need to take that up with the warden here. She's the one keeping us apart."

Kylie looked toward me, then back at Bo. She ran one finger slowly up his arm and leaned closer to him, letting the top of her T-shirt fall down slightly. "That's too bad. I've got some tricks I could treat you with." When I made a fake gagging noise, she looked back at me. "Anything you'd like to share, Kari?"

"A few things actually. First of all, ew. Also, Halloween is over and you're my little sister, so if I hear that trick and treat line ever again, it will be too soon." I waved my hand in the air in a circle in front of them. "All of this is also just way too hetero for me to handle."

Bo and Kylie exchanged a look and then burst into laughter. Once the laughter died down, Kylie grabbed my drink and sipped from it. "All right. Let's make this more homo. How's your girlfriend doing?"

I threw both hands in the air. "Why does everyone think Kacey's my girlfriend? We're just friends."

"Oh, I don't know. Maybe because you get all googly-eyed when you talk about her." My sister elbowed Bo and the two of them started to laugh again.

"I'm serious, guys. I'm not going down that road again. I can't. Being friends with her is fine. It's safe and it's comfortable and it's… it's fine."

My sister smirked and lifted an eyebrow. "Fine."

"Yep. Fine," Bo repeated.

I rolled my eyes at them. It didn't matter what they thought about mine and Kacey's friendship. I was perfectly happy with where we were at. *Perfectly happy…*

Chapter 8

I stared at my phone, contemplating whether or not I should call Kacey. We had been texting back and forth regularly, but hadn't seen each other in the two weeks since Halloween, and I missed her. I battled with myself over whether it was too desperate to call and ask to see her.

The sound of the doorbell ringing interrupted my internal struggle. When I opened the door to find Kacey standing on the other side, it took all of my self-control not to pull her into my arms. Instead, I leaned against the doorframe and crossed my arms in front of my chest. "Well, aren't you a sight for sore eyes?" I said as calmly as possible.

Kacey slowly rocked from one foot to the other as she rubbed her hands together. "Sorry for just stopping by like this. I just mi… Bailey is with a friend right now and it's unseasonably warm today, so I was wondering if you wanted to go for a walk." She moved her hands deep into her pockets and stared at the ground. "You probably have stuff going on. It was stupid to just stop by. Forget I asked." She went to turn around, but I grabbed onto her arm and forced her to look at me.

"Is the always-cool Kacey Caldwell nervous right now?"

I watched as Kacey's body began to relax with my joke. A small smirk settled on her face. "You always thought I was so much cooler than I actually was. I never understood that."

I moved my eyes to the sky as if I were thinking. "I think it was the tattoo. Nope. I don't think. I know. It was totally the tattoo. None of my other friends at the time had them and there you were with this mysterious symbol right in the middle of your toned bicep."

When I looked back at Kacey, her smile grew even wider. "So, is that a yes to the walk?"

"Absolutely. Let me just grab my coat and the dog."

Once Duke and I were back outside, I motioned for Kacey to lead the way and fell in step with her. Kacey nodded her head toward Duke. "So, how old is he?"

"He's six. I've had him for five years. The family who owned him before me apparently tied him up outside of the rescue with a note saying they didn't want him. It was late at night in the middle of winter and he was outside until someone came the next day. I'm honestly not sure how he did it. He's such a diva now. I'm surprised he's even out in this weather."

"And his name..." Kacey let her words trail off, but I knew what she was getting at.

"Are you asking if I named him that because of you?" I cringed when Kacey nodded. "If you would have asked me a few weeks ago, I would have vehemently denied it and acted like it was some weird coincidence, but since we're being honest—yes. I think I was trying to hold on to part of the life I thought I was going to have."

Kacey shook her head. "That's not true." Before I could fight her on it, she elbowed me playfully in the side. "Be honest. You would have never let us name our son Duke."

I chuckled. "I just feel like Duke is the kid that beats up other kids at recess."

Kacey pointed to the dog. "Does he do that?"

"Duke is too lazy to even acknowledge other animals, so no. Plus, he's a lover. Not a fighter."

"Our Duke would have been a lover too. Total peacemaker."

"Is that so?" I asked mockingly.

"Definitely. No question." Kacey stopped walking and turned to look at me. "Sorry. Is it weird that we're talking about this?"

I shook my head. "I'm strangely okay with it. It feels nice to talk about. I think it's good that we're at this point. It means we're comfortable being friends." *Was I comfortable being friends though?* I shook these thoughts from my head. Of course I was.

We continued to walk in a comfortable silence until we were out of the neighborhood. Kacey's hand bumped against mine as our bodies instinctively inched closer to each other. I looked down at our hands and thought about how easy it would be to grab hers. It used to be so natural. Touching her was like breathing, and right now, I felt like I was desperate for air.

"Good old Bellman." Kacey's voice interrupted my thoughts, and I realized we were standing in front of the entrance to campus. "Want to walk through?"

I tugged on Duke's leash. "I'm not sure if they allow dogs on campus."

Kacey scoffed. "You're Kari Adelberg. There's a dining hall named after your family. I'm pretty sure you could run across campus naked, and no one would care."

"Obviously, they wouldn't." I winked and nudged her in the side. "But, you're right. Let's do it."

As we walked onto campus, it felt different, yet familiar all at once. I had gone to Bellman a few times over the past few years and it didn't feel the same. Yet, having Kacey beside me changed that. Now I could see it as the place I loved. My oasis for those three years before it became my personal hell.

"So, do you still talk to any of the girls?" I was happy for Kacey's question. I didn't want to think about those dark days after Kacey left. She was back now, and I wanted to focus on the happy times.

"Alicia and I still talk regularly. She lives in New York now and we normally try to get together a few times a year. Sometimes Stacey and Heather meet up with us too. They live in Florida now and they're actually married. To each other."

This news caused Kacey to stop walking. "Wait. What? Stacey? As in, the girl who made her way through the whole football team?"

I chuckled. "That's the one. It didn't happen until after college. Stacey moved back to Florida and Heather stayed in Pennsylvania, and that's when they realized the extent of their feelings. Heather moved to Florida six months later and they've been together ever since. They even have two kids."

"Well, shit. Good for them. I never would have pictured them together, but now that I think about it, it makes sense."

I nodded my head as we started walking again. "It really does. They go well together. It's just crazy to think that they were around each other so much in college and nothing ever happened, yet a few months after being apart, they just knew."

"Life's funny that way. If it's meant to be, it's meant to be, and it's going to happen one way or another."

The weight of her words pushed down on me, but I decided not to think into it. I could tell by the relaxed grin on Kacey's face that she was being sincere and hadn't even thought about how that related to us.

This time, as we walked closer, I brushed my finger along the back of her hand. When she didn't seem to mind this, I hooked my pinky with hers. I watched as she took in a sharp breath, but didn't make any move to break the connection. Feeling confident and needing more, I slipped my pinky away from hers and took her whole hand instead.

Kacey looked down at our intertwined fingers and back at me but didn't say anything. As we continued our walk, I gently moved my thumb against hers, reveling in how good it felt. How right it felt. I refused to think about what it meant because I just wanted to enjoy the moment. A moment that felt more charged than anything I had experienced in years.

"So, what are you doing for Thanksgiving?" Kacey asked, finally breaking the silence, but keeping her hand tightly bound with mine.

"Just going to my parents' house. Thanksgiving is low key for us. Just my parents, sister, and me."

Kacey nodded her head. "It sounds nice. I always loved your family. Your mom was like the mom I never had."

"She loved you too. I think it took my whole family a long time to move on from you. They all thought you were pretty wonderful."

I meant it as a compliment but could tell my words made Kacey sad. She sighed and used the hand that wasn't holding mine to rub at her forehead. "I was an idiot. I should have reached out to your family. They did so much for me, and I just let them all down. I let all of you down."

I squeezed her hand. "It was a long time ago. You did what you thought was right."

104

"Does that mean you're not mad at me anymore?"

I looked at our hands, then smiled back at Kacey. "I think it's pretty obvious I'm not mad at you. Becoming friends again was the best thing to happen to me in a really long time. There's no need to be stuck in the past. I like where we're at right now."

The smile on Kacey's face was so genuine, it made my heart beat pick up and made me wish she was even closer to me. "I like where we're at, too," she breathed out. She held my hand even tighter and let out a contented sigh. "I really like where we're at."

"So, what about you and Bailey? What are you doing for Thanksgiving?" I forced myself to keep the conversation light, worried about where it would go if I said what was actually on my mind.

"We're just having a small lunch together, then putting up Christmas decorations while we watch *Elf*. It's our yearly tradition."

I pictured Kacey and Bailey inside their house, surrounded by boxes of decorations, while they laughed together and tried to decide the best place to put everything. The thought of it brought a smile to my face. "That's great. It sounds like a lot of fun."

"You know, depending on what time you get done with your family, you're welcome to come join us. I'm sure Bailey would love it. You *are* her second favorite person."

I bumped my hip against hers as we made our way back into our neighborhood. "Technically, she said we are her two favorite people. For all you know, I could be first."

"I changed her poopy diapers. That automatically makes me first."

Her lighthearted joke caused a feeling of longing deep in my gut. Longing for a life filled with things such as poopy diapers, scraped knees, and a child who needs you to tuck them into bed. "Noted. I don't want to intrude, though."

"You wouldn't be intruding," Kacey blurted. "Like I said, Bailey would love if you came. I would love if you came."

"I'll be there."

***

"Hold on a second." My mom looked around dramatically as she walked over to me, then placed a hand on my cheek. "You look like my daughter." She leaned in and sniffed. "Smell like my daughter too." She took one step away and acted as if she were studying me and trying to work out a puzzle. "You can't be my daughter though. I've barely seen or heard from her in weeks."

I laughed and pulled her into my arms. "I've missed you too, Mom."

When she pulled away from the hug, she continued to hold on to my arms, never taking her eyes off of me. "Why have you been so distant lately? Does it have something to do with a certain new next door neighbor that you don't want to talk to your old mom about?"

"So, Kylie told you? I swear that girl needs to learn how to keep her mouth shut."

My mom gave me her best "Mom" look and shook her head. "Don't blame your sister. Someone oughta keep me in the loop. Really though, honey, how are you doing?"

"I'm good. Great, actually. Kacey and I are friends, and it feels right."

My sister chose that moment to walk into the room. "Oh, yeah. *Friends*." She made air quotes when she said the word friends, her voice dripping with sarcasm.

"Just be careful, sweetheart. I don't want you to get hurt again. Kacey has a daughter. Her life is very complicated."

I glared at my sister. "You didn't spare any details, did you?"

Kylie shrugged. "She asked, so I told her. I also told her that Kacey adopted Bailey from her sister, and that's why she broke up with you. I didn't make her out to be a complete monster."

I put one hand up. "Wait a second. I didn't even tell you that part."

"Bo did."

Of course he did. "I swear, I'm surrounded by people who can't keep their mouths shut."

106

My mom rubbed her hand over my arm. "We all just care about you. I was sad to hear Kacey had all of that going on. Not very surprised, but still sad. I still don't think that gave her any right—"

"What do you mean you're *not surprised*?" I asked, interrupting whatever else my mom had to say.

My mom laughed as if my question was ridiculous. "Really, honey? Aside from your first semester, Kacey spent every holiday with us. It wasn't very hard to figure out that she had a rough upbringing."

Unless you were a naive college student, who thought everyone's life was just as perfect as yours. Reading my mind, my mom leaned in and placed a kiss on my cheek, then pulled back and gently squeezed my arm. "You were young. Or maybe it was just a mother's intuition. I don't know. That's all irrelevant. Even given all that, I'm still not happy that she hurt my baby the way she did."

I rolled my eyes. "I'm fine, Mom. I lived."

Kylie laughed, spitting out pieces of the cookie she was eating. "Barely."

"What did you barely live through?" my dad asked as he joined us in the kitchen.

"The Great Kacey Caldwell Incident of 2010," Kylie answered sarcastically.

My dad let out a low whistle. "That was a time. That's for sure. I'll tell you something, though. I think she was right to break things off. You were so caught up in her, you would have given up your own dreams for her. That wouldn't have been good for anyone."

My dad sounded like both Bo and Kacey, but I didn't want to focus on the what-ifs today. I just wanted to enjoy my time with my family and then my night with Kacey and Bailey. "Could we talk about something else?" I asked, feeling like a pouty teenager.

My mom put her hand on my back and directed me toward the kitchen table. "Of course. Lunch is ready. Sit down and we'll all say what we're thankful for." She took a seat and grinned so widely at all of us, it was almost scary. "I'll start. I'm thankful to have my whole family together."

My dad cleared his throat. "And I'm thankful to have one baby girl still living at home and the other just twenty minutes away."

"Sorry, guys. Love you, but I'm switching things up," Kylie said with a laugh. "I'm thankful for my students and the difference I get to make in their lives."

All three of them looked toward me, expectantly waiting to see what I would say. "I'm thankful for…" *Kacey. Bailey. Second chances. The way Kacey's lips curve just a little higher on the right than the left when she smiles.* "All of you. I'm thankful to come from a family where everyone loves and takes care of each other."

We spent the rest of the day eating and laying around watching football. When four o'clock rolled around, I stood from the couch and stretched out all the muscles that were sore from being in one position all day. "I'm going to head out, but thank you so much for everything, Mom and Dad."

My mom looked down at her watch. "Leaving so soon? You just got here."

I walked over and placed a kiss on her forehead. "I've been here for hours, Mom."

She kissed me back and kept a hand on my cheek. "But why rush out of here? Have somewhere else to be?"

All three members of my family stared at me and I had a feeling they knew what my answer was going to be. "Kacey invited me over to decorate for Christmas with her and Bailey."

"That sounds fun." My mom smiled her tight lip smile, which told me she was holding in what she truly wanted to say. "Let me walk you to the door."

Once at the door, my mom turned to me, concern written all over her face. "Remember what I told you. Please be careful."

"Remember what I told *you.* We're just friends. I can't get hurt if I don't give my heart away."

My words didn't seem to reassure my mom as her face dropped even more. "As long as you're happy, that's all I care about."

***

I didn't bother stopping at home before going to Kacey's. I was excited, almost giddy, about the night ahead of us and didn't want to wait any longer. Kacey and Bailey must have felt the same way because the door flew open before I even had a chance to knock.

A smile lit up Kacey's face as she opened the door for me. "We saw you pull in the driveway. Bailey has been watching for your car all afternoon."

Bailey nodded emphatically. "It's true. I was so excited when my mom told me you were coming over to help us decorate."

I bent down and held out my arms to her. "Come here, kiddo." When she hugged me, I pulled her in tight and spun us both around. Bailey laughed as I tickled her stomach, and the sound was like music to my ears. When I sat her back down, I booped her nose with my finger. "Happy Thanksgiving. Do you want to know what I'm thankful for?" Bailey nodded her head again, and I put a hand on her shoulder. "I'm thankful for you, and I'm thankful for your mom, and I'm especially thankful that you guys let me join in on your tradition."

When I finally turned my attention toward Kacey, she was already watching me. "That's really sweet," she said softly.

I took a few steps closer to her, then reached out and grabbed her hand, both of us smiling like idiots as we continued to keep our eyes glued to each other. "It's true. I'm so excited to help. I can't think of anywhere I'd rather be." Excitement bubbled through my chest, my eyes refusing to move from Kacey's, wanting to prolong this feeling for as long as possible.

Bailey cleared her throat, causing our eye contact to falter. I looked down to where she had her hands on her hips. "Can you two just hug already so we can start decorating?"

I laughed at the little girl's intuitiveness but wasted no time wrapping my arms around Kacey and pulling her in tight. Her hands instinctively moved to my hips as she

109

anchored herself against me. I let my head rest on her shoulder for the briefest moment and breathed her in. All too soon, we released each other.

Bailey gave us a satisfied grin and pointed toward their family room. "Christmas decorating time! Let's do this!"

Boxes filled the family room and a tall tree stood in the corner. "Where do we start?" I asked.

Bailey skipped to a box marked *pictures* and started pulling frames out of it. "We always start by putting our pictures with Santa up first." She moved her head from side to side as she scanned the room. "Where do you think we should put them?"

"Since those seem to be extra special, what do you think about putting them above the fireplace?" I suggested.

Bailey's already wide grin grew even wider. "I love that idea! And we can hang the stockings right in the middle of the pictures."

Kacey put an arm around Bailey and smiled down at her. "I think that's a great idea. What do you say you start unwrapping the ornaments while Kari and I get these set up on the mantel?"

I picked the pictures up one at a time, studying each one before setting it down. Kacey and Bailey had gotten pictures together every year since she was born. The Kacey in the first few pictures was the girl I remembered from college, while the last few years were the woman I knew now. Both felt so similar yet worlds apart, the lines between our past and our future blurred. As I stared at the line of pictures now all set up, I felt arms wrap around me from behind as a chin came to rest on my shoulder. I felt goosebumps form on my neck as Kacey spoke into my skin.

"I started doing the Santa pictures because they were the only professional pictures I could afford to get. Then it just became one of our traditions." She sighed and her breath on my skin caused my own breathing to stop momentarily. "I'm already dreading the day when she tells me she's too cool to get Santa pictures with her mom."

I leaned into Kacey and shut my eyes as I let the moment wash over me. "She's a good kid. Maybe she'll keep doing it just to make you happy."

Kacey hummed. "I can only hope."

Bailey joined us beside the fireplace leaned into me from the side, wrapping an arm around my waist. "Maybe someday you can get a Christmas picture with us, Kari."

"Oh, I don't think so, sweetheart. That's a tradition with you and your mom. It's special."

"You're special to us, though," Bailey said in a matter-of-fact tone. "I know you're special to me, and I can tell by the way my mom looks at you that you're *very* special to her, too." She put her hand over her mouth and giggled as if she had just revealed a big secret.

Kacey let go of me to move over toward Bailey. She took the little girl in her arms and began to tickle her as she held her upside down. "You think you're funny, don't you?" Bailey tried to wiggle out of Kacey's arms while she held onto her tightly. As they laughed together, I watched in awe and marveled over the two people who were quickly becoming my world.

I didn't have time to overthink it, because Kacey put Bailey back down, then whispered something in her ear and soon the two of them were attacking me. Kacey tickled me to the ground, where Bailey went after any free inch of skin she could find. "Uncle! Uncle!" I cried. "You guys win. I give up."

We all wiped the happy tears from our eyes and got back to decorating. We set up most of the decorations they had around the family room, then got started on the tree. Bailey explained every ornament to me before we hung them up, telling me about trips they took, shows they saw, and the people they met along the way. One ornament in particular, Bailey unwrapped really slowly. "This is my mom's favorite ornament, so I have to be very careful with it," she explained.

"Oh, I don't think we need to show her that—"

Kacey's words came too late, and my breath hitched when I saw the very familiar Bellman University ornament dangling from her fingers. "Could I see that?" I saw Kacey close her eyes in embarrassment as I took the ornament in my hand and turned it over. I ran my hand over the engraving that read *K₂ Forever*, then brought my eyes to Kacey's which were now open. "I always wondered what happened to this."

Bailey looked between the two of us in wonder. "You know what this ornament is?" she asked.

"I do. This ornament isn't just your mom's favorite. It's also very special to me."

Kacey led me to the bed in her dorm room and asked me to sit down. It was just a month into the second semester of our freshman year, and the way her hand was shaking when she took mine had my mind racing. Was she going to break up with me? I thought things were going really well between us, but now I was questioning everything that had happened since we got back. Did I say something wrong? Was she already sick of driving my drunk ass home from parties? I was ready to promise to change. Beg her to give me one last chance. We hadn't reached the six-month mark in our relationship yet. Hell, we hadn't even known each other for six months, but I felt a connection to Kacey I never felt before. There was also a certain something that I felt but hadn't found the courage to say yet. Were things really going to end before I had the chance to say it? Before she even met my family?

"Are you okay?" Kacey asked, interrupting my internal dialogue. "You look like you're going to be sick."

I laughed nervously. "I'm just going off your energy. Your hand is shaking."

Kacey looked to her hand and flexed her fingers. "Sorry. I'm just nervous about what I want to say."

"If you're going to break up with me, could you at least make it quick? I don't think I could stand to have it drawn out."

Kacey's head snapped up in response to my question. "Break up with you? God, Kari, it's not like that at all. It's the complete opposite of that." She let go of my hand and stood from the bed, picking up a bag that was sitting on her desk. "I got you a late Christmas present."

112

A slight smile came to my face. "But you already got me an on-time Christmas present."

"This one's… Umm… different." She held the bag out to me and nodded toward it. "Open it."

I removed the tissue paper, then pulled out a Bellman University Christmas ornament. Kacey took a deep breath and sat back down beside me. "I know it's strange to give you an ornament in February but I can explain. First off, I can't lie. The bookstore was selling them for almost nothing because of Christmas being over, and I figured I would just grab it because it was such a steal." She turned it over to reveal the engraving on the back. "Then a thought came to me. I wanted you to have an ornament to commemorate our first Christmas as a couple. The first Christmas that I was… that I was in love with you."

My vision blurred, and I realized I was crying as I looked at Kacey. She kissed my cheek, then pulled back to look me in the eye. "I am in love with you, Kari. I've been in love with you since that weekend we spent at your parent's house. I woke up the morning after we first had sex and watched you sleep and couldn't stop thinking about how lucky I was. Not because of the sex, but because of how safe I felt in your arms after giving myself to you completely. I never thought someone could make me feel that way, and I just knew."

Without a word, I put my hands on her cheeks and pulled her face to mine, kissing her with more abandon than ever before. I pulled back to wipe the tears from my face. "I love you too, Kacey. I know this is my first time being in love, but I don't think I'd ever be able to love another person the way I love you."

"Kari? Are you crying?"

I focused on Bailey who had her head tilted as she stared at me in confusion and wiped at my wet cheeks. "I think it's just my allergies acting up," I lied.

Bailey looked like she was considering this, then simply shrugged her shoulders and jumped up. "I'm going to finish hanging these ornaments so we can eat leftovers and watch *Elf*."

Bailey quickly put up the rest of the ornaments while Kacey set a blanket on the floor and prepared three plates of food that she placed on top of the blanket. "I forgot to tell you that we have a picnic while we watch *Elf*. I hope that's okay."

"Sounds pretty perfect to me." And it really was. Watching the movie with Kacey and Bailey was like getting a peak at what my life with Kacey would have been like, but the notion strangely didn't make me sad, because in a way, I could have that life now.

Just when I thought the night couldn't get any better, Bailey looked at me with tired eyes and asked if I could tuck her in. After she changed into her pajamas, I met her in her room and pulled back the pink and white striped bedding so she could hop in. I pulled the covers up to her chin, then pushed her hair out of her face and kissed her forehead. To my surprise, she wrapped her arms around my neck and pulled me into a tight hug. Her yawn gave way to a big smile as she closed her eyes. "Goodnight, Kari. I love you."

I had to blink back my tears to keep them from falling. "I love you too, Bailey."

When I came back downstairs, Kacey was standing at the bottom waiting for me. "Everything good?" she asked.

I rested my body against hers and sighed when her strong arms wrapped around my waist. "Everything is perfect."

Kacey pulled back and pushed a loose strand of hair behind my ear. "Any interest in staying for another movie?"

Of course I was interested, and Kacey knew that. Without waiting for a response, she took my hand and walked me over to the couch. As she scrolled through the movie selections, she hesitantly put one arm over my shoulder. "Is this okay?"

I snuggled close to her and draped one arm across her stomach as I laid my head on her shoulder. "This is more than okay."

Chapter 9

I blinked my eyes open, confused about where I was. I became even more confused when I felt the body heat from another person beside me. I rubbed my eyes and when I finally got my bearings, I realized I was in Kacey's family room. Kacey's arm was still around me and now her head was resting on top of mine. I could see the sun starting to rise through the window, and it took everything in me to pull myself away. Waking up in Kacey's arms was something I hadn't experienced in a really long time and it was even better than I remembered. Her grip was strong, but her touch was soft. It made me feel safe while also causing my heart to beat erratically. I tried to make slow, small movements so I didn't wake Kacey, but it didn't work. As soon as I broke the connection, her eyes shot open.

She looked around the room and smiled when her eyes landed on me. "It seems we fell asleep."

I tilted my chin so I could stare up at her, taking in the way her dark eyes somehow appeared even darker first thing in the morning. "It does seem that way, doesn't it?" My body stiffened when I suddenly became aware of just how close Kacey's mouth was to mine. I would only have to move a few inches to connect our lips, and in this moment, I couldn't think of anything I wanted more. I knew I couldn't, though. Holding hands and cuddling was one thing. Kissing would cross a line I knew I couldn't cross if I wanted to keep this friendship intact. I moved a few inches, but instead of placing my lips on Kacey's, I brought them to her cheek and kissed her there instead.

She leaned her forehead against mine and sighed. "I'd be lying if I said waking up next to you wasn't one of the better things to happen to me lately."

There it was again. That feeling in the pit of my stomach. The urge to do so much more than just cuddle. I stood from the couch before I ended up doing something we would both regret.

Kacey hopped up beside me and grabbed my hand. "I'm sorry. Was that the wrong thing to say?"

I placed my other hand on her cheek, then slowly shook my head. "Quite the opposite. It was exactly the right thing to say. I would say you make me feel things I've never felt before, but we both know that's not true. You're just the only person who could ever make me feel them." I groaned and laid my head in the crook of her neck. "Why is it so hard to be your friend? To figure out just where friendship ends and something else begins?"

Kacey pulled me closer and kissed my temple. "Maybe it's so hard because we're not meant to be friends."

I shook my head. "Don't say that. Please don't go there. I can't, Kacey. I just can't. Could we please just stay where we're at? I like where we're at." I knew I was contradicting myself, but I couldn't help it. My mind and heart felt like they were playing tug-of-war within my body.

"Of course, Kari. I like where we're at too. Never in my wildest dreams did I think you would ever talk to me again. I'm so happy with anything you're willing to give me."

I tapped my finger against her chin and gave her a flirtatious grin. "Well, in a little while, I'd like to give you some pumpkin pie, but that's not going to happen if I don't get home to bake it."

"Fine. I guess I'll let you go." Kacey slowly pulled her hand away from mine, letting her touch linger before she completely dropped her hand to her side. "Are you going to be okay getting home? I heard the driveway can be quite dangerous at this time."

I sighed dramatically. "I think I can make it."

Kacey laughed lightly. "See you soon, Kari."

"Yep. See you soon." Only, even the few hours when we would be back together at Bo's didn't seem soon enough.

***

I got to Bo's house an hour before everyone else was set to arrive and was greeted by an overly eager Duke. Bo pointed to him. "Remember this guy? I'm pretty sure you told me you were going to pick him up last night."

I rubbed behind Duke's ear as an apology for being away from him for so long. "Yeah. Sorry about that."

"No big. We watched porn and cuddled. Everything okay though?"

"Yeah. Umm… I just… fell asleep at Kacey's."

Bo smirked and lifted an eyebrow. "You sly dog."

I rolled my eyes at him. "It wasn't like that. We were watching a movie and fell asleep."

"That's lame. Let's get everything set up. Who knows. Maybe today will be the day you and Kacey make it to first base."

Kylie was the first to arrive. "What's up, bitchachos?" she shouted as she walked in holding a bottle of tequila in the air.

Bo wrapped her in a big hug. "My girl. Always bringing the good stuff." When he pulled away from her, he walked up to me and put an arm over my shoulder. "Did you know your sister had a not-so-adult sleepover last night?"

Kylie's face lit up. "No way! You and Kacey finally sealed the deal? Way to go, Sis."

She put her hand up for a high five, but Bo grabbed it instead. "Not so fast. I said not-so-adult. They fell asleep while watching a movie."

Kylie scrunched up her nose. "Yawn. How boring."

Bo grunted in agreement. "That's what I said." He pointed out the window. "Speak of the devil. Here she comes."

I looked out the window to where Bailey and Kacey were approaching the house hand in hand. Kacey had loose curls in her hair and was wearing a blue and white flannel under a form-fitting, cream-colored sweater. Her blue jeans were mouth-wateringly tight, and she topped off the outfit with a cute pair of boots.

"Did it hurt?" Kylie whispered from behind me.

"Did what hurt?" I asked, turning around to face her.

"When your jaw just hit the ground." Kylie laughed, then nodded her head at me. "By the way, you might want to wipe the drool from your face before your girlfriend gets in

---

117

here." I glared at her, but quickly ran a hand over my face just in case she was telling the truth.

"Well, if it isn't Kacey Caldwell," Kylie said as she greeted her at the front door.

Kacey's eyes went wide when she realized it was my little sister standing in front of her. "Wow, Kylie, I can't believe it's you. You look great." She looked unsure of what to do next, but Kylie reached her arms out to her.

"No reason this has to be awkward. Bring it in."

I could see Kacey's demeanor relax as my sister hugged her. After pulling away, Kylie knelt in front of Bailey. "And who are you?"

Bailey stuck out her hand. "I'm Bailey Caldwell. Nice to meet you. Are you Kari's sister? You're so lucky."

Kylie threw her head back and laughed. "How much did she pay you to say that?"

Bailey's face was serious as she shook her head. "She didn't pay me anything."

Kylie continued to laugh and put a hand on Bailey's shoulder. "If you think my sister's cool, just wait until you hang out with me."

I felt a little disappointed when I saw the other guests start to arrive. It would have made me happy to spend the day with just the five of us, but soon the house was filled. I was helping Bo carry food to the long table that extended from his kitchen to family room, when I felt a hand on the small of my back.

"Need any help?" Kacey whispered into my ear, causing goosebumps to form on my arms.

I turned around so I could face her completely and rested a hand on her hip. "We're good. Just finished up." I bit my lip as my eyes drifted over her body. "Have I told you how pretty you look today?"

Kacey swallowed hard as her eyes briefly landed on my lips. "You think I look pretty?"

The awe in her voice caused my stomach to do a flip. I didn't think there was anyone in the world more beautiful than Kacey, and the fact that my words meant that much to her, made me want to remind her of it every single day.

I jumped at the sound of a throat clearing beside us. Bo chuckled and shook his head. "If you two are going to rip each other's clothes off, could you at least go to the guest room to do it? I'm all about this. I just don't want to get anything on the turkey."

I slapped him on the shoulder and pushed him away from us as he continued to laugh. "We're just talking, Bo."

"Oh, I'm sorry. I could've sworn I saw you guys making sex eyes at each other. My bad. Keep *talking*." Bo turned his attention to the rest of the guests and spoke louder. "Lunch is served. Adult table is here. Kids table is over there. Enjoy. Mingle. Make new friends."

Kacey and I took a seat across from Joey and Faith Hopkins. Joey tapped her wife's shoulder and pointed across at us. "Honey, you remember Kari. This is her new neighbor Kacey. She also went to Bellman around the same time as us."

Faith smiled sweetly. "Would you look at that? Four Bellman alums. I'm surprised none of us ever ran into each other. I'm Faith."

Kacey reached a hand across the table for Faith to shake. "It's very nice to meet you, Faith. Always great to meet another Bulldog." She looked between Faith and Joey. "So, I take it you two met at school?"

Faith smiled lovingly at Joey, then looked back at us. "We did. We met our senior year when we both volunteered to deliver meals to shut-ins from our church."

Joey hitched her thumb toward Faith. "*She* was volunteering. I got stuck doing it after a big party at the track house got busted."

I laughed when I realized what she was referring to. "Wait a second. I was at that track party. It was my sophomore year. I was so wasted. Totally would have gotten busted if it wasn't for this one." I put my hand on Kacey's shoulder and squeezed lightly enough that only she would notice. "She snuck me out some window in the back, then ran about three blocks with me piggy-backing her."

My story made Kacey laugh as well. "Oh my God. That's right. I totally forgot about that, which is shocking, given how sore I was for like a month following that."

"So, you two knew each other back in college?" Joey asked.

119

Kacey gave me a smug grin that caused my stomach to do flips all over again. She continued to stare at me while she answered. "You could say that."

"Wait a second." Faith pointed between Kacey and me. "Were you two—?"

I nodded and let my eyes stay locked with Kacey's. I could feel my smile grow as I spoke. "We were together through college. Had a bit of a falling out and spent way too many years apart. Now we're getting reacquainted." I found myself lost in Kacey's eyes and the way they were focused so deeply on me. She always had a way of making me feel like we were the only two people in the room, and this moment was no different. Except we weren't the only two people in the house. We were surrounded by people. I shook myself out of my trance and looked back at Faith and Joey, who were both staring at us, a slight smirk present on each of their faces. "As friends. We're getting reacquainted as friends. That's what works best for us."

My rambling only caused the smirk on Joey's face to grow, and I could tell she wasn't buying a word I was saying. "Well, good for you guys. I could never go back to just being friends."

"It was a long time ago. I mean, college was ten years ago. A lot changes in that time. *Everything* changes."

I knew that was a lie before it even left my lips. So much was the same. Kacey still knew when I was flustered. She still had the ability to figure out exactly what I needed when I needed it. Like at this moment, when her hand slipped into mine underneath the table and she gave it the lightest squeeze. She didn't acknowledge the gesture, but also didn't let go, simply letting our hands dangle between us while we continued as if nothing was happening.

My attention suddenly snapped to the other end of the table when I heard Bo's boisterous voice shouting as he held my sister's phone up to his ear. "What's up, Mama A? I hear you're just around the corner. Get over here. I miss you."

Kacey removed her eyes from me to look at Bo. "What's going on over there?"

"I'm not sure. I think he's talking to my mom. I'm going to go see what's up." I reluctantly removed my hand

120

from hers, missing her touch as soon as it was gone. When I got down to Bo's end of the table, I put my hand on his shoulder to get his attention. "Was that my mom?"

"It sure was," he said cheerfully. "Your parents are on their way over here right now. They were at Bellman dropping off a check to the alumni association. They were already in the car when they called, so they should be here any minute."

Like clockwork, the doorbell rang at that very moment. I quickly made my way back to Kacey, since I figured she would want a warning, albeit a small one. "So, it turns out, my parents..."

"Mama and Papa A! So good to see you." Bo's shouting as he greeted my parents interrupted my warning.

Kacey's body stiffened as she turned her attention toward the door. I tried to reach for her hand, but she quickly pulled it away as if she suddenly didn't want anyone to see. I grabbed her chin and forced her to look at me. "Hey, it's okay. There's nothing to be nervous about."

She nodded her head, but I could tell she didn't believe me. "I have to run to the bathroom. Sorry. I just..." She closed her eyes and took a deep breath. "I need to calm myself down before I talk to them."

This time when I reached for her hand, she let me take it. "Take your time and just think about the first time you ever met them. You were so nervous that day, and it went great. They loved you then and they'll love you now. I promise."

I watched as Kacey walked away, her body language exuding much less confidence than usual, and my mind went back to the last time I had seen her this nervous.

"Would you stop pacing?" I put my hands on Kacey's shoulders to try to halt her movements.

"I just don't know if I can do this. I don't have a ton of experience with parents and this is so important. So, so important." Kacey pushed past me and continued to pace.

It was so crazy, and kind of adorable, to see her this worked up. Kacey was my cool, calm, and collected girlfriend. She talked me off the ledge every time I stressed about school or life. She also had a constant unintentional swagger in her step. Well, she normally did. Right now her body was so stiff, she almost looked robotic.

"As cute as this whole thing is, I really need you to sit down and talk about this with me." I sat down on my bed, then patted the empty spot next to me. When Kacey finally sat, I took her hand in mine and brought it up to my mouth to kiss her knuckles. "Do you want me to call my parents and tell them we can't make it to dinner?"

Instead of looking at me, Kacey stared at a spot on the ground. She shook her head so subtly that I almost didn't notice it. "No. That would look really bad. We have to go. We've been dating for months now. Your parents have been consistently inviting us over for dinner since we started this semester. That was two months ago."

"The only reason they keep asking is because they know how much you mean to me and they're trying to be supportive."

"I just really want them to like me."

I put my arm around Kacey's shoulder and pulled her tightly against me. "They're going to love you. Do you know how I know that?"

"How?"

"Because I love you, and I'm not sure how anyone in this world could meet you and not adore you."

This brought the slightest glimpse of a smile to Kacey's face. "I love you too, Kari. That's why I want this to be perfect. Are you sure my outfit is okay?"

I used her question as an excuse to check her out from head to toe. She was wearing tan corduroy pants and a long sleeve red and blue button up. Her blue shoes even matched the blue in her top. "Honestly, you look sexy as hell. Also, very presentable for meeting parents. It's impressive that you can pull off both of those at once."

"And you're sure your mom will like those flowers, and it's okay that I didn't get anything for your dad? I read you're supposed to give the father alcohol and I obviously can't do that."

I rested my head against hers. "You're overthinking this, babe. You didn't even have to get my mom flowers, but they're absolutely perfect."

"I got the peach roses because they represent gratitude, and I'm thankful for your parents having me over. I'm also thankful that they had you because you're the best thing to ever happen to me."

A smile bloomed on my face as her words gave me the butterflies I'd become very accustomed to since meeting Kacey. "There's my smooth-talking girlfriend." I put my hand on her thigh and slowly moved it higher. "I know one way I could calm you down."

Kacey breathed in sharply, but stopped my hand before it could get any higher. "We can't. They'll know."

"Oh, come on. It's not like I'd let you go there with sex hair and your shirt buttoned up wrong."

Kacey's eyes were wide. "It won't matter. They're parents. They'll still know somehow."

"Well, I guess we'll just have to save this for later." This time, she didn't stop me when I pushed her back onto the bed and kissed her slowly while grinding my hips into her. When I pulled back, Kacey looked much more relaxed. "Feeling a little better?"

"I'm feeling something," Kacey said with a laugh.

I hopped off the bed and reached my hand toward her. "Perfect. Let's go."

Twenty-five minutes later, we pulled up to my parents' house, and Kacey's nerves were back. I watched as she ran her hands over her pants, while reciting something under her breath. I got out of the car, then went around to her side to open the door for her.

She climbed out and grabbed my hand tightly. "Is this okay?"

"Aside from the fact that you're cutting off all circulation to my hand, it's great."

Kacey didn't even smile at my joke. "I mean, will your parents care that we're holding hands?"

"No, they won't," I reassured her.

Yet, when the front door started to open, she immediately dropped my hand. We were barely inside the door when my mom pulled me into her arms. She gave me an extra squeeze before letting go, then focused her attention on Kacey. "You must be Kacey. I've heard so much about you."

Kacey held out her hand. "That's me. It's so nice to mee—"

Before she could even finish her sentence, my mom wrapped her in a hug. "Handshakes are too formal. We're a hugging family." My mom pulled back and held onto both of Kacey's arms, a wide grin adorning her face. "Kari told me you were pretty. She wasn't kidding."

Kacey held out the flowers she was holding. "I brought these for you. Thank you so much for having me over. Kari's told me about how close the four of you are and how much you care about each other, and I just want you to know that I really care about your daughter too. She's the most amazing person I've ever met and I have to assume that's because of you and your husband. So, I guess I'm also saying thank you for raising her to be the person she is today."

I knew Kacey was only talking so much because she was nervous, but I could also tell my mom was eating it up. Once Kacey's rambling ended, my mom looked at me and blinked her eyes rapidly, the way she always did when she tried not to cry. "Well, that's just about the sweetest thing I've ever heard." She put one arm around Kacey and directed her toward the kitchen. "Tell me, dear, how do you feel about chicken pot pie?"

"It's one of my favorite meals." Kacey's answer was quick and I honestly didn't know if she was telling the truth. That didn't matter to my mom though. She turned around and her whole face was beaming. "You found yourself a good one, Kari. I think we're all going to get along really well."

When Kacey looked back over her shoulder at me, she was beaming just as much as my mom.

     I shook myself from my daydream and greeted my parents. My mom gave me a one-armed hug as she searched the room. "I thought I saw Kacey standing with you."

     "She had to use the restroom, but she should be back down soon." I felt Kacey's presence before I saw her and wasn't surprised when I turned around to find her coming up behind me.

     She nodded her head at both of my parents. "Mr. and Mrs. Adelberg. It's wonderful to see you. It's been a long time."

     "Way too long, if you ask me," my dad said cheerfully. "It's so great to have you back in the area. I know

Kari is very happy about that." He winked at me, and I had to wonder exactly what he was getting at

"I'm really happy to be back too. Everyone has been great, especially Kari." Her eyes lingered on me for a few seconds, before she turned her attention to my mom. "Mrs. Adelberg, do you think we could talk in private for just a few minutes?"

My mom's eyes went wide, but she recovered quickly. "Yes. I would like that."

Bo pointed toward the stairs. "It's pretty crowded and loud down here, so why don't you guys go upstairs to the guest room? It's the last room on the left."

We all watched as my mom and Kacey walked off together. Once they were out of sight, Bo leaned close to my ear to whisper to me. "So, are we going up there to listen?"

"You know, there is this crazy thing known as privacy."

"So, that means?"

"Of course we're going to listen. Let's go."

The door was partially open, so Bo and I stuck to the side of the hallway where they wouldn't see us and snuck just behind the door. I positioned myself right at a spot where I had a pretty good view of the room through the crack in the door. Both my mom and Kacey were standing in the middle of the room, but neither of them had started to talk yet.

Kacey ran a hand through her hair then stood up taller as she faced my mom. "I owe you an apology," she said firmly. My mom went to say something, but Kacey put a hand up to stop her. "You and the rest of your family did a lot for me. The whole time Kari and I were dating, you guys were like the family I never had, and I never thanked you for that."

"Oh honey, you don't have to—"

"I do, though. For years, I thought about calling you and saying something. Once I even had the phone in my hand with your number dialed, but I couldn't do it. I thought it might open stuff up with Kari again, and I didn't want to hurt her more than I already had. I also figured you had no interest in talking to the girl who broke your daughter's heart."

126

Kacey slowly shook her head and sat down on the bed. "I really thought I was doing the right thing. I don't know how much Kari told you."

"She told me enough. I'm sure that was a very difficult time for you. That was a lot to take on at such a young age, but you always were well beyond your years. I'm not going to lie and tell you I didn't feel slighted at the time all of this happened. But I don't blame you anymore. I know you were doing what you thought was right, and honestly, I think you made the decision you had to at the time."

Kacey looked at my mom and I could see a few tears running down her cheeks. It took everything in me not to run into the room and wipe them away. Kacey stood back up and faced my mom completely again. "It was the hardest decision of my entire life. Your daughter really was the best thing to ever happen to me and losing her was the worst. I don't want you to think I ever took her for granted. There wasn't a day that went by that I didn't think about her. I know people say that sort of thing all the time, but it's true."

Without saying a word, my mom pulled Kacey tightly into her arms. I motioned to Bo that we should go, and the two of us headed downstairs. As I walked, my head and my heart started another battle over what I should do with the words I just heard.

Chapter 10

Following Thanksgiving, Kacey and I continued to grow closer. Both of us were busy with the rush of the holidays, but we still found time to get together, usually later at night. I would have dinner with Bailey and Kacey or join them afterward as Bailey was getting ready for bed. Every night after tucking her in, Kacey would put on a movie and we would snuggle onto the couch together. Almost every night, we would fall asleep and wake up hours later, still wrapped around each other. Most of the time, I purposely tried to drift off just so I could wake up in Kacey's arms a few hours later and hear her say a sleepy goodbye.

One night in mid-December, I fell asleep and didn't wake until five the next morning. Instead of just slipping out, another idea came to me. I dug my hands into Kacey's sides to tickle her. She startled awake but smiled when she saw it was me.

I smiled a tired smile back at her. "Good morning, you."

Kacey rubbed her eyes and looked down at her phone. "Wow. It is morning, huh?"

My heart raced at the sound of Kacey's low, raspy voice and I couldn't stop myself from reaching out and running a finger up and down her arm. "It is. Since we're awake, I thought we could get ready and go to Emma's Twenty-four Seven Cafe before school and work."

"That sounds great, as long as I can get my daughter out of bed."

I leaned in and kissed her on the cheek before hopping off of the couch. "Perfect. You work on that and I'll go get myself ready. I'll be back in about a half hour."

Kacey chuckled. "You're giving me a lot of credit if you think I'm gonna have both myself and Bailey ready in a half hour."

"Well, lucky for you, I'm a morning person. It's when I thrive. So, if you guys need any help, I've totally got your back."

Kacey lifted an eyebrow at me. "Since when are *you* a morning person? I used to have to drag you out of bed in college."

"Since I stopped being in a committed relationship with tequila. Crazy what you can achieve when you're not up half the night. If I remember correctly, though, you always found creative ways to get me out of bed." My face heated at the thought.

Kacey stood from the couch and rested one hand on my hip. "I don't think I would say I got you *out of bed* exactly."

Now the heat traveled throughout my entire body, all the way down to my core. I stared at Kacey, the air suddenly heavy with sexual tension. Kacey took the hand that wasn't on my hip and used it to move a piece of hair behind my ear, then rested her forehead against mine. The moment was so charged, I could actually feel her lips moving closer to mine. I forced myself to look away and pulled out of her grip. "Sorry. I don't know why I brought that up. Probably not the best topic of conversation."

Kacey shrugged. "Old habits die hard, I guess." I could hear the pain in her voice as she stared down at the ground.

I put my hand under her chin to direct her eyes toward mine. "I'm sorry. I promise I'm not trying to play games. I don't want to hurt you. I'm just not used to being your friend and sometimes I slip up."

"Hey, we're both still trying to figure out how to navigate this relationship. It's okay. It feels like the more time that passes, it gets easier yet harder at the same time." She paused and looked deeply into my eyes. "You do know that I'm not going to hurt you though, right?"

I wanted to tell her that I knew that. There was a part of me that knew she wouldn't, but another part that was terrified of how she could destroy me if I fully let her in again. I cleared my throat and looked away. "I better get ready. I'll be back soon." I turned to walk toward the door, unwilling to face Kacey, knowing that the truth was written all over my face.

When I returned a half hour later, the tension had completely dissipated. Bailey was awake and greeted me at the door with a big hug. "Kari! This is going to be so much fun. When Mom told me we were going to breakfast with you, I hopped right out of bed."

Kacey shook her head as she joined us at the door and put one hand on Bailey's shoulder. "I guess I know the secret to getting her up now. Want to come over every morning?"

Bailey's face lit up. "That would be awesome! I would love it." Her eyes widened as if an idea had just popped into her head. "We should have a slumber party some night. You, me, and Mom. We could build a fort out of blankets and eat popcorn and watch movies until we fall asleep."

I had to admit it sounded pretty wonderful. I looked to Kacey who was shaking her head but had a twinkle in her eye. "Maybe we will have to do that someday, but for now, how about we get some breakfast?" I put my hand up and Bailey jumped to slap it, then opened the door and ran out to the car.

Kacey leaned against the door frame watching her daughter, a content smile on her face. "I can't remember the last time I saw her this excited, which is saying a lot, since she finds joy in the smallest things in life." She looked toward me, then reached out and squeezed my arm. "Thanks for suggesting this. You were always so good at taking an ordinary day and making it extraordinary. I missed that. I missed how fun it was just spending time with you."

"I haven't felt very fun the last few years," I answered honestly. "Then you came back here and suddenly I felt like I got part of myself back."

Kacey's face was serious as she looked over at me. "I will never let you lose that part of yourself again." The air was thick as we stared at each other. I could read the truth within her words and I knew she was promising not to hurt me, just as she had earlier. Her eyes said all of the words she was too afraid to speak, but I could tell they were begging me to believe her. Begging me to let her in fully and I wanted to. God, did I want to.

I opened my mouth to say something, unsure what words were about to come out, when my attention was suddenly pulled away by the sound of a loud car horn. Kacey and I both looked toward her car where Bailey was sitting in the driver's seat and rolling her eyes at us. When I looked back at Kacey, we both laughed.

"It looks like we're being summoned," she said. "One thing my daughter has yet to learn is the art of patience."

"Hey, can you blame her? We did promise her breakfast." At that moment, my stomach started to growl. "Which I could clearly use as well."

After climbing into the car, Kacey began to search her pockets. "Ah, shoot. I must've left my phone inside."

Bailey's hand reached through to the front holding Kacey's phone and when Kacey gave her a look, she shrugged. "You got a text, so I checked it. It was Kari's mom."

"My mom?" I asked, confused as to why she even had Kacey's number.

When I looked at Kacey, she seemed just as confused. "We exchanged numbers on Thanksgiving, but this is the first time she reached out to me." She turned toward Bailey. "What did she want?"

"She asked if we wanted to come over on Christmas Eve, so I said of course."

I couldn't help the laugh that escaped from my throat. Apparently, my mom had changed her mind since the lecture she gave me on Thanksgiving about being careful.

Kacey lifted an eyebrow at me. "I take it you didn't know about this." When I shook my head no, she began to chew on the inside of her lip as though she was concerned. "Do you... I mean... is it okay... if we come? It seems we already committed."

I smiled widely at her and grabbed her hand. "Are you kidding me? Christmas Eve with all of my favorite people just like the old days? Of course it's okay."

***

131

Late in the afternoon on Christmas Eve, Kacey and Bailey met me and Duke outside so they could follow me to my parents' house. Bailey's eyes went wide as soon as she saw Duke. "Duke is coming? Can I ride with you guys?"

"You're going to make your mom ride all alone?" I asked with a chuckle.

Bailey waved her hand nonchalantly. "She'll be okay. She's a big girl."

In the corner of my eye, I caught Kacey watching as I helped Bailey and Duke into the back of my car. I didn't dare to look at her because just the feeling of her eyes on me was almost too much for my body to handle. Instead, I got in the car and began to drive.

"So, are you my mom's girlfriend?"

I began to cough, shocked by Bailey's blunt question. "Excuse me?"

"You don't have to lie just because I'm a kid. I *am* almost ten. I know grown-ups who aren't married go on dates. My mom never has, but she acts different around you."

"How does she act around me?" I asked, unable to tame my curiosity.

Bailey shrugged. "Happy. Like really happy. Not in that grown-up way where they act happy so us kids won't think something's wrong. Just super happy. Like, as happy as I am when I wake up on Christmas morning. She also laughs at like everything you say, and no offense, but some stuff just isn't that funny."

I couldn't help but laugh. "Well, gee, thanks. But to answer your question, your mom and I are just really good friends."

Bailey seemed the slightest bit disappointed with this information but petted Duke instead of responding. She was quiet for a few minutes before she finally spoke again. "Welllll, if you wanted to be my mom's girlfriend, I'm okay with it. I would love it actually." She paused and brought her attention to Duke before making eye contact with me in the rearview mirror. "No pressure, of course."

Yep, no pressure. Except that it seemed like everyone in my life was plotting to get Kacey and me together. At this point, it seemed the only thing stopping us was my fear, but there was more than enough of that to keep us apart forever. Luckily, Bailey changed the subject, and we spent the rest of the car ride talking about the trip she and Kacey were going on to New York City the day after Christmas. Kacey had already told me about it and even invited me to come along, but I didn't want to intrude on that special time for her and Bailey.

After pulling into my parents' driveway, I asked Bailey to take Duke inside, then I walked over to Kacey's car. I opened her door and leaned up against it. "Hey, you."

Kacey looked up at me and I could tell the smile on her face matched the one on mine. We stayed like this for a minute, silently taking in the moment, happily lost in each other's eyes. After she removed her seatbelt, I reached out my hand to help her out of the car, but didn't drop it when she was standing beside me. Kacey smiled at our interlocked fingers, then smiled back at me. "So, how was your car ride?" she asked.

"Very interesting, actually," I said with a chuckle.

Kacey lifted an eyebrow. "Oh yeah? Do I even want to know?"

"Well, I hear that I make you very happy. Like Christmas morning level of happiness."

A slight blush came onto Kacey's face, and she shook her head slightly. "That's a lot of happiness. Did Bailey tell you that?"

"Well, it wasn't Duke, so I guess it must have been her."

Kacey used the hand that wasn't holding mine to playfully push me away, except she didn't let go and immediately grabbed my coat to pull me back to her. I stumbled into her, laughing as our bodies collided softly, and Kacey leveled me by placing her hands on my hips. Her face became serious as she stared into my eyes, her own becoming darker as they studied mine. "She's right, you know. You make me happier than I've ever been. You make me even happier now than you did in college, and that's saying a lot."

I sighed contently and wrapped my arms around her neck, resting my forehead against hers. "You make me happy too."

133

And she really did. Christmas Eve with Kacey, Bailey, and my family was better than any holiday I could remember. We all talked and laughed as if no time had passed at all since the last time Kacey was with my family. When my dad read *The Night Before Christmas,* Kacey snuggled into me from one side, while Bailey cuddled close on the other side. I tried to ignore the pull on my heart as I thought about how right it all felt. The pulling continued as I followed Kacey and Bailey out to their car. I helped Bailey into the back then rested my hand on Kacey's open door and looked between her and Bailey. "Tonight was wonderful. Thanks for coming."

Kacey grabbed my hand, immediately intertwining her fingers with mine, a motion that had become second-nature to us at this point. "Thank you so much for including us. It was perfect." She squeezed my hand one more time before dropping it.

I closed her door, then leaned up against my car to watch them pull away. I jumped when I heard someone laughing behind me and turned to see Kylie standing there. "You've got it bad, girl. I haven't seen you like this in years."

I shook my head. "It's not like that," I said, trying to convince myself just as much as I was trying to convince her at this point.

Kylie opened her mouth to say something, but I put my hand up to stop her. "Just drop it, okay?"

She put her hands in the air. "Hey, now. I was just going to ask if they were spending tomorrow with us too."

"No. They have their own Christmas traditions. Plus, Bailey is off from school for the rest of the week, so they are going to New York for a few days. I think they get back on New Year's Eve, but I probably won't see them since I told Bo I would go to his party that night."

"Speaking of which, Bo invited me to that. Do you mind having me tag along?"

"Someone's gotta keep him entertained. God knows I can't keep up with him."

***

134

"What's up, bitches?" Bo screamed as he opened the door for Kylie and me, a drink already present in the hand that wasn't holding the door.

I groaned. "I'm too old for this."

Bo gave me a look as he reached out to take my jacket. "You're thirty-one. You're not dead."

I looked past him to the bottle of tequila sitting on his kitchen counter with four filled shot glasses beside it. "I very well might be by tomorrow." I let my eyes search the house. "Is someone else here already?"

Right after I asked my question, I heard the toilet flush and watched Bo's friend, Derek, saunter out. I hadn't seen him in a while since he wasn't able to make it to Friendsgiving, but I could tell from one look that his nickname of Douchey Derek was still very fitting. His short brown hair was spiked up with way too much gel and it took everything in me not to remind him that his hairstyle stopped being cool after 1995. He was wearing skinny jeans that were way too tight and had a shirt on that said *I'm just here for the midnight kiss.* I was pretty sure he had worn that shirt every year and had yet to get a kiss. Not for lack of trying, though. I shuddered just thinking about how many times he had hit on me and tried to convince me making out with him would magically change my sexual orientation.

I shuddered again as he wrapped an arm around my waist and wiggled his eyebrows at me. "Ready to have some fun tonight?"

I slipped out of his grip and walked over to the counter to grab a shot glass. If I had any hope of making it through this night, I was going to need plenty of alcohol. I held my shot glass in the air. "Let's do this."

It didn't take long for me to develop a buzz that soon turned into a slurring, tripping, karaoke-singing level of drunkenness. Even though I was more drunk than I had been in a really long time, I still knew that keeping my phone with me wasn't the smartest plan. Still, this didn't stop me from slipping it out of my pocket a half hour before midnight to text Kacey. *I misssssss you. How was New York? Bo and I just sang karaoke.*

I stared at my phone, intently waiting for Kacey's reply, which came in less than a minute. *Ha. I'm sorry I missed that. New York was great. We had an amazing time.*

There was nothing special about her text, but it still had me smiling from ear to ear. I let out a sigh as I typed back my reply. *I'm sorry you did too. I wish you were hereeeeeee.* I thought for a moment, then sent a follow up text. *Actually, I wish I was there. This is lame.*

Doesn't sound lame. Karaoke sounds like fun. Bailey and I do a mean rendition of Let It Go.

I smiled as I thought about Bailey and Kacey singing together.

"Texting your girlfriend?" Kylie asked as she snuggled up next to me on Bo's couch.

I shook my head firmly. "Kacey's not my girlfriend."

Kylie groaned. "I don't understand why she isn't. Kacey is freaking sexy. Like ridiculously sexy."

I looked at my sister's half-lidded eyes and laughed. "And you're ridiculously drunk."

Kylie ran her hand over my face. "So are you, and I'm just saying, if I was gay, I'd be doing everything I could to get into Kacey Caldwell's bed tonight. I'm not sure why you're not."

I shook my head again. "Nope. Can't do that." I pointed down toward my crotch. "This is a Kacey Caldwell free zone."

Kylie laughed way too hard at my joke, throwing her head back as if it were the funniest thing she'd ever heard. "Okay, then. Keep that vagina lonely. But you have to agree that Kacey is sexy."

Even I was surprised when I shook my head no. "She's not. Okay she is, but sexy isn't the right way to describe her. She's beaaaauuuuutiful. God, Kylie, did you ever notice how beautiful she is? She radiates beauty. And not just on the outside. She's... ugh... she's perfect."

"And you're in lo—"

"Ladies and gentlemen! It's almost midnight! Anyone partaking in the midnight shot needs to come to papa." I was happy about Bo's voice interrupting Kylie's words, knowing I didn't want to hear something I was so unsure I could deny.

Kylie jumped from the couch. "That's my cue."

136

She was the only person to stumble over to Bo, the other party goers clearly just as over drinking as I was at this point.

I cringed when I felt an arm come around my shoulder, immediately knowing who it was. Derek smiled over at me, his perfectly straight white teeth glowing. "So, what do you say, pretty lady? Want to be my midnight kiss?"

I not-so-subtly inched away from him. "Nope."

He scooted closer to me. "Aw, come on. How many guys have you even kissed in your life?"

"Enough to know I don't like it."

Not deterred, Derek wiggled his eyebrows at me. "But you never kissed me."

The conversation was interrupted by Bo starting a countdown. When midnight struck, I watched Bo and Kylie click their shot glasses together and throw them back. I felt like my eyes were going to pop out of my head as Kylie pulled Bo close to her and started making out with him right there in the middle of the party. I shook my head as I made my way over to them and then pulled them apart. "Nope. Absolutely not. This. Nope. Not happening."

Kylie simply laughed as she wiped at her lips and Bo stared at her with a goofy drunk grin. Two arms wrapped around my waist from behind and started to pull me away. "Come on, babe. Let them have a little fun."

I whipped around to face Derek and removed his hands from my body. "Absolutely not. Not happening. This…" I pointed between the two of us. "Is also not happening. Not even if we were the last two people on this planet."

To my surprise, Derek simply smiled and shrugged. "Luckily, I have a backup plan. Tell me about your friend Kacey. Bo tells me you knew each other back in the day." The way he wiggled his eyebrows told me he knew about our past.

"Bo told you that?" I asked, becoming slightly annoyed that he would share my personal business with someone like Derek.

"Nope. Didn't have to. He told me Kacey was off-limits because of bro code or some shit like that, so I put the pieces together. Now you confirmed it. Seriously, though, that just makes her even hotter."

"You don't deserve to even think about Kacey Caldwell," I said firmly.

"Aw, come on. It's all in good fun. She has a daughter. She obviously swings both ways. So, what do you say?" He elbowed me in the side playfully. "Will you put in a good word for me? It's not like I'm looking for forever. Just a good time."

"Never," I said with a shaky voice. I couldn't stand to hear him talk about Kacey this way. I could blow off his advances on me, but something about hearing him objectify Kacey had my blood boiling. "Kacey is smart and funny and dedicated and the most caring person I've ever met. She deserves someone who sees all of that. She deserves someone who *does* want forever, because getting to spend forever with Kacey would be a dream come true."

I stormed away from him and was soon out the front door, slamming it shut so I didn't have to listen to his asinine explanation of how it was all just a joke and I was being too uptight. Without thinking, I pulled out my phone and clicked on Kacey's name.

After just three rings, she picked up. "Happy New Year!" she said cheerfully.

I scoffed. "What a start to the new year. First, Bo and my sister make out. Then, Derek tries to hit on me. *Then,* he has the audacity to ask about you."

"What about me?"

"Just some bullshit about how hot you are, which is true, but I told him you're so much more than that."

"You... you did?" Kacey asked a little more quietly.

"Of course. You're everything, Kacey. You're the whole package. All the funny and smart and caring wrapped up in one super pretty package."

Kacey laughed lightly, clearly becoming more aware of just how drunk I was. "Are you still at the party?"

I shook my head as if she could see me. "Nope. Walking home. Can't be there."

"You shouldn't be walking alone when you're wasted. Where are you?"

"Oh, come on. This is Bellman. Plus, I'm practically in the driveway."

I watched Kacey's door open down the street and saw her shake her head. "Practically in the driveway, huh?" she shouted.

I shrugged and continued to stumble down the street. Within a few seconds, Kacey was by my side with a hand around my waist, a touch I appreciated much more than Derek's. I stared at her as we walked together. "You're so pretty, like so so pretty. It's not fair for one person to be so pretty. Nope. Especially when it's the person I'm not supposed to be falling for. But, alas, you are. Your face should win an award. Most beautiful. Most kissable." I turned in her arms when we reached our driveway and stared at her lips, any control I was normally able to have over my body completely gone. "I want to kiss you right now. Derek wanted a midnight kiss. I would never. One because he's gross and two because I don't want to kiss anyone in the world but you."

I leaned in close and was surprised when Kacey pulled away. She cleared her throat and pointed toward her house. "We need to get you some water."

Once we were inside and I was seated on the couch, Kacey handed me a glass of water and Tylenol. I took the medicine and quickly drank the whole glass of water, then pushed my bottom lip out as I looked at Kacey. "Why won't you kiss me? Do you not want to kiss me?"

Kacey rolled her eyes at me. "I think we both know the answer to that, but you're drunk. I won't do something with you while you're drunk that you won't do sober."

I reached out my arms and pulled her down on top of me. "You always were so chivalrous," I said into her neck.

Kacey quickly stood and reached her hand toward me. "We should get you to bed."

In my drunken state, I almost started to cry at the thought of going home alone. "I don't want to be by myself on New Year's."

Kacey took my hand and directed me toward the stairs. "You can sleep in my bed. That way, I'm here to take care of you if you get sick." Soon, we were in her bedroom and Kacey sat me down on her bed, then headed to her dresser. She pulled out shorts and a T-shirt and threw them over to me. "Here. This will be more comfy to sleep in."

I didn't miss how she purposefully turned around while I changed. I giggled as I started to remove my outfit. "You know, there's nothing here you haven't seen before."

"Yep. So, there's no need for me to look."

"But you don't want to look?" I knew I was teasing her, but couldn't help it in that moment, a heat burning between my legs that I couldn't contain.

Kacey groaned. "Again, I think you know the answer to that."

Realizing Kacey wasn't going to be anything but respectful, I got myself dressed and crawled into her bed. After a few minutes, Kacey finally turned around and walked back to the bed. She bent down and ran a hand through my hair, then placed a gentle kiss on my forehead. "You're so beautiful."

Her words sent a whole new sensation through my body and I reached a hand out toward her. "Will you cuddle with me? Please?" I could tell Kacey was about to protest, so I put my hand up to stop her words. "I cuddle with you sober."

"But not in bed."

"I promise to keep my hands to myself." I gave her a look I knew she couldn't resist. It was the look that had convinced her to stay with me in my dorm room after many drunken nights and the look that could get her to bed when she insisted on staying up to study when we lived together. "Please?"

Kacey smiled knowingly. "That's unfair. You know I can't resist that face." Her smile grew as I pulled down the covers and motioned for her to get in beside me. "Let me get ready. I'll be out in a few minutes."

By the time she crawled into bed beside me, I was almost asleep. I naturally grabbed her arm and placed it around my waist so she could spoon me from behind. The sensation of her arm wrapped tightly around me as she held me close, brought back every memory I had been trying to suppress. I moved closer to her and allowed our bodies to melt together, the way they always did. I sighed contently as I drifted completely off to sleep. "I love you, Kacey."

Chapter 11

My eyes popped open, and I shot up as the memories from the night before came into my head. I looked toward Kacey who still had an arm wrapped tightly around me and knew I hadn't imagined it. I cringed as the ending to the night played out in my memory.

After getting in bed, Kacey had held me tight. Call it a reflex. Call it drunken truth. Call it sleepy confessions. No matter what you call it, I had told Kacey that I loved her as I fell asleep. But that wasn't the part that got to me. I wasn't freaking out over how true those words were, even if it was scary to admit. What really took me by surprise was what followed the long silence that lingered between us. The words Kacey spoke softly after she was sure I was asleep. "I love you too, Kari. I love you so much."

Her words sounded sad, as if loving me was the most painful thing in the world. And maybe it was for her. I had given her just enough of me without giving her the part she really wanted, and I hated the fact that I was hurting her, but I didn't know what to do. I didn't want to hurt her but was also terrified of getting myself hurt.

My stomach churned and I wasn't sure if it had to do with Kacey's confession or the tequila shots, but I knew I had to get it out. I quickly ran to the bathroom, making it just in time to hurl into the toilet. When I walked back out a few minutes later, Kacey was standing and watching me. "I was just about to come check if you were okay." She looked toward the ground, where she dragged one foot slowly across the carpet. "So, about last night..."

"Yeah, you might want to fill me in. What happened after I got here? It's all blank after the glass of water," I lied. I hated lying to Kacey, but I wasn't sure if I was ready to have this conversation.

Apparently, she wasn't either. I watched her body relax as she took a deep breath. "Nothing really. You insisted on staying here. We cuddled." She looked up at me.

"Is that okay? I wasn't trying to pull anything. You were just very persistent."

Before I could answer, Bailey ran into the room. Her eyes lit up when she looked at me. "Kari! What are you doing here? Did you come for breakfast?"

My eyes were wide as I looked between Bailey and Kacey. It seemed like lying was going to be a regular occurrence this morning. "I did, but I'm actually not feeling well, so I'm going to go."

I started to leave the room, but Bailey followed closely behind me. "Do you have a stomach ache? My mom is really good at taking care of stomach aches. She always makes me feel better."

I heard Kacey following us down the stairs and turned to face them once we were at the bottom. "I wouldn't want to get either of you sick. Plus, I'm sure you guys have New Year's Day plans, and I don't want to interrupt."

"Are you sure? We were just going to hang out. You wouldn't be interrupting. We would love to have you here." I couldn't miss the disappointment written all over Kacey's face, and it was almost enough to make me change my mind. Then I looked toward Bailey, who was equally disappointed and that *was* enough to change my mind. I couldn't let her down just because Kacey and I had unresolved issues.

"Okay. I'll stay. But only because I want to hear all about your trip to New York."

As we ate breakfast, Bailey spoke animatedly about their trip, but Kacey was quiet. Anytime I looked at her, it seemed like she was lost in her own thoughts, and I wondered if she was thinking about our late-night confessions. I knew I was. The few times she spoke during breakfast, all I could hear in my head was the way the word *love* sounded leaving her lips and how I wanted to hear it again and again. But I also couldn't shake the sadness in her voice and that made me question everything I had done with Kacey these past few months. How I treated our relationship that was constantly teetering between friendship and something much more.

Now, I really was feeling sick, so I excused myself and gave both Bailey and Kacey quick hugs before

142

practically running out the door. I had a lot to figure out and sitting at breakfast with Kacey wasn't going to help any of the questions running through my head.

***

When I arrived at my parents' house a few hours later, I immediately pulled Kylie aside. "Please tell me you didn't have sex with Bo last night," I said, trying not to make a face.

Kylie looked at me seriously. "Of course I didn't have sex with Bo. First of all, neither of us would pursue anything without talking to you first. Even drunk, we get that. Making out is one thing. Having sex is a whole other ball game. Second of all, I ended up throwing up like five minutes after we made out."

I laughed. "That's the reaction *I* would expect to have to making out with Bo. I wouldn't expect it from you."

Kylie smirked. "Oh, making out with Bo was great. I'm getting butterflies in my stomach just thinking about it. He doesn't kiss like other guys. It's like—"

I held up my hand. "Ew, stop. I can't listen to this."

"I don't know why you get so weird about Bo. I could honestly do a lot worse. He's a great guy."

I sighed. "Bo *is* a great guy. I obviously know that. He's my best friend. But because he's my best friend, I also know how he talks about girls. I wouldn't want you to be just another notch on his bedpost."

"Bo is a big teddy bear. I think he talks that way to you because he sees you as one of the bros. I don't even know if he means it. When was the last time you actually heard about him being with a girl? We're talking about the guy who held my hair as I threw up last night, then slept on the couch so I could have his bed. He didn't try anything. He was a total sweetheart. Speaking of which. I had to sleep at his house because a certain someone left me last night. Maybe *I* should be the one asking *you* if you had sex."

I rolled my eyes. "No. I didn't have sex. I did end up at Kacey's though. Figure I might as well tell you since I

143

know it'll be your next question. No sex. Just a lot of embarrassing myself."

Kylie laughed. "I don't understand why you and Kacey won't just face the fact that you're meant to be together."

"Because we're not," I answered a bit too quickly, trying to ignore the heavy feeling in my gut. "We're friends."

Kylie let out a low whistle and when I glared at her, she put both hands in the air. "I'm just saying. I wish I had a friend that looked at me the way Kacey looks at you."

I was about to answer when my mom walked over to us. "What are you girls talking about over here? It looks serious."

"Nothing," I answered at the same time Kylie said "Kacey."

My mom's face lit up. "Speaking of Kacey, I need to talk to you about something privately, Kari."

I swallowed hard as my sister walked away, leaving my mom and me alone, not sure where this conversation could possibly go. "What's up?"

"I need to apologize for something." My mom let out a long sigh, as though it was painful to say this. "I was wrong to tell you to be careful with Kacey. Seeing the pain you went through after she broke your heart was the hardest thing I've ever gone through. I hated her for doing that to you. But after talking to her and spending more time with her and Bailey, I get it. She was young and scared, but she's come a long way. Most importantly, she's every bit as in love with you as she was ten years ago and I know you'll try to deny this, but you're in love with her too. That's the real deal. If you can be apart from someone for ten years and still love them, that's real. Screw being safe. This is one time you're risking a lot more by playing it safe."

I opened and closed my mouth a few times, unsure what to say. Between Kacey's confession and my mom's speech, it was a lot to process. Why did everyone insist on making this something more? Why couldn't it just stay how it was? Wasn't it good this way? Before I could stop them, tears were streaming down my face.

———

144

My mom wasted no time pulling me into her arms and kissing my forehead. "Oh, honey, I'm sorry. I didn't mean to upset you. I just want you to be happy."

I pulled back and wiped at my eyes. "I am happy. At least, I think I am." I shook my head. "I don't know. Kacey makes me really happy. Ever since she came back into my life, everything just feels better. But do you know how scary that is? It's terrifying to know that someone has that much of a hold over my life. I can't give my heart to her, Mom. I just can't. It could hurt me way too much."

"You might get mad at me for saying this, but I think you already gave her your heart. You're trying to protect something that you're not even holding onto anymore. What you really need is the trust that Kacey isn't going to break what you've already given her."

"But how do I get that?"

My mom looked sad about my question. "I can't tell you that. That's something you need to figure out on your own."

I nodded my head, trying to decide what all of this meant. "I think I just need time and space."

"You do whatever you think is best, baby girl." Even though her words were supportive, I could tell my mom didn't agree with my methods, but she was right. It was my choice to make, and it seemed like the only choice, even if I didn't like it.

***

I let the space between Kacey and I grow even bigger in the weeks following New Year's. We still texted, but they texts became more sporadic and I kept coming up with excuses as to why we couldn't see each other. When January eighteenth rolled around, I knew it would be wrong to keep avoiding her. I was normally terrible at remembering special dates, but the eighteenth was one that I could never forget. I knocked on Kacey's door, worried about how she might react to seeing me after I had clearly been blowing her off the past few weeks.

Bailey opened the door and her eyes went wide when she saw it was me. "Kari! You're here." She wrapped her arms around me. "I missed you. Did you know today is my mom's birthday?"

I lifted up the gift bag I was holding. "I know. That's why I'm here. I brought her a gift."

Bailey opened the door even wider. "Come in. She's going to be so excited you're here. She missed you. I can tell. She's getting ready, so we can go to the movies. It's a tradition. Every year on her birthday, we go to the movies, then out to dinner, and then we both pick out a fancy cupcake at the bakery and bring them home to eat them. My mom said there is a bakery here too, which is good because I was worried. Do you have plans? You should come with us." When Bailey stopped talking, she took a deep breath as if she hadn't taken the chance to breathe.

"Bailey? Who are you talking to?" Kacey asked as she walked down the stairs.

My breath caught in my throat when I saw her. She wasn't wearing anything fancy—just a Bellman crewneck and jeans—but she looked fantastic. When her eyes met mine, I was hit with the realization of how much I missed her over the past few weeks. I had convinced myself I was okay pulling away, but being back in her presence felt like falling into bed after a long hard day. It felt like coming home.

"You came," she breathed, as if she was expecting it, but still surprised.

I held up the gift as I had to Bailey. "I couldn't miss your birthday."

Her smile was so sweet and sincere that I wanted to pull her into my arms and never let go. Instead, I closed the distance between us and held the gift out to her. "It's nothing big, but I thought you might get a kick out of it."

Kacey's smile grew as she pulled out the picture frame and stared down at the picture of us. "Is this...?"

"The first picture we ever took together. Yes."

She turned it so Bailey could see, and I looked at it for what had to be the millionth time since printing it out. We were lying close together on Kacey's dorm room bed. I was laughing at something she had said right before the picture was snapped and she was smiling over at me rather than looking at the camera. It had been my favorite picture up until the time we broke up.

"I always loved this picture," Kacey said, echoing my thoughts.

Bailey looked at the picture one more time, then her eyes darted between Kacey and me. A wide, somewhat malicious, smile spread across her face. "I actually better go to the bathroom before we leave." She skipped away and up the stairs. The fact that she chose to go upstairs when she was standing just a few steps from the downstairs bathroom wasn't lost on me.

Kacey took a few more steps toward me and hesitantly reached her hand out toward mine, smiling when I took it. I could feel a goofy grin taking over my face as I closed the space between us. "I've gotta say, thirty-two has never looked so good."

Kacey stared down at my lips as she ran a tongue along hers. My mind was buzzing with all the words I didn't dare say out loud. *Do it. Kiss me. Please kiss me.* Kacey closed her eyes and let out a frustrated sigh. "Please don't do this."

I pulled back so I could look her in the eye. "Do what?"

Kacey's face looked strained and I could tell she was trying not to cry. "Don't disappear on me for weeks, then come back here saying all the right things to make me feel special."

"But you are special," I said, my voice cracking.

"Stop." Kacey's voice was soft but firm, and it took me back to the way it sounded when she said she loved me. My heart hurt as the realization of how hard this was on her crashed into me. I might have been struggling with the feelings I didn't want to have, but Kacey was struggling just as much, if not more. She was along for the ride on the rollercoaster of my ever-changing emotions.

"I'm sorry. You're right. I shouldn't have come. It was wrong of me to strut in here as if I had the right."

I turned around and went to pull my hand away, but Kacey tightened her grip. "No. Please don't go. Please."

When I turned back around to look at her, I realized the desperation in her eyes matched her pleas. I turned so my body was facing hers completely and took her other hand in mine, hoping to convey the sincerity in my words. "I'm not going anywhere. I promise, Kacey. I'm not going anywhere." As the words left my mouth, the fact that I wasn't just talking about this moment hit me like a ton of bricks.

Kacey stared back at me, eyes unmoving, and something passed between us. Even though neither of us spoke of it, I knew we both felt it. There was a shift, and while I couldn't actually speak it out loud, I knew everything had changed.

"Will you spend my birthday with me?" Kacey asked shyly. It was so adorable the way her blushed cheeks led into a slight smile and her eyes darted away from mine, that I thought I might melt into a puddle right there on her floor.

I squeezed her hands and placed one lone kiss on her forehead. "Of course I'll spend your birthday with you."

Like clockwork, I heard the toilet upstairs flush at that very moment, almost as if Bailey had heard our whole conversation. But she couldn't have, right?

I didn't have much time to overthink it because soon she was running down the stairs and right past us. "We better get going or we're going to be late for the movie." When I hesitated for a moment, Bailey turned back to look at me. "Are you coming, Kari?"

By the time we arrived at the movie theater, I found out we were seeing the sequel to some kids' movie I had never seen, but now had the whole plot down thanks to Bailey. We bought popcorn to share and three sodas, then headed into the movie theater. Bailey insisted that Kacey should sit in the middle of us, which is how I found myself more focused on her every move than anything happening on the screen in front of us. I watched as she took the half empty popcorn bag from Bailey and put it between us. I willed my eyes away from her and tried to ignore how sexy she looked doing something as simple as eating popcorn. With my eyes on the screen, I reached into the bag of popcorn, surprised to find another hand already in there. It was like a cheesy scene from a movie when Kacey's fingers inadvertently brushed over mine, sending a chill down my whole body. When I looked over at her, her eyes were already on me, a slight smile adorning her lips.

I gave her a sheepish grin, then pulled out a handful of popcorn that I was suddenly self-conscious about eating in front of her, which was crazy. This was Kacey we were talking about. She'd seen it all when we were in college. I slipped the popcorn in my mouth and tried to ignore the eyes still burning into me.

When I focused my attention back on her, she let out a quiet laugh and shook her head. "Still just as messy, I see." She reached out and used her thumb to wipe what I had to assume was butter off the corner of my lip. It didn't matter what it was. I suddenly wished I had it everywhere so I could feel more of that touch.

I was torn from our shared gaze when a throat cleared beside us. Bailey grabbed her mom's hand, then leaned closer to whisper to us, holding their joined hands in the air. "This is how you do it. It's not that hard, or that big of a deal." She rolled her eyes at us before turning her attention back to the movie.

Kacey's eyes went wide in a combination of embarrassment and amusement, but it didn't stop her from reaching out and taking my hand. She continued to hold my hand throughout the movie and even as we walked out to the car afterwards. She even reached underneath the booth we were sitting in to hold it during dinner. This was something we had been doing for weeks, maybe even months but it felt different now.

She didn't let go for good until all three of us sat back inside the house eating the cupcakes we had picked out. Bailey smiled as she took a bite, and didn't wait to finish chewing before she started talking excitedly. "We never did our slumber party. I think tonight would be the perfect night, don't you, Mom?"

She looked at her mom expectantly, but instead of answering, Kacey turned toward me, using her eyes to ask if I was okay with that. I smiled over at Bailey. "I think that's an excellent idea. Let me just run home and put on my pajamas, and if it's okay, I'll bring Duke back with me so he can join us too." Bailey threw her fist in the air as Kacey nodded in agreement and I took that as my cue to head home.

Within a half hour, I was back, dressed in warm flannel pajamas and leading Duke on his leash. Bailey entertained Duke while Kacey and I worked to build a fort out of blankets in the family room. We placed a few blankets across the floor with a bunch of pillows for us all to lie on. Bailey laughed giddily when she saw what we had created and I couldn't help but lean into Kacey as we both took in her excitement.

After taking turns reading a few books, we put on a movie that Bailey quickly fell asleep to. I watched Kacey as she happily ran a hand through Bailey's hair while smiling down at her. "So, did you enjoy your birthday?" I asked quietly.

Kacey's eyes left Bailey's so she could focus on me. "It was honestly the greatest birthday ever. How couldn't it be? I got to spend it with my two favorite people." She sighed contently. "Never in my wildest dreams did I think I would ever spend a birthday with both you and Bailey. I thought about what it would be like to see you again, but never dreamed it could be like this."

"You thought about me?" I knew it was a pretty stupid question, given everything Kacey had told me, but I was still desperate to hear her answer.

"Kari, I thought of you every single day from the night I left Bellman. I never even tried to erase you from my mind because I knew it was useless. I knew no matter what, you would always be in my heart."

Instead of saying anything, I reached my hand up, placing it on the floor above where Bailey was lying between us. I wiggled my fingers and Kacey grabbed ahold of my hand for what had to be the thousandth time that night. I ran my thumb along her hand as I watched her eyes close slowly, a contented smile on her face as she drifted off to sleep.

For a minute, I looked between her and Bailey, my heart feeling more full than I could ever remember. When I couldn't keep my eyes open anymore, I let them shut. Before I could drift off to sleep, I whispered the words that had been on the tip of my tongue all day, begging for release even though I knew I wasn't ready yet. The whisper was so soft that even if one of the other occupants of the room was awake, they wouldn't have been able to discern my words. The words weren't a drunken ramble this time, but a sobering truth. "I love you so very much too, Kacey."

Chapter 12

A week after Kacey's birthday, I still felt like I was on a high from the time we had spent together. I was ready to stop being scared. Ready to give her more of me. How much more was the question, but that's something I would worry about later. For now, I was enjoying a Saturday night in with Bo. According to him, it was *boy's night*, but that just meant that the two of us ordered take out and watched movies with hot girls in them.

"What's going on with you?" Bo asked, raising an eyebrow as he stared at me from the other end of the couch, a slice of pizza halfway up to his mouth.

"What do you mean?"

He moved the pizza the rest of the way to his mouth and took a big bite, barely chewing before speaking again. "You're just all giddy and happy and shit."

I laughed. "Are you saying I can't be happy without having a reason for it?"

Bo shrugged. "It's a different kind of happy."

I couldn't hold back the wide grin that spread across my face. "Well, if you must know, I really think there might be something going on between Kacey and me."

Now it was Bo's turn to laugh. "No shit." When I rolled my eyes, he stopped laughing and took a sip of his beer. "I'm just saying, you don't see me walking around holding Derek's hand and undressing him with my eyes."

"Derek's an ass."

Bo gave me a look that said we weren't talking about that right now. "I told him he was an ass on New Year's Eve. Don't worry. I think he's going to chill out."

"He's an ass all the time."

"I get that, but he's still one of my oldest friends and would give me the shirt off his back. He's also all talk. I'm not saying that makes it right, and trust me, I told him that. But I honestly think he hits on you so much because he *knows* it won't actually happen. Same with Kacey. He wouldn't ever try to get with her. He just said that to get you worked up, because as we've already established multiple times, he's an ass. Speaking of Kacey, though, you're avoiding the real topic here. What changed?"

I was about to answer, happy to have someone to gush to, when my phone rang. I ignored it when I saw it was my sister, figuring I would just call her later, but when she immediately started calling back, I worried about what was going on. "Kylie, what's up?"

"Sorry. I know you're hanging out with Bo tonight, but I didn't want to call Mom and Dad. Could you… could you come pick me up?" Her voice was strained, and it almost sounded like she was crying.

"Of course. Are you okay? Where are you?"

"I'll send you the address. It's about fifteen minutes from you. I'll explain when you get here."

Bo was listening to the conversation and immediately stood from the couch to grab our coats. We were in the car in no time, and with Bo driving we made it there in just over ten minutes. I was surprised to find that the address was to a house and not a restaurant or bar. Kylie was sitting on the sidewalk in front of the house with her head in her hands. As soon as she heard us pull up, she jumped off the sidewalk and into the car.

"What happened?" I asked as Bo drove through the neighborhood to get us turned around.

Kylie shook her head. "I've been talking to this guy online for a few weeks, and he was super sweet. Always a gentleman. He asked me to go on a date tonight and even picked me up at Mom and Dad's house. He came to the door and everything. Even shook Dad's hand." She let out a frustrated groan. "Anyway, that's not important. I'm just trying to prove that I'm not a complete idiot. He took me to a nice restaurant and asked if I wanted to come over for a drink after. I agreed, and we came back to his house and started making out, but then he wanted to have sex and I told him to stop."

"Wait a second," I interrupted. "He didn't…" I couldn't even finish my sentence because it made me sick to think about.

"No. It was nothing like that. He just called me a tease and told me if I wasn't willing to put out that I needed to leave."

Bo slammed on the brakes, sending my body tight against my seatbelt, and then whipped his car around. I could see his chest moving up and down with deep, heavy breaths. Soon, we were back in front of the house we had picked Kylie up from and before I could comprehend what was happening, Bo was getting out of the car.

I ran after him as he made his way to the front door. "Do you really think this is such a good idea?" I asked as Bo pounded on the door.

Bo turned toward me with fire in his eyes. "Are you really going to let some scumbag treat your sister like that?"

I tried to reach out and touch his arm, but he tore it away from me. "Listen, I'm really pissed too, but I don't think we should do anything we might end up regretting."

"Oh, I won't regret this," Bo said with a snarl.

Before I could say anything else, a tall, brown-haired guy around our age opened the door. His face was riddled with confusion as he looked between Bo and me.

Bo stepped closer to him but luckily didn't touch him. "Listen, buddy, I don't know what your deal is, but I just wanted to tell you that you don't get to treat women the way you treated Kylie tonight." His voice was firm, but level.

To my surprise, the guy started to laugh. "Who are you? Her boyfriend or something? I guess I shouldn't be surprised."

Bo cracked his knuckles and I could tell it was taking everything in him not to take this guy down. "No, I'm not her boyfriend. But, let me tell you, if I had the chance to take Kylie Adelberg on a date, I would treat her a hell of a lot better than you did. Shit, I would treat any woman better. You don't treat someone like that. I would love to hurt you, but you hurt yourself enough tonight. You missed out on your chance with the most amazing woman in the world because you couldn't handle one more night with your hand. You're an idiot and deserve a lifetime of loneliness." Bo turned around and motioned for me to follow him. "Let's get out of here."

"Jackass," I screamed, waving my middle finger in the air as we walked away. I figured it was the least I could do after everything Bo had just said.

Once we were back in the car, Kylie looked at us with wide eyes. "What the hell just happened?"

Bo shook his head in frustration. "I just told that douche what I thought about how he treated you tonight."

Kylie sighed. "I guess I brought it on myself. I did agree to go back to his house, and I was the one who initiated the make out session."

"No," Bo interrupted sternly. "Don't say that. When someone says they don't want to do something, that decision needs to be respected." He reached his hand toward the back seat and took Kylie's, his demeanor becoming softer. "Are you okay?"

For the first time since picking her up, I saw a smile surface on Kylie's face. "I'm good. Thank you."

My heart swelled as I watched Bo's interaction with Kylie. I always knew he was a good guy, but this was a side of him I hadn't seen before. It was a more mature side and made me love and appreciate my best friend even more. I turned to Kylie, who now looked more than content. "What do you say we all go back to my place? We can watch a movie and then you can stay over."

As soon as we were back at my house, Bo asked if he could talk to Kylie alone and for once I didn't make a big deal over it. When they came back downstairs twenty minutes later, Bo pulled me into a hug. "I'm going to go home. You guys should have some sister time tonight."

Once he was out the door, I turned to Kylie. "What was that all about?"

Kylie closed her eyes and inhaled deeply as a small smile played on her lips. "It was really sweet, actually. He wanted to make sure Thad didn't force me to do anything I didn't want to and reminded me about thirty times that I deserved better than that."

I put an arm around her shoulder and walked over toward the couch, pulling her down beside me. "He's right, you know. You deserve much better than that, and I know you're going to find it."

"I think I al—" Kylie cut off her own words with a shake of her head. "I don't want to talk about this right now. Tell me about your love life."

For once, I wanted to gush about Kacey and the feelings I didn't want to hold in anymore, but I knew that wasn't what Kylie needed to hear after the night she had. "What do you say we watch a funny movie instead?"

Kylie smiled knowingly. "Fine. Tonight, we watch a movie. Tomorrow, you can tell me all about what's going on in that heart of yours because I can tell it's something."

***

There was definitely something big going on inside my heart and I could feel it as I sat with Bailey and Kacey the first weekend in February, playing a board game. Kacey laughed as her piece slid past mine, and my heart hummed with contentment. The sound of the doorbell interrupted her laughter. "Wonder who that could be," she mused as she stood to answer it.

When she opened the door, Bo slipped inside, looking slightly nervous. "Hey, buddy, what are you doing here?" I asked cheerfully.

Bo gave me a look I couldn't identify and shoved both of his hands into his jacket pocket, rocking back and forth on the balls of his feet. "I wanted to ask you something, but decided to do it in front of Kacey and Bailey so there would be witnesses if you tried to kill me."

I laughed awkwardly, unsure how I was supposed to feel about that. "Quite the introduction. What's up?"

Bo took a deep breath and whispered a few words under his breath as though he was giving himself a pep talk. When he looked back at me, his face was serious. "I'm just going to say it. I want to date your sister." He winced as though he was waiting for me to hit him, but when I didn't budge, he continued. "I know I've always joked around about it, but I meant it when I said how amazing she is. She really is. She's funny and nice and a hell of a good time. Plus, she just has this zest for life that is super contagious. It makes me want to be around her all the time. Since the incident last

156

week, we've been talking a lot, and I know she feels the same way. We just don't feel right pursuing anything without your consent."

I massaged my forehead, trying to take in everything Bo had just said and unsure how I felt about all of it. In all the time we had been friends, Bo had never been serious about a girl and I wondered if it was possible.

As if reading my mind, Bo moved my hand from my forehead and forced me to look at him. "I know what you're thinking. I'm the friend who always makes dumb jokes about hooking up with girls and not wanting anything serious. It's different with Kylie though. I'm willing to prove it to you. I actually thought the first time we hung out as more than just your sister and your best friend could be as a group. I just want to spend time with her. I'm not trying to take her home. I wouldn't. I want to do it right."

His words brought a smile to my face. I always knew deep down that there was something more between Bo and Kylie and hearing him talk about her that way was enough to convince me. Also, I had no question that Bo knew I would kill him if he ever hurt her, so that eased some of my worries. "All right. Let's do this. When were you thinking for this group hang?"

Instead of answering me, Bo looked toward Bailey. "When is that sleepover you've been talking about, kiddo?"

"Next Friday," Bailey answered excitedly.

Bo's lips curved into a smirk. "How funny. That's exactly when I was going to suggest we should all hang out. Perfect. Now Kacey can come too." He smiled even wider as he looked toward Kacey. "What do you say?"

"You don't have to ask me twice." Kacey sounded almost as excited as Bailey was about her sleepover and it made my own insides twist in excitement as well.

***

The excitement continued until the night of our hang out. Bo texted all of us earlier in the day to tell us to dress nice but didn't divulge any other information. When I walked out to the driveway where Bo was picking us up, my mouth began to water at the sight in front of me. Although it was covered by a jacket, I could still see Kacey's dress since the jacket wasn't closed. It was a black knee-length dress that was tight but still left a bit to the imagination. Although, it wasn't too hard to imagine since I had seen it all before countless times. That thought alone caused my heart to beat even faster. I moved my eyes up Kacey's body and stopped when they landed on her dark eyes, accentuated with a smoky eye shadow.

From the way she looked at me, I could tell that she liked the outfit I'd chosen as well. After much consideration, I had settled on a short red dress with black tights underneath, black boots, and a small leather jacket. As we met in the middle of the driveway, Kacey reached her hand toward me and I didn't hesitate to grab ahold of it. She used our intertwined fingers to pull me closer to her and when I was within inches of her, she ran her other hand over my leather jacket. "I see you still haven't started dressing for the weather."

I laughed lightly and ran a hand over her cheek. "I will risk my comfort to look cute for you. I thought we already established that." I looked over her outfit once again, running my eyes over each spot on her body. "Plus, I'm not the one wearing nothing on my legs."

Kacey smirked, and it made her even more attractive. "What can I say? It turns out I'm willing to risk my warmth to impress you too. Plus, the way you're looking at me right now is doing a good job of warming me up."

I felt the heat rising to my cheeks, but I wasn't going to let it throw me off, enjoying this back and forth too much to let it stop. I leaned in closer so my lips were just a breath away from hers. "I could say the same for you."

Kacey licked her lips as she stared at mine intently. I could have sworn she began moving the slightest bit closer when suddenly we were shocked apart by the sound of Bo's horn. When I whipped around to glare at him, Bo was pointing to his watch impatiently. I held onto Kacey's hand as we walked the few feet to Bo's car together. I only dropped it so I could open her door. I slid into the back seat beside her and was happy when she immediately reconnected our hands as Bo drove.

Bo turned to smile at us when he stopped at a red light. He had tamed down his hair and from what I could see, the outfit he was wearing was nicer than anything I had seen him in before. "Sorry for breaking up your little love fest," he said with a chuckle. "Our reservations are in forty-five minutes and the restaurant is fifteen minutes past your parents' house, which doesn't give me a ton of time to woo them when we pick up your sister."

"You're trying to woo my parents? I don't think that's necessary. They love you."

"They love me as your friend. I don't know how they will feel about me being the possible boyfriend of your sister."

It still felt weird to hear Bo say that, but I let it roll off my shoulders because I could tell how hard he was trying. "So, where are our reservations at anyway?"

I saw Bo's proud smile in the rearview mirror as the name rolled from his tongue. "Sapori D'Italia. Have you ever been there?"

I shook my head. "Can't say I have. I don't frequent super fancy Italian restaurants on the reg."

"Well, tonight is special." Bo's words were matter-of-fact, but his voice had the slightest bit of giddiness to it.

And he was right. Everything about the night felt special. The way he nervously made his way to my parents' door, then handed my dad the whiskey he had bought him and my mom the chocolate, finally relaxing when my dad put an arm around his shoulder and said something that made them both laugh. The way he awkwardly walked with his hands in his pockets and fumbled to open the door for Kylie. The way Kacey sat so close to me in the car that her leg brushed against mine, and the way she leaned in to whisper about how beautiful the restaurant was as we walked inside, hand-in-hand.

It wasn't the group hang-out I was expecting, but I found myself more than okay with that. By the time dessert came, we had all relaxed more and our conversation was light and fun. I leaned back in my chair and patted my stomach as I finished the last bite of the chocolate cake Kacey and I were sharing. "I think if I eat another bite, I might explode."

Seeing the empty plate, our over-attentive waiter immediately came back to the table. "Anything else I can get you tonight?"

"Just the checks. Could we do two and two please?" Bo pointed between him and Kylie, then me and Kacey. "You're okay with that, right, Kari?"

I sat up straighter, surprised by his question, having not really thought about the logistics of paying yet. Bo gave me a subtle wink that only I caught and I knew exactly what he was up to. This wasn't a group hang-out at all. "Of course I'm okay with that."

Kacey reached into her purse. "Are you sure? I don't mind paying for my half."

I put my hand over hers to stop her. "Yes. I'm positive. It's the least I could do."

"Least you could do for what?"

For leading you on incessantly, for playing with your emotions, for holding us back from something we both want so badly. I cleared my throat and playfully pointed toward Bo and Kylie. "For not leaving me alone with these two idiots." I leaned in closer and whispered so only she could hear, surprised when my voice came out much lower than usual. "And for being the most gorgeous woman in the whole restaurant. I've done a full inspection. No one even compares."

Kacey bit her lip, then seductively ran her eyes over my whole body. "I think you may have missed someone."

Her words, paired with that look, were enough to get my whole body buzzing. I was thankful for the cold breeze as we left the restaurant a few minutes later cooling my skin that was hot with anticipation. I was in a daze as we drove back to my parents' house, focused only on the way Kacey's fingers were tracing circles along my knee, and was surprised when Bo's car came to a stop and I realized we were already there.

Bo ran around to open Kylie's door, then motioned with one finger for her to hold on. He ran back to open the driver's door again and grinned into the back seat. "Will you kill me if I kiss your sister goodnight?"

I laughed and shook my head. "Get it, buddy. Just keep your hands to yourself."

160

Bo nodded his head, then joined Kylie back outside the car. I leaned my head on Kacey's shoulder as we watched the two of them walking to the door. Once at the door, they talked for a few minutes before Bo leaned in for a brief hug. As soon as he pulled away, Kylie wrapped her arms around his neck to pull him back in and kiss him. Even though Kylie moved her hands from his shoulders and down his arms, until they rested at his hips, Bo kept both of his rooted firmly to his side.

Kacey chuckled, causing her whole body to rock against me in the best way possible. "You gotta hand it to him. He follows directions very well."

When Bo got back into the car, he had a big goofy grin on his face that had both Kacey and me chuckling in the back seat. Bo's smile only grew wider as he watched us make fun of him. "Next stop—Driveway di Adelberg-Caldwell."

"Actually, Bo, you can just drive to your house and we'll walk from there." I winked at Kacey as I squeezed her hand that was still resting on my leg. "I could use the cool air."

Bo agreed, and after another dazed drive and a few goodbye hugs, Kacey and I were hand-in-hand walking through the neighborhood. We were both quiet, but it was a comfortable silence. I thought about our night and how perfectly romantic it had been.

As we walked up to Kacey's door, I couldn't help but laugh. "Did we just get tricked into a double date?"

Kacey lifted one eyebrow in the way she had to know I couldn't resist. "I don't think friends go on dates."

I looked down at my feet and kicked at some non-existent object on the ground. "You were never my friend, Kacey."

"I… I wasn't?"

I looked back up at her and had to smile. Her suddenly timid demeanor was ridiculously cute. I shook my head. "No. From the moment I bumped into you at the beginning of freshman year, I knew you would be more to me. Then when you came back into my life, I wanted to act like I could see you differently, but I think we both know that's a lie. So, I want you to think long and hard about this

---

161

question because it's going to determine my next move. Was this a date?"

The smile on Kacey's face grew wider than I had ever seen it before when realization hit her. She took a step forward and rested her hands lightly on my hips. "Yes. This was definitely a date."

Not needing anymore prompting, I leaned in and kissed her. As soon as I felt her lips on mine, I couldn't imagine why I ever went without them. I wrapped my arms around her neck to pull her closer to me. Kacey took this opportunity to open her mouth to mine, and I thought I might collapse as our tongues reunited for the first time in way too long.

I forced myself to pull away. As much as I wanted to kiss her, there was something else I wanted to do even more. "Would you like to go on an official date with me?"

Kacey's smile somehow grew even bigger. "There's nothing I want more than that."

"Perfect. Just let me know what day works for you and I'll take care of the rest."

Kacey's smile dropped slightly. "I'll have to figure it out. It's tough with Bailey. I know we've been here a few months, but she's still adjusting and I don't want to leave her with just anyone."

"I'll do it."

I jumped in the air as a dark figure emerged from the shadows. "Shit, Bo. What the hell are you doing here?"

Bo's boisterous laugh echoed throughout the neighborhood. "I followed you. I wanted to know what happened."

Kacey cackled beside me. "Privacy *is* a thing. You know that, right?"

Bo slipped his hands in his pockets and took a few steps closer to us. "Yes, but can you really be mad at me when I'm about to offer to watch Bailey next Friday? Valentine's Day to be exact."

"Don't you think you should talk that over with my sister first?" I asked. "You guys did technically have your first date tonight. She might expect a Valentine's Day date."

Bo shrugged slightly. "Already talked to her about it. We agreed that if you guys finally embraced your feelings, we would offer to watch Bailey on Valentine's Day."

"And when exactly did you talk about this?"

"When I walked her to the door tonight." Bo stated it as if it were the most normal thing in the world that my best friend and sister were meddling in my love life.

I looked toward Kacey. "What do you say? Do you trust those two fools to watch Bailey?"

"Oddly enough, I think I trust them more than most people." She focused her attention on Bo. "If you're sure that's okay, I'm going to take you up on that offer."

"It's a date," Bo said excitedly while clapping his hands together. We both stared at him until he finally got the hint. "Right. I'll go now. You ladies enjoy the rest of your night."

I watched him until he became a shadow and disappeared into the night, then turned back to Kacey. I put my arms around her neck, pulling her tight so our bodies were as close as possible, reveling in the way it felt. I wasn't scared like I expected to be when I finally gave in. It was the complete opposite. I felt safe. I felt like I was right where I belonged and that nothing could hurt me.

Kacey laughed a hearty laugh, and I realized we had both just been staring at each other, caught up in our own thoughts. "What's going inside that head of yours?" she asked with a slight tilt of her own.

I placed a quick kiss on her lips, then rubbed my nose against hers. "Just thinking about how ridiculously happy I am right now. What about you?"

"Honestly? I'm thinking about how much I want to invite you inside, but I don't trust myself to behave."

I leaned back just enough for her to see the smirk on my face. "Who said you have to?"

Kacey groaned playfully and threw her head back. "I said so." Her face became more serious as she ran a finger along my cheek and I instinctively leaned into her hand. "Seriously, I don't want to rush things. I want to do this right and show you just how serious I am."

"You always were the chivalrous one."

"And you always deserved it."

I ducked my head so Kacey couldn't see just how much her words were affecting me. "I better go. I'm not so chivalrous. If you keep talking to me like this, I might have my way with you right here in the driveway."

Kacey placed one kiss on my forehead, then pushed me away. "Goodnight, Kari."

"Goodnight, Kacey."

When I got into my house, I leaned against the door and squealed. Even our *goodnight* felt like it was laced with promises. Promises I couldn't wait to see through.

Chapter 13

On Valentine's Day, I heard a knock at my door at precisely 6:30, which was the exact time Kacey said she would pick me up. Even though the date was my idea, she insisted on planning it. When I opened the door, I couldn't control the wide smile that spread across my face. Kacey was holding a single red rose and a big bottle of my favorite wine.

"You remembered," I said breathlessly.

Kacey stepped closer and moved the rose to the hand that was holding the wine. She ran the hand that was now free through my hair, causing goosebumps to rise on my arms. "I couldn't forget anything about you, Kari."

I pulled her into me and crashed my lips into hers, enjoying the familiar tingle it sent throughout my body. When I pulled back, I laughed at her wide eyes and red cheeks. "Sorry. I've been holding back kisses from the moment I first saw you. The way I see it, I owe you a bunch."

Kacey smirked and leaned into me again, stopping when her lips were just barely grazing mine. "And how many is a bunch exactly?"

I closed one eye as if I was considering her question. "I'd say approximately five-hundred seventy-two."

Kacey placed one kiss on my lips, then pulled back slightly. "That's a lot." Leaning in, she kissed me quickly three more times.

After the third kiss, I wrapped my arms around her neck and nuzzled into her. "You know, we don't *have* to go out. I could repay my debt."

Kacey shook her head slowly. "Absolutely not. I have a full night planned for us." She looked down at her watch. "Starting with dinner reservations that we're going to miss if we don't go now."

Less than ten minutes later, we pulled up to the town's newest restaurant, The Bulldog Bistro. The parking lot was packed which wasn't surprising since a new restaurant was like a gold mine to a small town with not much else to do.

"How did you get a reservation here?" I asked as Kacey struggled to find a parking spot. "I heard they were booked like a month out."

Kacey shrugged. "I pulled some strings." When I tilted my head, a smirk came to her face and she let out a slight chuckle. "I helped them put their website together, so they owed me one."

Of course she did. "Nerd," I said with a laugh.

"But I'm a cool nerd, right?" Kacey asked playfully.

"The coolest nerd I know, babe."

"You just called me babe," Kacey said quietly, sounding surprised.

I reached across the car and squeezed her arm. "Is that okay?"

"Yeah. Of course. It just feels so surreal. For years, I dreamed of a night like tonight. I just never thought it would actually happen."

"Well, get used to it, you cool nerdy babe you," I joked to keep myself from getting choked up.

Kacey rolled her eyes and shut off the car. "Let's get inside, weirdo."

"So, what do you think Bailey, Kylie, Bo, and Duke are getting up to right now?" I asked once we were seated.

Kacey laughed as she took a sip of her water. "I don't think I want to know."

"Don't worry. I'm sure Bailey will take good care of them." I reached my hand across the table to take Kacey's and became more serious as I ran my thumb along the back of her hand. "I know I've said it before, but she's a really good kid, Kacey. You've done an amazing job with her."

Kacey swallowed hard and got a far off look in her eyes. When she focused back on me, it appeared she was trying to hold back tears. "Thank you for saying that. Seriously. I've tried so hard to give her a better life than I had growing up. Even though I tell myself that it wasn't my fault, I feel like I failed my sister. No matter what I did, it was never enough to get her on the right path, and God knows I tried. I tried to the point where it just became too much. She had to be willing to help herself, and she wasn't. But I wanted it to be different for Bailey. I want her to succeed, but most of all, I just want her to be happy."

"Well, you're doing a good job of both."

Kacey smiled, but it didn't reach her eyes this time. "She's the one thing I did right."

"The one thing?" My tone was more tense than I expected it to be, but Kacey's words had taken me by surprise. "Kacey, you've done so much right."

Kacey shrugged. "I guess I just feel guilty about my sister."

"You shouldn't. You are, what? Five years older than her? You shouldn't have been expected to raise her. It seems like you did everything you could given the circumstances."

Kacey shook her head slightly. "I could have stayed home for college instead of going to Bellman so I could keep a closer eye on her. I needed to get away though."

I felt like I might cry hearing about all the guilt Kacey carried with her. "As you should have. You deserve to be a little selfish. You deserve to do what you need to do. Plus, I'm very happy you came to Bellman."

Kacey smiled slightly, and this time I could see her face brighten the tiniest amount. She ran her fingers along mine and stared into my eyes. "I could never regret going to Bellman because it led me to you. But it still doesn't take away the guilt." She cleared her throat and wiped a hand over her eyes. "I took care of her when she was pregnant and was able to control her enough to keep her safe and healthy. I thought maybe things had changed, but as soon as Bailey was born and the adoption went through, she fled. She left me a note saying she needed to live her life and wouldn't be back." She let out a frustrated sigh. "I almost wish that had been the case. She came back three years later when she needed money and I let her move back in with us, just to have her take off a few months later. She did the same thing a few times throughout the years and I finally put my foot down and told her it needed to stop. I cut her off because I couldn't have her waltzing in and out of Bailey's life. It was too confusing for her to have someone who was there one day and gone the next. So, I told her she wasn't

---

167

getting anymore money from me, and I haven't seen her since. Now she doesn't even know where we live." Kacey took a gulp of water and forced a wide smile onto her face. "Anyway, sorry. Tonight is supposed to be about new beginnings. Let's forget about all of that."

There was so much I wanted to say to Kacey. I wanted to tell her how proud I was and how she did everything she could, but I could tell she was struggling, so instead I simply held my wine glass up to her. "To new beginnings."

"To new beginnings," she repeated softly.

The rest of dinner carried on as if Kacey hadn't made a big emotional confession, and the conversation was light and fun. Once we were back in the car, I excitedly asked what we were doing next.

Kacey pointed to the bottle of wine she bought me. "We're doing one of those wine and paint things."

I clapped my hands together. "We've never done anything like that before."

Kacey simply smiled and grabbed one of my hands. "I know."

Halfway through the wine and paint, it was very obvious that I was much better at the *wine-ing* part than the painting part. Kacey laughed as she looked from me to my painting, which was supposed to be a sun setting over a mountain, but looked more like an abstract of colors.

"I think you got more paint on yourself than on the canvas."

I looked down at the smock that I was thankfully wearing and noticed all of the fresh paint, then looked toward Kacey who was perfectly clean. I smirked as an idea came to me, and I grabbed my paintbrush, then pointed it to her canvas. "You missed a spot, you know."

Confusion was written all over Kacey's face as she turned to study her painting. I used her distraction to run my paintbrush down her cheek, leaving a long red streak. She closed her eyes and shook her head when she realized she had been played. "So, that's how it's going to be, huh?" Instead of picking up her paintbrush, she ran her hand through the paint on her cheek and then rubbed it on my nose. "There. Now we match," she said proudly.

I shook my head and leaned in close to her. "Not quite." I rolled my nose along hers, leaving some red remnants behind. "Much better."

To my surprise, Kacey closed the distance between us and placed two chaste kisses on my lips, as if it were the most natural thing in the world. Then again, it kind of was. Everything was natural with Kacey, and years apart hadn't changed that. I sighed as she pulled away, wishing we could deepen the kiss, but knowing it was inappropriate to do in a room full of people.

I got my chance to do just that an hour later as Kacey and I stood outside her door. She wrapped her arms around me tightly and kissed me as though it was the end of the world and she needed to soak in every last bit she could. When she pulled away, she slid a piece of hair behind my ear, and even something so simple sent a chill down my spine. "Wanna come in and see what Bo and Kylie are up to? You can also take Duke with you if he's willing to leave Bailey."

I agreed and when we walked inside the house was dark and quiet. Kacey whispered their names as we walked upstairs but got no response. When we got to Bailey's room, Kacey threw a hand over her chest, and I leaned up against her to take in the view. Bo, Bailey, Kylie, and Duke were all asleep in her small twin-size bed. Kylie had a book resting on her stomach and Bailey's head on her chest. Bo was on the other side of her, where Bailey's tiny hand was resting on his big one. Duke was asleep at their feet. "This might be the most adorable thing I've ever seen," Kacey whispered. She placed a kiss on my forehead then studied my face. "Well, the second most adorable."

I wanted to stay lost in this moment forever, standing next to one of my favorite people while I watched the rest of my favorite people sleep contently, but after a few minutes, we woke up Kylie and Bo. They yawned dramatically as they stumbled down the stairs and toward the front door.

Kylie looked at me through blinking eyes and mumbled a quick, "You have paint on your face," before slipping out the door.

Kacey closed the door and leaned against it, letting out a sigh as she stared over at me and took my hand "Tonight was amazing."

I ran my thumb along her hand and relished in the way her skin felt under mine."It was. You are quite the date planner. But what do you say I plan the next one? Next weekend?"

Kacey sighed and looked toward the stairs. "I have to see about Bailey. I feel guilty leaving her with other people."

I shook my head. "That's not necessary. I want to take both of you on a date." When Kacey looked at me with a mixture of confusion and appreciation, I added, "I don't want to just date you, Kacey. I want your whole life. Every part of it, especially Bailey."

Kacey crashed her body into mine so hard that it knocked the air out of my lungs as she pulled me into a tight embrace. "I don't know how I ever lived without you," she whispered into my hair.

"You never have to worry about that again," I whispered back.

***

A week later, it was my turn to knock on Kacey's door. My heart melted when Bailey opened the door with Kacey standing close behind her, both wearing matching sweaters. I held a bouquet of flowers out to Kacey and handed Bailey a rose-shaped chocolate. "Well, don't I just have the prettiest dates in the whole wide world?"

Kacey looked toward Bailey and pushed out her bottom lip. "No fair. Why does she get the chocolate?"

"Because I like her better." I smiled widely as Kacey tried and failed to glare at me, and settled for shaking her head as a smile spread across her face.

"Shall we go?" I asked as I reached one hand toward Bailey and the other toward Kacey. They followed me out to the car where I opened both of their doors before getting into my side and starting the car.

"So, where are we going?" Kacey asked as I pulled out of the driveway.

"You'll see soon enough," I answered, trying to hide the wide grin that was coming to my face just at the thought of where I was taking her.

Less than five minutes later, Kacey's smile matched mine as we pulled into the Bellman Bar and Grill for the first time in ten years. As I parked the car, I spoke to Bailey. "The first time I ever came to this restaurant, it was with your mom. Actually, I don't think I've ever been here *without* your mom."

"So, it was a special place for you?" Bailey asked curiously.

"Very special," Kacey answered, her tone nostalgic.

I looked between the two of them, unable to stop the warmth that was spreading throughout my body more and more with every passing minute I spent with them. "Now it can be a special place for all three of us."

Without saying a word, Bailey unbuckled her seatbelt and hopped out of the car. She closed her door, then opened Kacey's and put her hands on her hips. "Well, what are we waiting for? Let's go!"

The food was just as good as I remembered it and the company was even better. When the waiter came to collect our plates and ask if we saved room for dessert, I asked for one milkshake with three straws. It was hard to ignore the way Kacey's eyes were burning into me with more passion than I'd ever seen in them before as I explained to Bailey that it was our tradition to split a milkshake, and my body buzzed with this awareness. It didn't take us long to finish the milkshake and then we were off to the second part of the date, which was just a few more minutes down the road.

Kacey shook her head and laughed when she saw the ice skating rink. "You always loved this place, didn't you?"

I shrugged. "What can I say? It was always an adventure to come here with you."

"Yeah. An adventure of me trying to stay on my feet."

Bailey leaned forward so her head was sticking into the space between Kacey and me in the front seat. "Don't worry, Mom. Kari and I can hold your hands so you don't fall."

171

I made a fist so Bailey and I could pound our knuckles together, then raised an eyebrow at Kacey "Bailey gets it. She figured out my secret. That's exactly why I always loved coming with you."

And that hadn't changed. As we made our way onto the ice, Kacey gripped my hand so tightly, I was pretty sure I had lost all circulation. Bailey's eyes went wide as she looked at her mom's death grip and the way she was desperately reaching for the wall with her other hand. "On second thought, I'm going to just hold your hand, Kari. Sorry, Mom. You need that wall." She giggled as she skated to the other side of me and grabbed my hand lightly, an extreme contrast to Kacey.

As we made a few laps around, Kacey began to loosen up a little and actually took her hand off of the wall. Unfortunately, she misjudged her balance and almost immediately started to fall. I somehow kept one hand in Bailey's, while I moved my other hand around Kacey's waist to draw her closer to me and keep her from falling. Her body hit mine with a thud and her lips stopped just inches from mine. I wasn't sure how I was supposed to act in front of Bailey, so instead of kissing her, I gave her a knowing smile and reluctantly pulled away, slipping my hand back into hers. To my surprise, Kacey leaned in and placed a kiss on my cheek.

"My hero," she mused as she pulled away.

Bailey's eyes moved between Kacey and me, an amused look on her face, before she settled her stare on me. "So, does this mean you're my mom's girlfriend now?"

I felt Kacey's body go stiff beside me. "Bailey Grace! We're not at that point. I mean, it's not—"

I cut Kacey off by squeezing both her and Bailey's hands as I focused my attention on Bailey. "Don't listen to your mom. She's totally my girlfriend." I added a wink, then gave Kacey a nervous smile, hoping I hadn't overstepped. The way her face glowed as she moved in even closer to me told me I hadn't.

"Well, I for one, am very happy about that," Bailey said with a slight giggle that caused Kacey and me to chuckle as well.

As the night continued on, it quickly became the best night of my life, only getting better when Bailey asked if the three of us could read a book together before bed. As Kacey lay on one side with me on the other, we listened to Bailey read out loud. While I watched Kacey run a hand through her daughter's hair, I realized this is all I wanted, moments like this for the rest of my life. I might have been getting ahead of myself, but I couldn't help it. Kacey was my future. That's how it was always meant to be.

I could tell she felt the same way as she pulled me from Bailey's room once she was asleep and stopped just outside her bedroom door to stare at me, her dark eyes looking straight into my soul. She ran a finger down my cheek, then leaned in to give me a slow, sensual kiss that had me ready for whatever came next.

"Spend the night with me," Kacey said breathlessly as she pulled away from me.

I nodded my head and swallowed hard as I followed her into her bedroom, understanding the implications of her invitation. Neither of us had to say anything. We both knew what was coming, so it was no surprise when her mouth crashed back into mine. Quiet moans escaped from my throat as our tongues brushed against each other, doing a dance inside our connected mouths.

My hands went into Kacey's hair as hers came to rest on my hips. I took in a sharp breath as her fingers slipped underneath my shirt and pushed into the skin just above the waistline of my jeans.

I removed my lips from hers and began placing kisses along her neck. She tilted her head back to give me more space to kiss as her hands continued to move higher, first tracing circles along my stomach then moving over my bra. When she gave my breasts the slightest squeeze, I instinctively sucked at her neck, which elicited the sexiest moan I had ever heard.

I forced myself to pull back so Kacey could lift my shirt over my head. It was her turn to kiss my neck as she reached behind me to unclasp my bra. Her kisses moved from my neck, down to my chest, until she finally sucked one nipple into her mouth, rolling it around on her tongue in a

173

way that had my whole body going so weak that I had to lean into her to stay upright.

I ran my fingers along any inch of skin I could find while she moved her attention from one breast to the other, giving it the same care and attention. As I moved my hand to the bottom of her sweater, she pulled away so I could remove it, and the desire I saw burning in her eyes was enough to wipe all thoughts from my mind. The only thing that remained was her and me and this moment we were sharing.

Once her shirt was off, I made quick work of her bra, marveling in the perfection that was Kacey Caldwell. I moved my thumb along her peaked nipple and enjoyed the hum of pleasure that escaped from her lips. I licked across her collarbone as my other hand moved to the breast that hadn't gotten attention yet. My hands trembled as they moved over her body, part of me still in disbelief that this was finally happening. It had been years since I had experienced something like this. No one else had come close to eliciting the feelings that Kacey could bring out in me. Even the sex that we had months ago was nothing like this. While that was hurried and desperate, this was slow and passionate. That had been fueled by desire, while this was fueled by nothing but love.

Okay, desire was present too. The desire to make Kacey feel everything I was feeling. The desire to show my love by giving myself to her completely. The desire to become one with her and remain that way forever.

My thoughts were interrupted by the feeling of Kacey's hand on the button of my pants. She paused to stare into my eyes and when I nodded my head, she undid the button, then slid the zipper down at a teasingly slow pace. She knelt down in front of me as she pulled my pants down inch by inch, following the path with her lips until my pants were low enough for me to step out of them. Then she kissed her way back up my legs, pausing before placing one last kiss on the inside of each thigh before standing back up and joining her lips with mine once again.

As our mouths moved in tandem, I worked to remove her pants as well, pulling back just long enough to completely remove them. We continued to kiss as I traced my fingers over her center, turned on by the wetness I felt through her underwear.

"God, Kari," she said breathlessly as my fingers continued to touch her until I moved them to the top of her underwear and pulled them down little by little while also digging my nails into her skin.

Once she was naked, I stepped back and took her all in. I studied every inch of her body, wanting to re-memorize every single spot. Kacey's eyes studied my body just as intently and when they met mine, I bit my lip and raised a seductive eyebrow before doing a striptease with the one piece of clothing remaining on my body. Kacey repaid me by placing one hand on my chest and pushing me backward until the back of my legs hit the bed. She directed me the rest of the way down, then crawled on top of me, my breaths ragged as I felt her body connect with mine in all the right places.

Once we were face-to-face, I couldn't hold in my feelings any longer. I put a hand on one of her cheeks and placed a light kiss on the other before pulling back to look into her eyes again. "Kacey, I love you. I'm not sure I ever stopped, but one thing I am sure of is that my feelings are even stronger today than they ever have been before. I'm so incredibly in love with you."

Kacey nodded her head and I could have sworn I saw some wetness forming at the corners of her eyes. "I'm so incredibly in love with you too, Kari." She chuckled softly. "But you already knew that, didn't you?"

When I tilted my head, she rolled her eyes at me. "Come on, we both know you heard my confession on New Year's Eve. That's why you disappeared, isn't it?"

I swallowed hard, now embarrassed by the way I had acted following that night. "I didn't disappear because of your confession. I disappeared because of how scared you sounded to say it."

Kacey ran a hand through my hair and twirled the end between her fingers. "I was scared you would never be able to love me fully, the way I need you to."

"Well, I do. I love you with all my heart, Kacey. I'm all in."

Kacey nodded her head, a serious look surfacing on her face. "Do you trust me?"

"With my life."

That's all she needed to hear to continue what we started. She kissed me desperately as her body began to grind against mine, already causing stars to appear in my vision from the pure ecstasy of the moment. She pulled back after a few seconds, looking breathtaking with her chest heaving up and down and dots of sweat forming on her forehead. "I need to taste you. I want to feel you come apart below my mouth."

That was everything I wanted too, and as usual, Kacey just knew and didn't waste any time on kissing a path down my body. She started with my jawline, then worked her way down my neck and across my chest, causing my body to roll up into hers as she lightly bit down on my nipple. Just as quickly, her lips moved down my stomach. She skipped the spot where I really needed her and licked a path up my thighs, one at a time, starting at my knees. Then with one long sweep of her tongue, she began to lick at my center. My hips pressed upward and my hands settled in her hair, encouraging her to continue. And she did.

If Kacey hadn't confessed that I was the only person she had ever been with, I would have believed she had a lot of practice over the past ten years with the way her mouth knew exactly where to go and which spots to pay extra attention to. And when her tongue dipped inside of me, I felt my whole body begin to tingle, making me lose control in the best way possible. When I was about to reach my limit, Kacey pulled back enough to look me in the eyes. She moved one hand up the bed until it reached the spot where one of mine had dropped to. She intertwined her fingers with mine and squeezed gently as she whispered the words, "I love you" one more time, her breath sweeping over the area her tongue had just been.

My body writhed below her as she dove her tongue back inside of me, sucking me completely into her mouth until my body melted into a puddle on the bed, completely spent. She kissed me once more before moving her body back up mine to be face-to-face once again. She simply stared at me as I struggled to catch my breath.

"Kacey, shit, that was… that was just… wow." My words were just barely a whisper between my gasps of air.

Kacey's face was serious as she ran her thumb across my sweaty forehead and rested her hand on my cheek. "Was it okay?"

I laughed louder than I expected, surprising both of us with the sound. "Okay? That was so much more than okay. That was the most earth-shattering orgasm of my entire life. I'd like to repay the favor if that's okay."

Kacey seemed nervous as I flipped myself on top of her then slid my body down hers, never taking my eyes off of her. I was just about to situate myself between her legs when she grabbed ahold of my shoulders to stop me. "I'm probably not going to last very long," Kacey said softly, almost looking embarrassed by that fact.

"Kace, I don't care if you last ten seconds. It will still be the best ten seconds of my life. I've waited years to be with you like this again."

Kacey gave a subtle nod, and I took that as my cue to continue on. One taste and I was completely hooked. My mouth moved on Kacey as if I had been starving, and in some ways I had. I was starved for her. For her love. For her affection. For all of her. For her part, she held on much longer than I expected, releasing the words "I love you" once again through strangled gasps as her body gave out below me.

"I love you too, Kacey," I whispered as I snuggled my body into hers. "I'll never stop loving you."

Chapter 14

I woke the next day to Kacey's strong arm wrapped around me from behind and sighed as I scooted back closer to her, relishing in the feeling of her naked body against mine. She pulled me even tighter against her and whispered a tired "Good morning" as she placed a kiss on my temple.

I turned in her arms so I could face her and smiled when I saw that she was already smiling back at me. I leaned in and brushed my lips with hers. "Good morning." I shook my head back and forth. "This isn't a dream, is it?"

Kacey slipped a hand between my legs and slowly moved one finger over me. "If it was a dream, would that feel so real?"

I bit my lip and reluctantly pushed her hand away. "If you start that, I'm not going to be able to stop, and I really should get going."

"So soon?" Kacey asked, pushing her lip out slightly.

I couldn't resist placing another kiss upon those lips but left it at one so I didn't end up getting carried away. "I think it's for the best if I'm not here when Bailey wakes up. I know she's happy with everything, but this is a lot of change to throw at her all at once. I just want to ease her into things, you know?"

Kacey laid her head on my chest as she let out a content sigh. "I swear. Just when I think you can't get anymore perfect, you go and prove me wrong."

I pulled myself from the bed and put my clothes back on, then slipped from the room before I changed my mind and jumped back in bed.

Once outside, I was surprised to see an old car sitting in the driveway that I didn't recognize. I looked around and noticed a girl a few years younger than me. Her hair was blonde, but I could tell from her dark roots that it wasn't her natural color. "Can I help you?" I asked, unable to hold back my gasp when the girl turned to look at me. The hair might have been different, but there was no way to mask those distinctive dark eyes and the face that was an almost exact replica of Kacey's.

"I'm looking for Kacey Caldwell," the girl answered, almost looking annoyed that I would even ask. "I'm her sister, Ariana."

I swallowed hard. I knew this was the case just by looking at her, but hearing it confirmed sent a chill throughout my body. I had to think quick and choose my next actions wisely since I knew this was going to have a big impact on both Kacey and Bailey. I put one finger in the air. "Give me a moment. I'll see if I can find her for you." Before she could say anything else, I turned back on my heels and let myself back into Kacey's house, locking the door behind me. I leaned against the door and took a deep breath, my heart now beating out of my chest.

When I opened them back up, I noticed that Kacey was standing in front of me, confusion written all over her face. "Kari? Everything okay?" I shook my head but wasn't able to answer. Kacey took my hand in hers and rubbed her thumb over the back of my hand. "What's going on?"

My heart broke when I looked into her scared eyes. She probably thought I was having second thoughts or maybe even regretting our night. Although, I wasn't sure if what I was about to tell her was going to be easier or harder for her to swallow than that would be. "Your sister is here. She's right outside."

Kacey's face turned a ghostly white. "Ariana is here? But how does she even know where we live?" I shrugged and was about to say something when a knock sounded on the door. It started off soft but was quickly becoming louder. "Shit," Kacey whispered, running a hand through her hair. "She's not going to leave without a fight, but I can't let Bailey see her."

I put a hand on her cheek and placed a soft kiss on her lips. "Do you want to talk to her outside and I'll stay here to make sure Bailey doesn't catch on to what's going on?"

Kacey leaned into my hand and shut her eyes for a moment. "You would really do that for me?"

"I wasn't lying last night when I told you I'm all in. We're a team, Kacey."

179

Kacey nodded her head then placed one more quick kiss on my lips before reaching for the door. She turned once more before opening it, her eyes burning into mine as she spoke the most sincere "I love you," I ever heard.

If the moment wasn't so overtaken with anxiety, I probably would have melted to the floor from all of the emotions I was feeling. Instead, I headed up the stairs while Kacey slipped outside.

Bailey walked out of her room, rubbing her eyes sleepily. "Is someone at the door?" she asked with a big yawn.

"Sorry, sweetheart, that was me. I was just coming back to have breakfast with you guys, but I didn't mean to wake you."

Bailey looked me up and down, blinking rapidly as though she was still trying to wake up. "Why are you wearing the same clothes as last night?"

I looked down at my outfit and could feel my face turning red with guilt as I thought about all of the lies I was telling. "I was too tired to change when I got home last night and this morning I was just too excited to get back over here to take the time to do it."

Bailey shrugged, but I couldn't tell whether it was because she believed me or thought I was losing my mind. "I heard people act crazy when they're in love. Guess it's true."

Well, that answers that question.

"Your mom had to run to the store to get a few things to make breakfast," I lied once again. "Want to snuggle in her bed with me and watch cartoons until she gets back?"

Bailey's face lit up. "Do you even have to ask?" Without waiting for a reply, she skipped down the hall into Kacey's room.

Once we were both in the bed, Bailey scooted close to me and laid her head against my shoulder. "My mom really likes you, you know," Bailey said without removing her eyes from the TV. "You're not going to break her heart, are you?"

Her question took me by surprise, but I'm not sure why. Bailey was wise beyond her years. I ran a finger through her hair and gave her a reassuring smile. "No, I'm

180

not going to break your mom's heart. You don't have to worry about that. I just want to make her happy."

Bailey nodded her head slowly as if she were considering my words. "That's good. I think she got her heart broken before. She always said that all she needed was me, but I think that's because she was scared." Bailey looked up at me and stared intently as if she were considering something. "You knew my mom before. Do you know who broke her heart?"

I swallowed hard as I thought about what to say. How do you explain the complexities of life and love to a nine-year-old? "I think it was life. I think life broke both of our hearts, kiddo."

Bailey's eyes went wide, and I worried I was a bit too honest. "I hope life doesn't break my heart."

"It won't. You know how I know?" When Bailey shook her head, I continued. "Because your mom loves you and I love you and we won't let anything or anyone hurt you." My mind flashed back to what Kacey was dealing with outside and I hoped I could stick to my word.

Bailey snuggled into me again and sighed. "I hope you're not my mom's girlfriend forever." *Not exactly what I was expecting to hear.* "I hope you become her wife, then we can be a family."

I put an arm around Bailey and pulled her closer to me, barely able to handle how full my heart felt and praying Ariana's unexpected return didn't put a wrench in things. "We are family, and no matter what happens, that won't change, okay?"

"What are you two talking about?"

Both of our heads turned to the bedroom doorway where Kacey was now standing, a strained smile on her face. "Just talking about life, family, and broken hearts," Bailey answered nonchalantly.

Kacey laughed and a sincere smile spread across her face. "Quite the loaded conversation to be had over Saturday morning cartoons."

"So, what did you buy for breakfast?"

Kacey's eyebrows knit together curiously. "For breakfast?" I gave her a look to try to convey the lie I had told. "Oh... umm... I didn't end up getting anything. I decided we should go out to eat instead. Want to go get changed and use the bathroom, so we can head out?"

Bailey hopped off of the bed but whispered something to Kacey before leaving the room that had Kacey gripping her side with laughter. I lifted an eyebrow at her once she was gone. "What was that all about?"

Kacey let out a few more chuckles. "She said I should make you change too since you've been wearing the same outfit since yesterday."

I put a hand over my heart. "Ouch. Tough crowd. I'll do that in a minute, but first..." I patted the spot beside me on the bed and Kacey sat down, laying her head on my shoulder just as Bailey had done.

"Apparently, I'm ridiculously predictable. When Ariana showed back up at our old house and realized we had moved, she knew this was where I came, then a few questions around this small town was all it took to figure out where we live."

"And what does she want?"

"She claims she wants to see Bailey. She said she misses both of us. I wish I could believe it, but I've heard it all before. Once she gets what she comes for, which is usually money, she leaves. And she slipped in the fact that she got fired from her last job multiple times during our conversation, so I don't have the utmost confidence that she's telling the truth."

I ran a hand through Kacey's hair as she scooted even closer to me. "So, what did you tell her?"

Kacey took a deep breath, then pushed all the air from her lungs in one long exhale. "I told her to prove it. I said if that's what she really wanted, she would put in the time and energy to show me. So, I called the cheapest motel in town, got her a room for the next week, and told her I'd be in touch. I don't have much of a plan beyond that. Am I a complete sucker?"

"She's family," I breathed out.

"She's blood. She's not family. At least not until she proves otherwise." Kacey let out another breath and looked up at me. "Still all in?"

Instead of answering, I leaned in and gave her a kiss that I hoped would convey everything I was feeling. Kacey deepened the kiss, and it took all of my willpower to pull away a few seconds later. I put my hand on her chest and pushed her away from me gently. "Bailey is going to come barreling back in here any minute now."

Kacey groaned, then ran her eyes over my outfit. "That means you need to get changed." She nodded her head toward the closet. "Help yourself to whatever."

When I emerged from the closet moments later, Kacey looked me up and down as though I had chosen a short skin-tight dress. She stood from the bed and walked over to me, wrapping her arms around my waist and spinning me around. "I really like how you look in my clothes," she whispered into my ear.

I looked down at the jeans and Bellman University sweatshirt I was wearing and laughed. "They look just like my clothes."

Kacey kept her mouth close to my ear, her breath against my skin giving me the impression that I could feel her throughout my whole body. "But I know they're mine and I love it."

I buried my head in the crook of Kacey's neck. "I love it too. They smell just like you, so it's like you're constantly wrapped around me. Makes me want to never take them off."

"Good grief. What is it about being in love that makes you not want to change your clothes?" Bailey asked as she walked back into Kacey's room.

Kacey pulled away from me to look me in the eye, lifting one eyebrow and looking so very sexy. "You told her you were in love with me?"

Bailey shook her head as she walked closer to us. "She didn't have to. Your effulgent glances gave it away. You're both totally done for."

Kacey laughed and slipped away from me to put a hand on Bailey's shoulder. "I'm not exactly sure what that word means, but I'm going to bet you're not wrong, kid. Let's go to breakfast."

And so we went. As if this had always been our life. As if it always would be.

183

***

Two weeks into Ariana being in town and it felt like I saw Bailey more than I saw Kacey. Okay, so that wasn't exactly true. Kacey was good at assuring her time with Bailey wasn't compromised because of her sister. She would see her some mornings after dropping Bailey off at school, before she had to be at work, but mostly it was at night. We would both tuck Bailey into bed, then Kacey would sneak out once we were sure she was asleep. As for me, I would lay in Kacey's big bed alone, until she crawled back in sometime in the late hours of the night and we would make love until we couldn't keep our eyes open anymore. It wasn't ideal, but it was what Kacey needed right now and I wanted to support that.

One night after having another mind-blowing orgasm, Kacey ran her hand along my stomach and stared into my eyes as if she were longing to say something. I stopped the path of her hand and reached up to twirl a piece of her hair between my fingers. "What's up? You look like you have something to say."

"I think…" Kacey sighed then took a deep breath as if it were hard to get the words out. "I think I want you to meet my sister. Bailey was invited to a slumber party next weekend, so we wouldn't have to worry about explaining it to her or lying about where we were going. I just… things are going okay and I'm cautiously optimistic, so I want to know how you feel." She stopped to stare at me for a few seconds, looking at me as though she was trying to read into the words I hadn't said. "Would you be okay with that? You don't have to do it if it makes you uncomfortable."

I pulled her close to me, bringing our lips back together for what had to be the fiftieth time that night. When I pulled back, I placed one more kiss on the tip of her nose before looking into her eyes. "I'll do whatever you want me to. If you want me to meet your sister next week, I'm in. I love you, Kacey."

Kacey let out a long breath as though she had been holding it all night in anticipation to my answer to that question. "I love you too, Kari. God, I love you."

184

***

A week later, Kacey and I drove to the old motel at the edge of town where her sister was still staying and picked her up. Ariana was quiet during the car ride and continued her silence throughout most of dinner, only speaking when she was addressed directly.

When Kacey excused herself to use the restroom, I let my eyes wander around the restaurant, ready for a few minutes of awkward silence. To my surprise, Ariana's eyes fell on me and she continued to watch me as she took a sip of her water, a smirk appearing on her face. "She's not like you, you know."

"Excuse me?" I asked, surprised to hear her speak.

"Kacey. She's not like you, and no matter how much she pretends to be, she's never going to be. We come from a different world. A world where mommy and daddy don't just dish out what we need. A world where people work hard to barely scrape by."

I picked up my water and took a large sip, surprised that this was the direction our conversation had taken. "I think you may have gotten the wrong impression of me. I'm not some trust fund baby living off of my parents' money."

"You're also not white trash." Ariana laughed as if referring to herself this way was normal. "You didn't grow up in a house that was too small for the amount of people living in it. You didn't live in a neighborhood that was known to be the bad part of town, even if there really weren't any *bad* parts where we grew up. You couldn't just do whatever you wanted, whenever you wanted without repercussions." I wanted to point out that Kacey *didn't* do whatever she wanted growing up, even if she could have, but decided to let her continue to talk instead. "In our world, you fend for yourself. You look out for number one and that's it. It's ingrained in us because that's what we know."

"I could easily argue that Kacey is the opposite of what you're describing. From what I've learned, she was about as unselfish as they come growing up, looking out for anyone but herself, especially you." I gave her a pointed look

185

that told her I didn't appreciate the way she was speaking about my girlfriend.

Ariana shrugged. "Kacey was always under the false impression that she was better than us. She only did that stuff because she felt like she had something to prove."

I sat my hands down hard on the table, my knuckles turning white from the impact, my words dripping with all of the anger I was feeling inside. "Kacey did everything she did because she thought you guys deserved a better life than what you were given. Not just a better life for her, but for both of you, and now for Bailey."

To my surprise, Ariana's smirk grew with my words. "Maybe that's true. Who knows? But if it is, it only furthers my next point. While Number One might come first in our parts, blood comes second. She'll never choose you over me."

"I'm not asking her to choose," I said stiffly.

Ariana laughed once again. "You don't have to. She just will. And when she does, it will be her blood. I mean, come on, she already chose me over you once, right?"

"I'm not sure—"

"I'm not an idiot," Ariana said sharply, cutting me off before I could say anything else. "I know you're the girl Kacey was head over heels for in college. The reason she never came back to see us. The one who made her believe she was somehow better than us. She had pictures of the two of you all over her room when she moved back home and would spend hours staring at her phone, waiting to talk to you. None of that mattered in the end though, did it? She cut you off like you never even mattered. It's cute that you seem to think you're getting a second chance, but you're only setting yourself up for the same disappointment."

Anger coursed through me. I wasn't angry about the thought of Kacey choosing her family over me. I was angry that her sister would talk about her this way. Angry that she would try to sabotage something that clearly made Kacey happy. I wasn't sure what her angle was, but I knew for a fact that she didn't have her sister's best interests at heart. I opened my mouth to voice all of this, but was stopped by the feeling of a hand on my shoulder.

"Did you guys find something to talk about while I was gone?" Kacey asked cheerfully as she sat down beside me.

"We sure did," Ariana answered sweetly.

Kacey looked between the two of us and squeezed my shoulder that her hand was still resting on. "You okay, babe? You look like you're going to be sick."

"I'm fine. I just need to run to the bathroom." I stood from the table abruptly and quickly made my way through the restaurant, splashing my face with cold water as soon as I was in the bathroom and trying to wrap my mind around everything that was happening.

When I returned to the table, Ariana was talking animatedly as if her conversation with me had rejuvenated her. The rest of the dinner continued this way, only now I was the quiet one, ruminating on everything that had been said.

I was happy once the night was over and we were back in Kacey's bed, far away from Ariana and all of the drama she brought along with her.

"So, what did you think? I think it actually went better than expected. Hopefully you agree?" Kacey looked at me with so much hope in her eyes that I couldn't bear to break her heart by telling her everything Ariana had said.

"It was good, babe," I answered softly.

Kacey's face fell as though she noticed my trepidation. "Why do I not believe what you're saying?"

I sighed and forced my eyes away from hers. "I just want you to be careful, okay? I don't want you to get your hopes up and then be disappointed."

"I know. I keep telling myself that too. I don't know why I even care at this point, but something feels different this time. Maybe it's just because things have been going so well for me that I finally believe they could." She studied my face as she ran a finger down my arm. "Did she do something to make you say that?"

I swallowed hard and hoped Kacey didn't notice my anxiousness. "There were just a few red flags."

Kacey kept her eyes on me as if she were waiting for me to elaborate, but I didn't want to go into more detail than that. I knew what Ariana said would hurt Kacey for so many reasons and hoped I could make my point while scooting around the truth.

"What were the red flags?" Kacey's body became a little stiffer and she removed her hand from my arm. "Because you can't expect it to be the way it is with your family. Even at her absolute best, Ariana isn't going to be like your sister." There was the slightest bite to Kacey's words that I had never experienced before, and it made my mind flash to what Ariana said about where her loyalties lay.

I shook these thoughts from my head. Thinking like that was exactly what Ariana wanted. Instead, I put my hand on Kacey's cheek and forced her eyes that had now wandered away to focus on me. "I love you, Kacey. I just want you to be happy and I support whatever it is that makes you happy, one hundred percent."

My words caused Kacey's demeanor to soften, and she sunk back into me, crashing her lips into mine for a mind-blowing kiss. When she pulled back, the smile had returned to her face. "I love you too, Kari. Forever."

Chapter 15

"Why do you look so sad?" Bo asked a few days later at breakfast. "Aren't newly in love people supposed to be glowing and shit like that?"

"You mean like you two?" I asked as I looked between him and Kylie, both holding tightly to each other's hands as they ate their breakfast with the other.

"Yes, just like us," Kylie said dreamily. "Your best friend is quite the gentleman. He also does this thing in bed where—"

I put my hand up to stop her before I had to hear anything else. "Please stop. I have enough on my mind without having that picture in there as well."

"What's going on?" Kylie asked, becoming serious.

I sighed and took a sip of my coffee, relishing in its warmth. "Things have been strained between Kacey and me ever since I met her sister. Last night was the first time in weeks that we didn't spend the night together. Things felt off, so I told her I was going to leave and she didn't stop me."

Bo raised both eyebrows. "What happened when you met her sister?" I told them the whole story from Ariana's words at dinner to the small tiff Kacey and I had when we got back to her house. Once I was done, Bo sat back and let out a low whistle. "Wow. That really is a lot to take in. Why didn't you just tell her the truth?"

I shrugged. "It wouldn't have done anything but hurt her. If Ariana is the jerk she seems to be, she's going to slip up and Kacey will see it. I'd just like her to see it without having to be subjected to the degrading things said about her. Plus, maybe Ariana isn't trying to sabotage things. Maybe she just doesn't like me."

Kylie shook her head emphatically. "I disagree. If she cared about Kacey, she wouldn't have done that. Remember your girlfriend Tenley? She chewed like a cow and I couldn't stand her. But did I ever tell you that? No, because she made you happy, at least happier than you had been. So, I dealt with Miss Cow Lips just for you." I opened my mouth to argue about the differences, but Kylie put up her hand to stop me. "I also never told *her* that her chewing made me want to fake my own death just to get out of eating dinner with her, so if you were going to make that point, you can forget it."

"Has anything been said about when she's going to be allowed to see Bailey?" Bo asked, clearly trying to avoid a sister fight.

"No. Thank God. Kacey is still really leery about that."

Kylie reached across the table and took my hand in hers. "I'm not trying to give you a hard time. I just care about you and want you to be happy. You were given a second chance with the love of your life. Most people don't get that. I don't want you to lose it because of some loser who doesn't deserve either of your time."

I squeezed her hand and forced a smile onto my face. "This is just a bump in the road for us. Trust me, I know I can't live without Kacey. I'm not going to let anything tear us apart."

Both Bo and Kylie looked relieved at this reassurance. Bo joined his hand with ours on top of the table. "On a happier note, it's your birthday in a few days. Are you excited? What do you want to do?"

I shrugged. "Something small would be great. Maybe everyone could just go to Mom and Dad's on Saturday and by everyone I mean you guys, Kacey, and Bailey. I think a nice relaxing day with all of my favorite people is just what I need." *And hopefully it will help Kacey and me get back on track.*

***

I woke up on the morning of my birthday to the feeling of kisses being peppered across my skin. When I opened my eyes, I smiled up at the dark eyes already focused on me. Kacey slipped her naked body on top of mine and began kissing my neck while grinding her hips into mine. "So, I thought your first birthday present could be me," she said between kisses.

"I think you already gave me that last night," I flirted, happy about the light air surrounding us, so different than how it had been lately. I ran my hands down her bare back, then grabbed her ass in a way that had her squirming on top of me. "See. Already unwrapped and everything."

Kacey laughed as she slipped her hand down between our bodies. "Well, since I'm totally re-gifting, I guess I better make it worth your while." She moved a finger inside of me while running her tongue from my jawline and down my neck to my chest, stopping only to suck on my pulse point. She pulled back just enough to move her mouth to my ear, running her tongue along the outside before taking it between her teeth. "Tell me what you want, baby," she whispered breathlessly.

I could barely form words because I was already so turned on. "I want... I want you to... make love to me."

"Obviously," Kacey said with a slight laugh. "Isn't that what we've been doing?"

I didn't want to tell her that it hadn't felt like that lately. That since the awkward dinner with her sister, while the sex was great, it still felt like just sex. I was desperate for that connection that I had only ever had with her. "Please, Kacey. Make love to me."

This time, she nodded her head seriously as if she understood exactly what I meant. She moved against me more slowly, connecting each part of her body with every piece of mine as she rolled up against me. This time when she leaned down to whisper in my ear, it was sweet rather than heated. "I love you, Kari." She kissed my forehead, then moved her lips to my temple to place another kiss there, then her tongue traced a path along my neck and up to my ear once again. "You make me feel stronger and weaker all at once. You make me feel like I'm floating away and at the same time, keep me grounded."

She kissed her way across my cheek, before settling her lips over mine and kissing me deeply. When she pulled back, she looked into my eyes once again. She positioned herself so she was now situated between my legs, her center pressed hard against mine, her wetness combining with mine. She let out a gasp that matched exactly how I was feeling from the unexpected contact. Without looking away, she began to rock against me, barely able to get her words out anymore. "You're the only woman I've ever loved and the only one I ever will and..." *Gasp.* "God, I just... This is all I want for the rest of my life."

I wrapped my arms around her, desperate to bring our bodies even closer. I pushed my hips up into her, relishing in the feeling of connecting with her at every level—body and soul.

I knew neither one of us would last much longer, but Kacey tried to get the last of her words out between shallow breaths. "I...love...you...happy...birth—" Her words were cut off by the orgasm that seemed to shoot from her body right into mine, both of us writhing together before melting into a single puddle on her bed.

Kacey laid her head against my chest and I took this opportunity to run a hand through her hair while I tried to steady my breathing. After a few minutes, Kacey lifted her head to look at me, her face serious and eyes sad. "I'm really sorry if it hasn't felt like I've been making love to you lately. I know things have been strained with Ariana being back here, but I still see you, Kari. That will never stop and I hope I don't make you question that again."

I shook my head and pulled her back into me. "It's not just you. I've been distant too. But that... wow... that was a birthday present."

I could feel Kacey smiling against my chest. "So, it was a good gift to start with?"

"I'm honestly not sure how you'll top it."

Kacey brought her face up to mine once again, a sexy smirk now adorning it. "I could just top you again."

"Mommy? Kari?" Bailey's voice called from down the hall.

I slapped her back end and pushed her off of me. "It looks like we might have to postpone that."

We each quickly put on a set of pajamas that hadn't made it onto our bodies the night before and headed down the hallway to her room. As soon as she saw me, Bailey jumped out of bed and ran across the room to wrap me in a hug.

"Happy birthday! I'm so excited to celebrate today!" She pulled back and skipped to the other end of the room, picking a piece of paper up off her desk and skipping back to me with it. When I looked down at the picture now in my hands, I saw a drawing of three girls holding hands, which Bailey labeled as me, her, and Kacey. At the top, she had written *family* with a heart. She smiled at me proudly as I tried to blink back tears. "So, what do you think?" she asked, her voice oozing with excitement. "Is it the best gift you've gotten today?"

"Absolutely," I answered while giving Kacey a knowing smile. "It might just be the best gift I've ever gotten."

Bailey shook her head, a serious look on her face. "I don't think that's true." I swallowed hard wondering what Bailey might have heard when she woke up. My anxiety eased up when a sweet smile spread across her face. "I think your best gift ever was me and Mom."

"You're right. You guys are the greatest gift I could ever ask for." When I looked to Kacey, she was already smiling at me and a silent moment passed between us.

The morning started with breakfast at the same cafe we had all eaten at together a few months ago, followed by a chilly walk around Bellman and board games back at Kacey's house. After a lunch of grilled cheese sandwiches and tomato soup, courtesy of Kacey and Bailey, I went back to my house to shower and change. Later in the afternoon, we got in the car to head to my parents' house, Kacey whispering that she would give me my last gift once we were back home.

My mom opened the door for us with an excitement that I knew had nothing to do with my birthday, but rather the fact that it was the first time she was seeing Kacey since I had told her we were officially back together. "Happy birthday! It's so nice to see all of you!" She was speaking to all three of us but her eyes were focused on Kacey. I was surprised when she pulled me into a hug first, then Bailey, and then finally Kacey. She held onto Kacey a little longer, giving her an extra squeeze as she loudly whispered into her ear. "I'm very happy that my daughter finally came to her senses. This is how it's meant to be."

193

When they pulled apart, Kacey looked between my mom and me, a look of surprise on her face. "I'm just happy to be given another chance." She reached out and grabbed my hand as my mom beamed at us as if she had just been given the greatest news in the world.

"Where's Kylie?" I asked as my eyes searched the house.

My mom's smile grew even wider now, to the point where she looked almost crazy. "She's at Bo's house. Been spending a lot more time there lately. The two of them should be here soon. What a nice young man he is. I always liked him, but he's even more of a gentleman now that he's dating Kylie."

I had to hold back my laughter at Bo being described as a gentleman. No matter how good he was to my sister, I didn't think I would ever see my crazy best friend that way. When my dad came into the hallway, he had a serious look on his face. "I don't care how much of a gentleman he is. I don't know if Kylie really needs to be spending every night there."

My mom laughed and gave him a kiss on the cheek. "She's twenty-six, sweetheart. You have to let go sometime."

"I'm not so sure I do," he answered seriously before softening as he looked toward me. "There's my birthday girl. How does it feel to be thirty-two?"

I shrugged. "Just about the same as it felt to be thirty-one." I looked toward Kacey, unable to stop the smile that blossomed across my face. "Although, I am much happier this year, but I don't think that has anything to do with my age." Kacey squeezed my hand, and I leaned into her, enjoying the heat from her body that was now enveloping me.

"They're in love," Bailey announced, causing all of us to laugh.

My mom smiled at Bailey, then back at Kacey and me. "They sure are. Now, the only question is when they are going to get me some grandbabies and you a sibling." She winked at Bailey, making her giggle.

I cleared my throat. "Slow your roll, Mom. Let us enjoy our time together a little before you start putting all of this pressure on us."

"I'm just saying. I'm not getting any younger. None of us are." She lifted both eyebrows and smirked as she looked between Kacey and me.

My mom's eyes diverted from us when Bailey tapped on her arm. Bailey looked up at her, a serious look on her face. "A sibling would be nice, but I've also always wished I had grandparents." She continued to stare at my mom expectantly.

"And now you do," my mom answered, her voice cracking slightly as she pulled Bailey into a tight bear-hug.

The moment was interrupted by Bo and Kylie's arrival. Once we said our hellos, we enjoyed the homemade pot pie my mom had made, then spent the night watching home videos. Bailey was excited when my mom put one in from Christmas my junior year of college, because Kacey was in it. I stole glances at Kacey while I watched our younger selves laughing together, so unaware of all of the hardships we had ahead of us. I nudged her side at a part where the camera caught her staring at me, her eyes full of love as I opened one of my presents. "You were quite smitten back then," I teased.

Kacey looked at me with the same love, but I could see so much more behind it now, years of longing and adoration that hadn't faded over time. "I'm still quite smitten."

I put my hand on her cheek and kissed her softly, but quickly. When I pulled away, I noticed that my mom was watching our interaction, looking just as smitten as Kacey did in the video. I saw something flash in her eyes as though a lightbulb had gone off and she looked past us at Bailey. "Hey, Bailey? I was just wondering how you would feel about spending the night here tonight. We could make popcorn and watch a few movies. Your mom and Kari can come back in the morning to pick you up and I'll make a big brunch."

"Really?" Bailey asked excitedly. "I would love that. Can I, Mom? Please?" She looked at Kacey with big puppy dog eyes, but we all knew that wouldn't be necessary.

195

"Of course. That's very nice of Mrs. Adelberg to offer. I'm sure you guys will have a great time." She gave my mom a grateful smile, then gave me a look that had me ready to leave immediately.

We made it another hour before we said our goodbyes, both itching to get back to Kacey's to spend some time alone. "When we get back, I can give you your big present," Kacey said once we were close to our neighborhood.

I wiggled my eyebrows at her. "Can't wait."

Kacey laughed and shook her head. "Get your mind out of the gutter. It's not that kind of gift." She looked me up and down and licked her lips. "Although, I must say that I'm very thankful to your mother for giving us a free pass to have a long night of loud, unencumbered sex."

"Normally, she just gives money, but this is much better. Although, I really am going to miss tucking Bailey in and reading a book together."

"You're so incredibly adorable. I love how much you love her." Kacey stared at me lovingly and ran a finger over my arm.

"I love both of you." I gave Kacey a quick smile before returning my eyes to the road, my focus immediately going to the extra car in our driveway. The car was just inches from Kacey's and almost sideways. "What the hell?"

Kacey took her eyes off of me to see what I was responding to. "You've gotta be kidding me," she said with a strained huff.

Once we parked and got out of the car, Ariana's voice cut through the darkness. "My, my, my, isn't this cute?" I looked toward the sound to find Ariana leaning against Kacey's garage door, arms crossed, eyes hooded as if opening them was too much work at the moment.

"What are you doing here, Ariana?" Kacey asked sternly, also aware of how drunk her sister was.

"Just thought I would stop by and see the child I created," she slurred.

Kacey took a few tentative steps and tried to reach her hand toward Ariana, who quickly pulled away. "You know you can't just show up like this. Especially when you're wasted."

Ariana's eyes burned as she focused on Kacey. "You're not better than me. You can't control what I do or who I see."

"No, but I can control who I let into my daughter's life."

Ariana scoffed. "Oh yeah. Hero Kacey. Always swooping in to save the day. But you know what? You adopting Bailey was never supposed to be part of the plan. I was going to give her up and then we'd never have to see her again. It's your fault she's still dealing with our family's shit. You had to take control. Prove that you're better than the rest of the family."

Kacey shook her head, tears now running down her face. "Stop. Don't you dare say anything about Bailey. I kept her because I loved her from the moment I laid eyes on her and have grown to love her more and more with every passing day. You can say a lot about me but don't even think about trying to say that I had any motive other than love for adopting her."

I put my hand on Kacey's arm to show my support, and Ariana's eyes immediately bounced over to me. "And you. Don't even get me started. I've heard all about your family. Spoiled rich people with so much money you throw it away to have a dining hall named after you. I'm sure your parents like to act all high and mighty, act like they're doing it to further the education of poor college students. But really, they just want to look good. Have something to brag about at the town country club."

Kacey took a step in front of me, protectively shielding me from Ariana's wrath. "You don't even know them. Don't you dare talk about them that way. The Adelberg family is the most loving, sincere group of people you'll ever meet. They welcomed me with open arms from the moment they met me. Same with Bailey. It's a lot more than I can say for you."

"Oh really? Is that how it is? You spend the last few weeks acting like you're happy to have me back, then throw me away the moment I speak a few inconvenient truths about your new *family*." Ariana did air quotes as she spoke the word family, her voice now coming out as a snarl.

Kacey lightly grabbed ahold of her arm and motioned for me to follow as she walked her toward the house and opened the door. "We're not having this conversation outside."

"Oh yeah? What's wrong? Are you afraid that your neighbors are going to figure out where you came from? That you're nothing but trash dressed up in nicer clothes?"

"I can't believe that I actually thought you changed." Kacey's words were barely a whisper and her shoulders slumped as she said them. It was heartbreaking to see, and I felt helpless, standing there with nothing more to give than a supportive touch.

"You always did see the best in people. Like your little girlfriend here. You actually believe she won't break your heart. But she will. Just like I told her that you will always choose your actual family over her, she'll eventually choose a better life over slumming it with you. You'll never be able to escape your past. She'll choose someone with a better family. Someone who doesn't come with baggage. And you'll choose me."

Kacey shook her head, a look of confusion taking the place of her sadness. "What do you mean *just like you told her?*"

I wanted to jump in and explain, but Ariana began to cackle loudly before I could. "She didn't tell you, did she? I thought you guys told each other *everything*. Anyway, I just let her know where your loyalties would always lie. How you'll always go back to your roots."

Kacey locked her eyes with mine and I tried my best to express everything I was feeling with just one look. "I didn't tell you because I didn't want you to get hurt. She said some pretty terrible things that I was hoping you wouldn't have to hear." Tears started to roll down my cheeks, but Kacey put a hand on my cheek and used her thumb to wipe them away.

Our moment was interrupted by Ariana's terrible cackle once again. "I don't get it, Kacey. I really just don't understand what you see in this girl."

Kacey's body went rigid as she turned to look at her sister. "I don't need to explain that to you. In fact, I don't have to explain anything to you ever again. I don't know what your angle was coming here and acting sweet, just to blow up like this, but I'm done. I mean it, Ariana. You can't just show up and put down all of the people I care about. My family. Because that's what they are. *They're* my family. Not you."

Ariana stuck her nose up in the air, a smug look on her face. "You'll regret this. You will."

"The only thing I regret is giving you another chance." Kacey nodded her head toward the stairs. "There's a guest room upstairs. You can sleep in there since I don't want you to be driving when you're drunk. But tomorrow morning, I want you to leave and never come back."

Without saying another word, Ariana stomped away and up the stairs. After a minute, a door slammed, causing Kacey to flinch before looking back at me. "I'm so sorry about that."

"I'm sorry too. I should have told you about what your sister said at dinner that night."

Kacey sighed. "I wish you had told me, but I get why you didn't."

"You do?"

Kacey nodded her head. "I know all about doing what's hard, and might even be wrong, to try to protect the person you love."

I thought about her words, struggling with voicing what had been on my mind for a while now. "I have to tell you something else. I hate to admit it, but I think you were right to break up with me all those years ago. You were right. I would have given everything up for you. I wouldn't have gotten my master's degree or gone on to become board certified. I probably would have resented you eventually, no matter how unfair that would be. I also didn't have the maturity level that you did to be a mom. I'm not sure if I could have done it. I'm not questioning whether I would have loved Bailey with all of my heart, because I know I would have. But I'm just glad I came into her life at a time when I was ready to be everything she deserves."

Kacey's lips curved into a slight smile for the first time since arriving back at her house. "Thank you for telling me that. Seriously. It means a lot to me that you're able to see that." Her smile dropped as she looked away from me. "Tonight isn't about me though. It's about you."

Before I could argue, she walked away and came back a minute later holding a small wrapped box. "This is your birthday present." Her hand shook as she handed it over to me, and when I looked into her eyes, I saw that she was trying to fight back tears.

I put the gift into the pocket of my jacket that I was still wearing, then put my hand under Kacey's chin, directing her eyes toward me. "Hey, just because it's my birthday doesn't mean you have to act strong. Let's go up to bed. You could use some sleep. That was a lot to take in." I pushed a lock of hair behind her ear and placed a kiss on her forehead before taking her hand and leading her upstairs.

We both changed and got ready for bed. Kacey looked at me with tired eyes as she lay down beside me. "I'm really sorry the night didn't go as we expected."

"Stop. Anytime with you is perfect, Kacey. I promise."

Kacey nodded her head, then burrowed it into my neck, clinging to me like a child to a parent. I ran a hand through her hair and tried to will myself to fall asleep.

Sleep didn't seem likely though. First there was Kacey's constant tossing and turning, with little bouts of tears and asking why she had been so wrong. When we finally fell asleep, we were startled back awake to the sound of sirens not very far away that seemed to last forever. I was drifting off to sleep again when the faint sound of my phone vibrating woke me back up. I pushed the side button to stop it, then tried to ignore it when it started up again. After it repeated several times, I ripped it from the nightstand and found missed calls from both my parents and Bo, as well as a text from my mom telling me to call her right away.

"Mom, what's going on?" I asked sleepily when she picked up the phone.

My mom's voice was so shaky, it was almost hard to discern the words she was saying, but when they registered, it felt like my whole world came crashing down. "You need to come to the hospital. It's your sister. She's been in an accident." The phone dropped from my hand at the same moment I felt my stomach drop.

Chapter 16

Kacey and I rushed around the room putting on clothes and grabbing anything we might need at the hospital. Once downstairs, I tried to catch my breath while Kacey frantically searched for something. "I can't find the small backpack I wore to your parents anywhere. It has my car keys, license, and all of my cards in it." She took a deep breath and ran a hand through her hair. "I'm too overwhelmed to remember where my spare keys are." She shook her head and groaned. "My car is blocked anyway. Give me your keys. I'll drive us in your car. You're in no condition to drive right now."

I fumbled with my keys as I tried to focus on Kacey through my tear-filled eyes. She wrapped her arms around me and pulled me tight against her. "She's going to be okay. She'll be okay." The tone of her voice made it sound like she was trying to convince herself just as much as she was trying to convince me and even her strong arms couldn't ease my anxiety.

I gently pushed her away and started to walk toward the door. "We should go." I couldn't focus on anything as I crawled into the car, but Kacey's whispered expletives caught my attention. "What's going on?"

"My sister's damn car is gone. I have a feeling that's where my backpack got to." She forced a smile and squeezed my hand. "It's not worth worrying about right now. Let's just make sure your sister is okay."

I looked at my phone and found another desperate text from Bo. "Bo hasn't left yet. Could we pick him up?"

Without saying a word, Kacey nodded her head and directed the car toward Bo's house. When we arrived, he was already waiting outside, pacing back and forth while he talked to himself. As he slid into the back seat, he ran a hand through his hair and let out a low growl before breaking into tears. "I should have been with her. She told me she wanted to stay at your parents' house longer, and I decided to go home. I just wanted the chance to shower and clean up a little before she came back over. It was so stupid. Why am I so stupid?"

Kacey kept one hand on the wheel while reaching the other back to take Bo's. "You can't think like that. Beating yourself up isn't going to help anything. All we can do now is to be there for her, okay?"

I reached my hand back so all three of our hands were connected and we rode to the hospital like this, no one speaking for the duration of the drive.

Once we were inside, Kacey led the way until we arrived on the floor that we were told to go to. As soon as the elevator doors opened, I saw my parents and ran to my mom, collapsing in her arms. "What's going on? Is Kylie okay? Mom, please tell me she's going to be okay. Please."

I could tell my mom was trying to stay strong for me, but was barely hanging on. Her face looked tired and tear-streaked and it was covered in worry. "We don't know, sweetheart. We don't know anything. They said the injuries were extensive and that she needed emergency surgery, but that's as much as we know."

"But she's going to be okay, right?" My voice was desperate and I couldn't stop the tears that continued to run down my face.

"We can only hope," my mom said solemnly. "Come on. Let's go sit down, and I'll tell you everything we know."

We walked over to where Kacey and Bo were sitting on each side of my dad, each holding one of his hands. They all looked just as scared as I felt, but Kacey tried to give me a reassuring smile. I sat down beside her and laid my head on her shoulder and Bo moved over so my mom could sit beside my dad. "What happened?" I asked, almost afraid to hear the answer.

My dad cleared his throat and looked out into the distance. "We don't know much. She was hit head on coming into your neighborhood. They think the other driver ran a red light, but they aren't sure because it was a hit and run. Most likely a drunk driver."

I looked at Kacey and I could tell she was thinking the same thing I was by how pale her face became from learning this new information. I had to look away because the thought was too upsetting. She ran her fingers over my hand, trying to encourage me to take hers, but I couldn't will my hand to move. Her touch no longer felt comforting and even though I could feel her eyes burning into me, I couldn't force myself to look at her, afraid of what I might feel if I did.

My eyes shot up at the sound of footsteps approaching. A doctor who looked way too young to have gray spots in his hair, but still did, stopped in front of us. He looked between my parents, avoiding eye contact with me completely. "Are you the parents of Kylie Adelberg?" he asked, the tone of his voice giving nothing away. When my mom nodded, he took one more step toward us, dropping his voice slightly. "I'm going to need you to come with me."

As my parents started to follow him out of the waiting area and into a different part of the hospital completely, all of the worst thoughts came to my head. "He took them back to tell them something. Oh God. Isn't that what they do when they need to tell someone that..." I couldn't even say the words because speaking them out loud made it feel too real and I didn't want to believe it. I couldn't even begin to imagine a life without my sister. Never again hearing her laugh. No longer enduring hours of teasing. Losing the simple things that I always took for granted, but meant so much to me, like her hugs and the way we could talk for hours about nothing at all.

Kacey moved from her chair and squatted in front of me, placing both hands on my knees and tilting her head at an angle that forced me to look at her. "It's going to be okay, baby. You're going to be okay. I promise. I'm here. I love you and I'm not going anywhere. No matter what happens, we'll find a way to get through this together."

Her words fell on deaf ears and I felt an anger building up inside of me as I stared back at her. When I looked at those eyes and her lips and the way her eyebrows curved slightly in concern, I no longer saw the love of my life in front of me, but someone else entirely. Someone I had no interest in seeing. I tore my eyes away and tried to move away from her touch. "God, I can't even look at you right now. All I see is… is… *her*."

Tears came to Kacey's eyes, and she laid her head on my lap, her body shaking with emotion. "I know. I know.

I'm sorry. I'm so sorry." She lifted her head and tried to look at me, but I moved my eyes to the ceiling, looking anywhere but at the woman sitting in front of me. "Please, Kari. I'll take care of this. I'll go to the police. If Ariana had anything to do with the accident, I'll make sure she gets caught."

"*If?* Really, Kacey? There's no *if* about it. Your sister. She caused the accident. And now my sister might be… well, she could be… God, I can't even say it."

Kacey leaned her forehead against mine, putting her hand at the back of my head so I couldn't pull away. "We don't know anything yet. There's no need to believe the worst right now. All we can do is hope and pray that it's not as bad as it seems."

So many thoughts ran through my mind, but even I was surprised by the words that slipped through my lips. "Leave."

"Wh-what?" Kacey asked softly, just as surprised by my words.

"Leave," I answered more firmly. "I can't be around you right now."

Kacey reached for my hand once again, but I quickly pulled it away. "I'm not leaving you, Kari. I love you. I'm going to be here for you no matter what."

"If you really wanted to be there for me, you'd leave me alone. You're making everything worse right now."

Kacey nodded her head and slowly stood. "If… if you insist. Your dad told me they had a neighbor come to the house to watch Bailey. I guess I'll go there. I'll probably go to the police station first though." She looked to me for a response, but when I didn't say anything, she reached into her coat pocket and handed me the keys to my car. "I'll call a ride. I hate leaving you, but I also want to do what's right for you. I wish I knew what that was." She cleared her throat and looked away from me. "Please call me if you need anything. I love you."

"I won't," were the only words I could push out, too emotional to even fathom how hurtful they were.

Kacey's shoulders slumped as she walked away and got onto the elevator. I didn't look up until I heard the elevator doors close, feeling a strange sense of relief wash over me. Bo sat silently beside me, not making any comment about the scene that had just played out right in front of him. My heavy eyes started to close, and I couldn't stop the sleep that washed over me. I wasn't sure how much time had passed when I felt a tap on my shoulder. "Sweetheart. Sweetie, wake up."

I blinked my eyes at my mom, then rubbed them to try to bring her into focus. "Mom? What happened? Did she…? Is she…?"

My mom nodded her head, but I had no idea what she was agreeing to. "She's going to be okay, Kari. She has a lot of broken bones and the swelling and bruising are really bad, but she'll be okay."

I swallowed hard. "She's going to be okay?" I pictured the doctor who came out to grab my parents and a new anger settled over me. "That asshole."

"Excuse me?" my mom asked, completely thrown off by my response.

"The shitty doctor. He's such an asshole. Why wouldn't he say something? Why would he pull you away like the worst had happened?"

"He wanted us to be aware that it would be a long recovery process and warn us that she didn't look like herself right now. That way we wouldn't be surprised when we saw her."

My head spun from all of the emotions I was feeling, the most prevalent being anger, which even I couldn't explain. "You saw her?" I snarled. "You knew she was okay and didn't think that *maybe* it would be a good idea to come out and tell us that?" My mom opened her mouth to answer, but I fell into her arms before she could, sobbing harder than I ever had in my entire life. "I was so scared, Mom. I'm sorry. I was just so scared. I thought… I thought… oh my God. I'm just so happy she's going to be okay." I pulled away and wiped at my eyes, my anger replaced by relief and just a tinge of sadness for what could have been. "I think I know who did it," I said quietly. My mom stared at me intently, so I continued. "I think it was Kacey's sister. She showed up at Kacey's house tonight drunk out of her mind and Kacey told her to stay, but when we woke up, she was gone."

My mom put one hand over her mouth. "Oh, dear. Does Kacey know? Is she okay?" She looked around the waiting room as if she were watching for Kacey to appear.

I shook my head. "She's not here."

My mom sighed and placed a hand on my shoulder. "I'm sure this was all very hard for her. I know she wants to be here for you. She's probably just trying to sort everything out. Heck, knowing Kacey she probably went to the police station to tell them her suspicions."

My mom's worry for Kacey's well-being caused guilt to take over. Anger wasn't even a consideration to her, and I was starting to realize it shouldn't have been for me either. "I... I told her to leave. I was so mad and I told her to go. Shit, I made a big mistake, didn't I?"

"We all do things we shouldn't when we get emotional. Kacey will understand." My mom pushed my hair back, massaging the top of my head as she did, and the sensation was enough to elicit a big yawn as I struggled to keep my eyes open. "Get some sleep. The doctor said no one else will be able to see Kylie until the morning, so there's no reason to force yourself to stay awake. I'll call Kacey for you."

I was too tired to argue, so I let myself drift back off to sleep. When I woke up a few hours later, still slouched down in the hard waiting room chair, my eyes instinctively searched for Kacey. Disappointment coursed through me when I realized she wasn't there. Bo was asleep next to me, his head resting on my shoulder, and my mom was standing across the room, talking to one of the nurses. I carefully extracted my body out from under Bo's and made my way over to my mom. "Is Kylie awake yet? Did you talk to Kacey? Is she coming back?"

My mom turned to look at me and I felt guilty when I saw the tired look on her face. She clearly hadn't slept at all, doing everything to take care of the rest of the family. "Your dad is in with her now. They think more than one person at a time will be too overwhelming for her."

I nodded my head, itching to hear the answer to my other question. "And Kacey?"

My mom shook her head. "I couldn't get ahold of her. It went right to voicemail." When my lip started to quiver, she put an arm around my shoulder. "Give her time, sweetheart. What you said was hurtful, but Kacey's a smart girl. She'll realize the words were said out of fear instead of anger."

I took a deep breath and stood up taller, trying to put on a brave face. "When can I see Kylie?"

At that moment, my dad walked back into the waiting room, looking just as worn out as my mom. My mom nodded her head toward the hallway he had just walked out of. "You're next." I started to walk away, but she grabbed my hand before I could. "Just be prepared. Her injuries are extensive. She'll be okay though. Just remember that she's going to be okay and that's all that matters." The look on my mom's face told me that she was trying to convince herself just as much as she was trying to convince me.

I followed a nurse down a long hallway until we reached the room at the very end. I took a deep breath before entering and had to do a double take to make sure I was in the right room. Kylie had tons of machines attached to her, a big cast on her leg, and her face was so bruised, it was almost unrecognizable. "Hey, Sis," she said weakly, a small smile creeping onto her face. "You didn't expect me to let your birthday weekend be all about you, did you?"

I laughed through my tears. Of course Kylie would find a way to make a joke out of a terrible situation. I walked across the room and sat down in the chair beside her bed, taking her hand in mine. "I'm just so glad you're okay."

"Okay? I had a plate put in my leg and my face looks like I starred in a Freddy Krueger movie." She laughed slightly at her own joke.

I squeezed her hand gently. "But you're here."

"Of course. You're not getting rid of me that easily." She scanned the room, sighing dramatically, before looking back at me. "At least tell me you and Kacey got in a few rounds of birthday sex before being interrupted."

It was my turn to let out a dramatic sigh. "We didn't. We actually had drama of our own earlier in the night."

"Tell me about it."

I shook my head. "You have more important things to worry about."

Kylie gave me the look she always did when she thought I was being ridiculous. "All I've heard about since getting here is my accident and my injuries. It would be really nice to be filled in on someone else's drama instead."

"Our drama might actually be your drama though," I said quietly, feeling ashamed, both for what Kacey's sister had done and also for how I had treated Kacey.

"Now you have to tell me."

I blew out a long breath, contemplating where I should start. "Well, Kacey's sister showed up at her house last night."

Kylie's eyes went wide and looked like they might bulge out of her head. "No shit."

"Yep. She was super wasted and said some terrible things, so Kacey told her she was done with her."

"Good for her." Kylie slowly moved her hand and weakly tapped me on the knee, while lifting both eyebrows. "See. I told you Kacey would figure it out. You have a very smart girlfriend."

"That's not the end of it." I put my head down and ran both hands through my hair. When I looked back up, Kylie's full attention was on me. "Kacey told her to stay until the morning because she didn't want her driving drunk, but she didn't listen. She snuck out sometime after we fell asleep and we think…" I let my voice drift off rather than finishing my sentence.

"Shit. That bitch messed with your head, screwed over Kacey, and then put me in the hospital? What an asshole." She shook her head. "I gotta say though. I never would have taken her for the type of person to drive a truck and a fairly nice one at that."

"Wait, what? Ariana doesn't drive a truck. What are you talking about?"

Kylie closed her eyes as though she were thinking about something. "I could have sworn it was a truck that hit me, but what do I know? Everything that happened past dinner is super fuzzy. I can't even remember you leaving Mom and Dad's." Kylie opened her eyes and studied my face. "You're not somehow blaming yourself for what Kacey's sister did, are you? Because it's no one's fault, but hers."

I hung my head, ashamed that even my sister who had just experienced the scariest moment of her life could acknowledge that. "No, but I did blame Kacey. Well, kind of. I didn't think you were going to make it and she tried to comfort me, but all I could see was Ariana, so I told her to leave."

"If I could slap you right now, I would. You're a dumbass."

"And you're pretty mean for someone who almost died."

"Well, thank God I didn't. Someone has to be here to tell you when you're being an idiot." She shook her head, cringing from the pain it must have caused. "Just make things right, okay?"

Before I could reply, there was a knock on the open door. I looked up to see Bo standing there, an unsure look on his face. "Is it okay if I interrupt?"

Kylie's smile grew bigger than I had seen it since walking into the room. "There's my sexy boyfriend." She motioned to where I was sitting. "Switch places with my sister. She has damage control to do. She's been stupid."

Bo looked between us and a small smirk came to his face. "Yeah, I witnessed the whole thing. It wasn't good."

Kylie glared over at him. "And you didn't stop her?"

Bo shrugged. "I kind of had a lot on my mind."

Kylie looked at me and then Bo. "You leave. And you, come give me a kiss and I'll forgive you for not being a good watch dog."

I slipped from the room and immediately took my phone from my pocket and dialed Kacey's number, my heart dropping when it went right to voicemail. "Kacey, listen, I'm sorry. I didn't mean anything I said. Please call me back, okay? I love you."

I ended the call then sent a few desperate text messages before pushing the doors open to the waiting room. I was surprised to find two police officers standing by my parents, all of them with serious looks on their faces. "What's going on?" I asked once I reached the group.

The female officer turned to look at me. "We know who's responsible for the hit and run. He turned himself in this morning."

The sickness I had felt in my stomach ever since my mom called to tell me to get to the hospital became ten times worse. "He?"

The male officer shook his head. "Yeah, a kid on the Bellman football team. Fled the scene because he was afraid of losing his spot, but I guess his conscience got the best of him. Thank God. I'm just glad we have some answers for your family."

"I need to sit down," I said softly, before stumbling over to one of the chairs.

My mom followed behind me and sat down beside me, placing a hand on my arm. "Doesn't it make you feel better knowing it wasn't Kacey's sister? That's something neither of you should have had to live with."

I shook my head and started to cry for what had to be the millionth time in the past twenty-four hours. "I pushed Kacey away. I blamed her for something that wasn't her fault after making an assumption that wasn't even true."

My mom moved her hand up and down my arm, the same way she used to when I was a little girl. "Kacey loves you, sweetheart. She'll forgive you."

I scoffed through my tears. "The crazy thing is I don't even think she's mad at me. She probably understands, because that's just how Kacey is. She's the most understanding person in the world. But I confirmed all of her fears from college. I made it seem like her family and her past caused me pain. Like it was somehow her fault. What if she decides it's too much? What if she walks away again because she's trying to protect me? I can't do it, Mom. I barely got through it the first time. Losing her. God, losing Bailey. No." My tears turned into sobs and I put my head on her shoulder, leaving it there for what felt like hours.

My mom eventually stood when Bo came back out, switching spots with him as she went back to have her time with Kylie. "I told your sister I loved her," Bo said as he sat down beside me. When I looked at him, he gave me a shy smile. "I know it's probably too soon to say it, but I figured if I felt it, there's no reason to hold it in. I could have lost her and she never would have known how I felt. I didn't want to waste another minute."

I reached out and took his hand in mine. "That's sweet, Bo. What did she say?"

His smile grew bigger than I had ever seen it in all of our years of friendship. "She said she loves me too."

I bumped my shoulder against his. "That's awesome, dude. I'm really happy for both of you." I hoped he didn't notice the way my smile faltered, but I could tell by the way he was looking at me that he did.

"Things will be okay with Kacey. I've shipped you guys from the beginning. I know you won't let me down now."

I removed my hand from his so I could run both of mine up my arms, the chilly hospital air becoming too much for me. Bo motioned toward my coat that was sitting on the chair next to me. "You look freezing. You should put that back on."

I grabbed the coat and put it on, quickly shoving my hands in the pockets, surprised when my hand hit a small object. I pulled it out and realized it was the gift from Kacey. I swallowed hard and looked over at Bo. "This was from Kacey. I never got the chance to open it."

He put a hand on my shoulder, squeezing gently, then stood up. "I'm going to go talk to your dad so you can have some privacy to open that."

My hands shook as I removed the wrapping paper and opened the small box. My vision blurred once again as I stared down at the beautiful gold bracelet that had *K₂Forever* engraved on the front. When I turned it over, I read the back which was inscribed with the words, *I never have and never will stop loving you.*

I took out my phone and called Kacey, groaning when her voicemail picked up once again. "I'm sorry," I cried into the phone. "Please don't pull away from me, Kacey. Living without you isn't living at all. Please. I'm begging you. I can't lose you again."

A few hours and countless calls and texts later, I had yet to get through to Kacey. My dad sat down beside me and gave me a tired smile. "You and Bo need to go home for the night. You both look exhausted and could use some sleep."

I shook my head. "No, that's okay. I'll stay here."

My dad chuckled lightly. "That wasn't a question. It was a demand. You guys look awful, and honestly, you don't smell very good either. I can't have the hospital staff thinking I raised a dirty daughter." He winked at me and pushed his shoulder against mine playfully.

Bo and I listened to him and the two of us drove home from the hospital mostly in silence. The only reason I was looking forward to getting home was so I could talk to Kacey, so I was disappointed when I pulled into the driveway and realized her car wasn't there. I walked Duke so he could go to the bathroom, surprised by how calm he was for going so long without being taken out. I took a long hot shower, which I had to admit felt really good, then called Kacey one more time before falling into bed.

I was shocked when I woke up in the early hours of the morning and realized I had slept for over ten hours. I quickly got dressed, then left the house to head to the hospital, once again disappointed to find that Kacey's car was still missing. I did the walk through the hospital on autopilot and only looked up when the elevator doors opened, expecting to see my parents sitting in the waiting room. Only, it wasn't them. It was someone else entirely.

"You came back," I whispered before running into Kacey's arms.

She held me tightly for a few minutes before pulling back to look into my eyes. "Of course I came. I love you, Kari. I love you so much." She placed a kiss on my forehead, then stared into my eyes once again. "I'm sorry I missed all of your calls and texts. My phone died and I didn't have a chance to charge it. After my phone died, I went to your parents' house and stayed there so I didn't have to wake Bailey. Then, in the morning, I went to the police station to report Ariana, and they told me that the drunk driver had turned himself in. The one officer mentioned how he was lucky that the victim was okay so he couldn't be charged with vehicular manslaughter. Anyway, after hearing that, I decided to go back to your parents' and clean up a bit, so they wouldn't have to worry about doing that before bringing Kylie home."

"You cleaned my parents' house?" I asked, completely swooning over the perfect woman standing in front of me.

Kacey shrugged. "I just made the beds and did the dishes. Stuff like that. Bailey drew Kylie a few pictures that she hung on her wall. Then Bailey and I used your spare key to get into your house so we could take Duke out. After that, I finally charged my phone and was shocked to see all of the calls and texts from you. Instead of calling you back, we hopped into my car and headed right to the hospital and when we got here, your mom told us we had just missed you. Your parents looked exhausted so I offered to stick around the hospital, so they could go home and get some sleep. I didn't call or text you because I knew you would come right back, and I wanted you to get sleep as well."

I pulled Kacey close to me again, completely breathing her in. "I don't deserve you. I was terrible to you and you still did all of that for me."

Kacey gave me a quick kiss on the lips then brought her hand to my jaw to force me to look at her. "You were scared. I get it. So was I. You have nothing to feel bad about."

"I was so worried when I didn't hear back from you. I thought maybe history was going to repeat itself and you would decide pulling away was what was best for me."

Kacey pushed out a deep sigh. "I'm not going to lie. I thought about it. Because you were right—that easily could have been my sister. And she might be gone for now, but who knows if she'll show up again." She stared into my eyes, silently reiterating all of our promises to each other. "But that's not my choice to make. It's yours. I made the mistake of choosing for you once and I wasn't going to do that again."

I took her hand in mine and held it tightly. "I choose *you*, Kacey. I meant it when I told you that I want every single part of you. I want your past, present, and future. I want every single piece that makes you you, because frankly, I've never met a better person than you. Your past—the life you left behind—I hate that you went through that, but I'm also so damn proud of you. You beat the odds. Life gave you lemons and you told life where to stick 'em. I'm just in awe that someone like you sees something in me. I have been since the day I met you. If your sister shows up again, we'll face it together, because that's all I want. To experience every part of life, the good and the bad, with you by my side."

To my surprise, Kacey picked me up and twirled me around, both of us laughing when she sat me back on the ground. "I'm really glad to hear that, because it's honestly the only choice I was going to accept. I never knew what home felt like until I met you. Everytime I see you, it's like coming home all over again, and I love that feeling."

I put my hands in Kacey's hair and pulled her lips to mine, not worried about the other people in the waiting room who were getting a free show. I deepened the kiss and relished in the feeling of Kacey's hands resting on my hips. When I finally forced myself to pull away, I rested my forehead against hers and took in those dark eyes, the ones that had me mesmerized from the day I met her, and spoke the words we both needed to hear. "Welcome home, sweetheart."

Epilogue

The months following Kylie's accident were long and hard. Her recovery was slow and it took the whole family to get her through it. Kacey was by my side every step of the way, the voice of reason who kept not just me, but my whole family on track. She encouraged Kylie to stay positive, cooked meals for my mom when she was too tired, had a drink with my dad when he needed an escape, and even convinced Bo to take care of himself every once in a while when he was draining himself by pouring everything into my sister.

After Kylie's last day of physical therapy, my parents had a big party at their house to celebrate. Kylie invited all of her friends and we spent the day laughing and reminiscing on how far we had come. When the party came to an end and it was just my parents, Kylie, Bo, Kacey, and Bailey left, Kylie gave me the signal to go ahead with what we had been planning together the past few weeks. Even though I told her I shouldn't do it on her special day, she insisted, and her stubbornness won out in the end.

So, I stood from the table and tapped on my wine glass, signaling a toast. "I just want to say how happy I am that we're all here together. A few months ago, we almost lost a very important person." I looked toward my sister. "Kylie, I can't even begin to express how much of a blessing it is to be your sister. The strength that you have shown since your accident is mind-blowing. I always thought you were amazing, but wow. You're my hero. And Kacey," Kacey was surprised when my eyes met hers, "I think we can all agree that you played a pivotal role in keeping every single one of us positive and sane. I know I tell you this everyday, but I don't know what I did to deserve you. My whole family agrees, which is probably why they keep insisting I tie you down. And you know what? They're right. It's been almost fourteen years since I decided you were the person I wanted to spend the rest of my life with, so it's about time we make it official." Kacey put a hand over her mouth as tears began to run down her cheeks. "I have a very important question to ask you, but there's someone else I need to talk to first."

I got down on one knee in front of Bailey and pulled a jewelry box out of my pocket, showing her the bracelet that had three birthstones on it—hers, mine, and Kacey's. I cried as I slid it onto her wrist, laughing at my own shaky hands. "I'm going to ask your mom to marry me, but first I wanted to ask you something. Are you ready to officially become family?"

Instead of answering, Bailey jumped out of her chair and into my arms, causing both of us to stumble backward. "Can I take that as a yes?" I asked with a chuckle. Bailey nodded her head and I realized that she was crying too, so I held her tightly and placed a kiss on her cheek before pulling away. Still down on one knee, I turned my body toward Kacey. "I kind of gave a little spoiler there, but what do you say? Kacey Grace Caldwell, will you marry me?"

Just like Bailey, she nodded her head as the tears streamed down her face. I slipped the ring onto her finger, then stood and took her into my arms, letting go just long enough to pick up Bailey so she could join us in the family hug. As we all held each other tight, my mind was already buzzing with dreams of how our wedding day would go.

***

Two years later, those dreams became a reality. I stared at myself in the mirror as I ran my hands over the long white dress and took in my hair that was curled and partly pulled up. "You look great," Kylie said as she walked up behind me.

I smiled at her in the mirror. "You have to say that. You're my maid of honor."

Kylie rested her head on my shoulder and raised an eyebrow. "But have I ever lied to you? Why would I start now?"

"True. You have always been brutally honest."

A smirk broke out on Kylie's face. "Exactly. So, you'll know it's the truth when I tell you that both of your girls look absolutely stunning. You're one lucky lady."

I couldn't have stopped that wide smile that spread across my face if I tried. "I really am. Your man looks rather dapper today too."

"I do clean up well," Bo said as he joined us in the room. He looked between Kylie and me, his smile matching both of ours. "I must say you two look ravishing. Two of the five most gorgeous women here."

Kylie put a manicured hand on Bo's chest and leaned in to kiss him. "I'm sure you told my mom she was the most gorgeous."

Bo tilted his head and squinted one eye, a guilty look on his face. "Actually, no. I saved that one for Bailey."

Kylie laughed. "Be careful. If you keep saying these things, she might get a crush on you."

"Oh yeah, you're like number twenty on her list of favorite people now so it could totally happen," I joked.

Bo crossed his arms over his chest. "I'm higher than that."

Kylie put a hand on his arm. "It's okay, babe. You made my top ten."

"Stop being so hard on him," my dad said, walking in and putting a hand on Bo's shoulder. When his eyes met mine, the tears immediately started to fall. "My beautiful girl. When did you become such a stunning woman?" He shook his head and walked toward me, reaching his arm out when he got close. "Ready to get married?"

I looped my arm with his. "I've been waiting for this day for over a decade. Of course I'm ready."

We walked down a long hallway, then waited by the door as Bo and Kylie slipped by us. I felt a touch on my arm and my mom looked at me with tears in her eyes. She pulled a tissue out of her purse and hid it in my flowers. "I just spent the whole morning with Kacey. Trust me when I tell you that you're going to need that." She winked at me, then walked out the door behind Bo and Kylie. I could hear the music change in our outside ceremony space and at that moment, two of our wedding coordinators opened the door for my dad and me. All of our family and friends stood as I walked

217

toward them, then down the aisle. Bo and Kylie stood at the end, each on a different side. Once we reached them, my dad gave me a kiss before taking a seat beside my mom. I stood beside Kylie and took a deep breath as I looked down the aisle.

As soon as the doors opened, I pulled the tissue from my flowers, and Kylie rested a hand on my back, clearly noticing that the sight in front of me had made me weak in the knees. Kacey wore a tight white gown and her long, dark curls were resting on her back just below her shoulders. Right at her side was Bailey, wearing a cream-colored knee length dress, high boots, and a crown made out of sunflowers. Both of them were wearing the most beautiful smiles I had ever seen and I thought my heart might explode with love before they even made it to me. Kacey stopped at the end of the aisle to give both of my parents hugs before turning to me. "You are so beautiful," she mouthed as she took my hand and stood across from me.

Joey Hopkins stood between us, excited to be officiating her first wedding since becoming ordained for the occasion. She began to speak and everything around me faded away as I stared into Kacey's eyes. The eyes that first attracted me to her. The eyes that still had me captivated. I was surprised when Joey announced it was already time to read our vows to each other. With a shaky hand, I took the paper from Bo that I had my vows written on. I took another deep breath before I started to speak. "Just over fifteen years ago, I quite literally ran into you for the first time. I thought my dignity was the only thing I lost that night, but it turns out I also lost my heart. Without even realizing it, I gave my heart to you and never got it back. The years we spent together in college were some of the best years of my life, but they don't even compare to the past few years we've spent together. You and Bailey are the greatest gift I ever received and I'm so happy that I get to spend the rest of my life with you guys. I can't wait to make our little family even bigger and to fall more and more in love with you every single day. I promise to love and support you for the rest of our lives. You're my past, present, and future. I love you, Kacey Grace Caldwell. I always will."

I watched as Kacey took her own vows from Bo and stared down at the piece of paper in her hands. She looked up and scanned the crowd, laughing slightly. "Before I start, I just want to say that I promise I didn't sneak a peek at Kari's vows. Any similarities are an absolute coincidence." Her eyes went back to the piece of paper and she cleared her throat. "Kari, a kiss wasn't the only thing I gave you that first night we met. I also gave you my heart. I went to college searching for a fresh start and ended up finding my soulmate. We were destined to be together and the fates were going to assure that happened. In college, it came in the form of you clumsily running into me a few times. As adults, we miraculously became next door neighbors. If that's not fate, I don't know what is." She studied the paper for a few seconds, then rubbed her eyes before focusing her attention on me. "You've given me so much throughout the years. But above all else, you gave me a home and a family. Getting to fall in love with you, not just once or twice, but every single day, is one of life's greatest blessings. Watching you love my daughter and accept her as your own has been the greatest blessing of all. I'm so excited for everything the three of us have to come. I don't know what the future holds, but I know I can face it with you two by my side. I love you, Kari. Forever and always."

We exchanged rings and shared a kiss before heading back down the aisle and into the refurbished barn where our reception was being held. The night was filled with singing, dancing, and lots of love. When the time came for the bouquet toss, I gave Bo a knowing smile as the DJ asked for all of the unmarried people to come out to the dance floor. Kacey and I turned our backs to the crowd and acted like we were winding up to throw the bouquets, but instead, I walked my bouquet over to Bo and she gave hers to Kylie. Kylie looked confused as Bo dropped the bouquet and walked toward her, fishing for something in his pocket. The DJ handed him the microphone as he pulled out the ring box. "Since Kari used your big day to propose, we both thought it was only fair that I should use hers to do the same. I never thought it would happen, but the day Kari gave me permission to date you, I knew I would never date another girl for the rest of my life. We've been through a lot together in the time we've been dating, and I can honestly say that I love you more every day." He dropped onto one knee and held out the ring. "Kylie Bree Adelberg, will you marry me?"

"Isn't love sweet?" Kacey asked as she sidled up beside me and put an arm around my waist.

I stared at the love of my life, then leaned in close to breathe her in. "It sure is."

Kacey kissed my forehead then let out a sigh. "K Squared forever, babe."

My smile grew as I stared into my future with my wife. "K Squared forever."

About the Author

Erica Lee finished writing her first book, Dear Santa: I'm Gay, in December 2016. Since then, she has published a total of eleven books.

Erica currently lives in Pennsylvania with her wife, dog, chinchilla, and bunny. She spends her days working as an optometrist and her nights snuggled up on the couch with her furry family, binging on netflix or youtube.

Made in the USA
Coppell, TX
07 May 2021